A TALE OF MIRTH & MAGIC

KRISTEN VALE

FOREVER

New York Boston

This book is a work of fiction. Names, characters, places, and incidents are the product of the author's imagination or are used fictitiously. Any resemblance to actual events, locales, or persons, living or dead, is coincidental.

Copyright © 2025 by Kristen Raddatz

Cover design by Daniela Medina. Cover illustration by Luciana Bertot. Cover copyright © 2025 by Hachette Book Group, Inc.

Hachette Book Group supports the right to free expression and the value of copyright. The purpose of copyright is to encourage writers and artists to produce the creative works that enrich our culture.

The scanning, uploading, and distribution of this book without permission is a theft of the author's intellectual property. If you would like permission to use material from the book (other than for review purposes), please contact permissions@hbgusa.com. Thank you for your support of the author's rights.

Forever
Hachette Book Group
1290 Avenue of the Americas, New York, NY 10104
read-forever.com
@readforeverpub

First Edition: August 2025

Forever is an imprint of Grand Central Publishing. The Forever name and logo are registered trademarks of Hachette Book Group, Inc.

The publisher is not responsible for websites (or their content) that are not owned by the publisher.

The Hachette Speakers Bureau provides a wide range of authors for speaking events. To find out more, go to hachettespeakersbureau.com or email HachetteSpeakers@hbgusa.com.

Forever books may be purchased in bulk for business, educational, or promotional use. For information, please contact your local bookseller or the Hachette Book Group Special Markets Department at special.markets@hbgusa.com.

Print book interior design by Jeff Stiefel

Library of Congress Cataloging-in-Publication Data

Names: Vale, Kristen author
Title: A tale of mirth & magic / Kristen Vale.
Description: First edition. | New York : Forever, 2025.
Identifiers: LCCN 2025009172 | ISBN 9781538771822 (trade paperback) | ISBN 9781538771839 ebook
Subjects: LCGFT: Fantasy fiction | Romance fiction | Novels
Classification: LCC PS3622.A42525 T35 2025 | DDC 813/.6—dc23/eng/20250306
LC record available at https://lccn.loc.gov/2025009172

ISBNs: 9781538771822 (trade paperback), 9781538771839 (ebook)

Printed in the United States of America

LSC-C

Printing 1, 2025

A TALE *of* MIRTH *&* MAGIC

*Here's to all who still believe in true love and magic,
despite everything.*

A TALE *of*
MIRTH
& MAGIC

1
Elikki

"There. It's almost perfect." With a satisfied smile, I placed the final pair of earrings on the deep purple velvet of my booth's tabletop.

I surveyed my work—shining pieces of jewelry spread out in front of me in an alluring mix of metals, stones, gems, and crystals. The brass hairpins looked particularly pretty today, glinting in the bright daylight. Not to be outdone, the quartz and silver necklace shone brighter, stealing my glance with a cheeky sparkle. "Show-off," I muttered fondly.

After a couple more minor adjustments—straightening a bangle here, shifting a pendant there—I let out a contented sigh and looked up from my display for the first time in a half hour. The market wasn't in full swing yet. I had arrived early for once. Early enough to snag a prime spot by the town square's central fountain, thank the goddesses. I desperately needed to make a few solid sales today.

With sunshine starting to poke out from behind the morning's fluffy clouds and not a hint of rain in sight, it was shaping up to be a beautiful day. The town of Povon, compact and tucked into the western edge of Willowisp Woods, was distinctly average in most ways. But every day I'd spent here this week, I noticed more and more pops of unexpected beauty. A bright mural of a lake in an otherwise drab alley. Clusters of planted daffodils scattered throughout the town, poking up cheerily into the early spring air. Intricate engraving around the whole of the square's fountain, clearly the work of many days.

A handful of people walked about the square now. Some picked up freshly baked loaves for their breakfast from the yawning bread maker. Some headed straight to the fountain to wash clothes, pleasant chatter filling the morning air. And some—the ones I had my eye on—wandered aimlessly around, browsing the vendors' morning wares. Those were the ones I wanted to draw over to my booth.

"Okay, girl. You've got this," I told myself after taking a quick breath in and out. I adjusted my red embroidered corset over my thick curves. A glance in a hand mirror at my auburn hair and rosy cheeks, a second coat of pink lipstain, and a minor straightening of my booth's wooden sign—now I was ready: Jewelry by Elikki was open for business.

Smiling politely at each townsperson who came within a fifteen-foot radius of my booth, I threw out compliments like my life depended on it.

"Look at you, shining like a new gold coin today! Love your energy!"

"A goddess walks among us! Your hair is stunning, wow."

"Uh-oh, are you a thief? Because you're stealing my breath away with that smile!"

I got laughs, grins, and more than a few pleased blushes for my efforts. People started to wander over and peruse my pieces. I sank into the rhythm of my favorite activities—making strangers happy and matching the right piece of jewelry to the right person.

First I sold an intricate gold cuff earring to a cute dwarf, discounting it heavily for the joy of her shameless reciprocal flirting. And I thought *I* was good at pickup lines! She outcharmed the charmer, and I adored it. With a wink and a "Maybe I'll see you at the tavern later?" she strode off with a confident smirk, leaving me chuckling after her.

A set of musical copper bangles went to a shy young human next, his face lighting up at the sound they made as he jangled his wrist. The smile faded when I told him the price, making my heart squeeze. So I told him it's his lucky day—today was my monthly and definitely very real Half-price for Humans Deal! Delighted with his find, he thanked me repeatedly and headed out in a happy daze.

The morning passed in a busy blur. Townspeople filled the square until it was a lively, bustling crowd. Folks browsed booths like mine, travelers selling specialty pieces or practical homewares, while others gathered provisions for the week ahead. Friends and couples strolled around companionably. A few well-dressed, harried servants were shopping for their well-to-do employers. A group of children played next to the fountain, where their parents could easily keep an eye on them.

It was loud and sometimes raucous—arguments breaking out here and there over high prices or unpaid accounts—but lovely all the same, and I soaked up the feeling of a new place, a new town. The baker sold all his loaves by midmorning and packed up, but no matter—there were more vendors peddling delicious wares. Carts and booths sold steaming hand pies, fruit-studded scones, and some kind of messy, mouthwatering local fried dough treat on a stick, swiped with a thick glob of dark jam.

I had just started to consider taking a break for my midday meal when another customer ambled up. A short human, he had greasy hair and a sneer that looked permanently fixed on his face.

"So how much for this?" he grunted, grabbing one of my pewter cuff bracelets. They were a costly new design I was particularly proud of. I'd inlaid the thick metal of each with large flat agate stones and carved runes of protection on the underside. They took painstaking work to finish. I'd made only three so far, each one taking days to create, and had sold…zero.

"Five gold for that," I replied with a sunny smile. Out of the corner of my eye, I noticed an extremely tall, broad person dressed in drab brown clothing, complete with a thick hood that hid their face. For a moment I thought they were watching me. But they were just carefully inspecting the hilt of a broadsword, nodding occasionally at the smithy's sales pitch.

"Five?!" My customer's loud scoff drew my attention back. "This isn't worth five. I'll give you one gold."

He slipped the cuff on his hairy wrist, and I checked my urge to lunge across the table and snatch it back. It was not only an expensive piece, but it was also my favorite of the cuffs—a lovely cerulean agate that reminded me of the sea. I'd just finished it yesterday.

I took a calming breath.

Injecting a drop of venom into my normally sugar-sweet voice, I said, "The price is five. Five gold coins. With the high materials and labor cost that it takes to produce this kind of metalwork, I cannot accept less than that. The delicacy of the stone and the complex detailing of the runes takes—"

Clink. Clink.

"All right, enough." He placed two gold coins on the velvet in front of me. "I've been watching you barter all day. How about I give you two, and you give me some of that cutesy shit you've been doling out to everyone else?"

I stared at him, momentarily stunned.

"I've seen you flirting, pushing up your tits, giving out discounts and smiles to everybody who bothers to throw some coin for the scrap metal you've got here." He leered at me with a grin, eyes moving down to my chest. "Where's my discount, huh?"

Suddenly a shadow fell over my booth.

"I think you should leave," said a deep bell of a voice.

The hooded person loomed over us, focused intensely on the rude man. They shifted from side to side a bit, as if uncomfortable with speaking out loud. If they were trying to be intimidating, they weren't doing a great job at it. The man barely glanced at him.

"Mind your own business, pal."

Still ogling me, he picked up his two coins and grabbed my arm with his other hand, another oily smile plastered on his face.

Everything slowed down. As if from a distance, I heard the tall person shout brusquely and start reaching out as if to tear the customer's hand off me. Half frozen, I felt a trickle of fire sparking in my chest, tendrils burning their way to my brain, down my legs, through my arms.

Fury. Burning fury shot through my veins.

With a half step, I yanked out of the rude man's grasp. Inhaling a sharp breath through my nose, I swept my right palm in an arc that came to a halt by my wide hips. My gesture had raised every piece of jewelry on the velvet tabletop two feet into the air. They hovered there, at the man's eye level. He paused, stock-still. Glancing around him at the metal, he hissed, "Calm down, elf."

I raised my palm and squeezed it into a fist. My jewelry snapped to attention, soldiers to their general's call, moving a few inches closer to the man and sparkling with malicious intent. The hairsticks looked particularly menacing, sharp points directed right at his sweating face. He backed away with a slow step. I smiled.

"Time for you to go." I flicked the fingers of my other hand, sending his two gold coins back at him. He grabbed at them, missing, and they fell to the cobblestones.

Clink. Clink.

Then I twisted my wrist slightly, the motion tightening my pewter cuff that still encircled his wrist. Obeying the pounding drum of my fury, I twisted more…more. I could feel my power so acutely in the man's panicked face, his fragile limb in my invisible grip. When I heard a small *crack* of splintering bone, I released my magic's hold.

I gestured toward myself, and the cuff flew happily into my hand. "Good work!" I told it, and it warmed at my touch. I swept my right hand in a reverse arc, and all the jewelry drifted softly back onto their velvet.

The man had paled to a parchment white, gasping at the pain. He scrabbled at the ground for his coins. Staring around at the passersby, he shouted in disbelief, "Did you see what she did?! Did you see that nasty elf attack me?" Some watched him in disgust—they had seen the whole interaction. Some began to look at me with suspicion. Most passed by with indifference.

I smiled sweetly at all of them. The crowd moved on. The man gave me one last look of hatred and fear, then staggered off out of the busy square. Once I knew he was gone, I let out the breath I'd been holding.

I began packing up my wares quickly, fingers shaking a bit. I tucked the three cuffs away first. Then the hairsticks, taking comfort in their solidity and sharpness. Then the earrings, the pendants, chains, bracelets, necklaces, and rings. Mind racing, I rolled up the velvet cloth and secured my coin purse in my skirts. Someone cleared their throat nearby. I looked up.

It was the tall one again. I hadn't even noticed them still standing there. They were like a big brown boulder, quiet and forgettable. Even with my height of nearly six feet, they still towered over me and everyone else in the square. They were at least seven feet tall, likely more. A half-giant, perhaps? Sparks of my anger still lingered, and I glowered at them. What had they been trying to do? Rescue me from that doofus? Play the big strong protector? Thanks, but no thanks.

Now that they stood in front of me, only part of their face hid in the shadow of the thick hood they wore. I peeked up curiously.

Warm brown eyes gazed back, a deep smoky quartz. Soft lips, now wearing a slight frown, were a muted violet a few shades darker than the lavender skin. Yes, a half-giant man, from the looks of it. My mind blanked for a few moments.

As I came back to, he cleared his throat uncomfortably

again and looked away. I shook myself and tried to rouse the annoyance I felt a minute ago. It didn't come, but I snapped anyway, "You didn't have to step in, you know. I was handling myself fine."

He considered me quietly for a moment. "You're right. I should have asked if you needed assistance first. I apologize."

"Well…good," I replied.

"Good," he repeated.

We stood there awkwardly, seconds passing. He looked at me with a steady gaze, as if he wanted to say something else. My skin prickled with sudden warmth as we watched each other. I felt aware of my breath, the tight stays of my corset, my palms still tingling with magic. Our eyes were caught. The noises of the marketplace faded, and I felt like one of my jewelry pieces just minutes ago—frozen in the air, poised to fly.

As I opened my mouth to introduce myself, he blinked rapidly and strode away.

After a second of shock—and perhaps a small twinge of disappointment—I shook myself into action again. I gathered my things, did a last visual sweep of the booth, then headed in the opposite direction with a huff, in search of a well-deserved meal.

2

First, though, I needed to stop by the Artisans Guild to restock my metalsmithing supplies. It was basically on the way to the tavern where I was staying anyway. To appease my rumbling stomach, I grabbed one of those dough sticks that had been tantalizing me—appropriately called sticklers, according to the street vendor. Then I set my boots toward the guild, tallying up a mental list while I wove around people through the busy square, trying and failing to eat the deliciously sweet fried confection before the jam ran down to my fingers.

Silver, definitely. I barely had enough left to make a thin ring or two. A new file, since the handle on mine had broken clean off and was rusting to boot. More spare chains, particularly the long dainty ones that were in style and too tedious to make myself. I'd much rather have more time and creative energy to spend on my pendants that hung on the chains.

Twisting to avoid passersby, I turned left down a quieter side street that led to the guild, wiping the last of the sticky jam off my fingers with a handkerchief. Spotting a couple of the town's many stray cats lazing on a stoop, I placed the stick between them so they could enjoy the remaining tidbits of dough. After a few quick pets, I moved along. The sun was still shining, and the townspeople of Povon strolling through the streets seemed in high spirits.

Most of them anyway, I thought, the rude man's angry face flashing in my mind. Hopefully he'd learned his lesson, and I wouldn't have to see him again. But it might be time to move on soon.

As I reached the wide, welcoming entrance of the Artisans Guild, my thoughts strayed from that dickhead to the mysterious lavender-skinned half-giant who'd tried to intervene. I wished he hadn't rushed off so soon. I passed underneath the open stone archway and walked through the small courtyard, its floor inlaid with rustic mosaic tiling, and headed toward the main hall where the vendors would be setting up for market day. Inside, it was nearly as bustling as the square. This wasn't a large town, so its guild buildings were modest. The Artisans Guild of which I was a longtime member, occupied this cozy spot consisting of a central main hall where artists displayed and sold their works, a few tiny side rooms used for meetings, a long shared underground room filled with cots for starving artist types, and a small outdoor forge tucked in the back. I was welcome to sell my wares here in the hall—and had a couple times so far, making some new friends with fellow artisans—but I'd opted for the square today to take advantage of the general town market. It was wonderful to see, however, this turnout in the guildhall. Povon seemed to have a deep appreciation for art and culture, I'd already gathered from my short time here—rare for such a small town, but always gratifying to discover.

I spotted Shree, a friendly middle-aged human vendor I'd met a few days earlier, and beelined to her table in a corner of the hall. Her warm brown face cracked in a smile as I approached.

"Morning, dear!" she chirped.

"Good morning, ma'am! I'm on the hunt for a new eight-inch hand file," I said, returning her grin before scanning the wares laid out across her space. "And I know you're the best woman to come to for tools around these parts. Got some I could look at?"

She chuckled, pulling over a wooden box. "You flatterer. Yes, dear, I've got some. Coarse or fine?"

"Fairly fine. A half-round if you have it," I said as she laid out a few. "Oh, these are perfect!"

We talked through options, gossiping about guild drama all the while. After a time, I settled on a file, and we pleasantly haggled a bit just for the sake of it.

The steady buzz of voices in the hall suddenly dipped, and I looked round to see what had drawn people's attention.

Him. It was the half-giant from the square, so tall he had to duck slightly under the doorway. *What was* he *doing here?*

The noise filling the hall went mostly back to normal, the nosy but mostly kind people of Povon not outright staring at the massive man towering above the crowd. He slowly made his way through the room, waiting for folks to move or carefully shifting around them rather than pushing through like I'd seen many big men do.

As he grew closer to Shree's table, stopping at a couple of other vendors to check out their wares, I passed her my payment and quickly ducked into the neighboring stall of a tapestry artisan before he could spot me. My heart thudded uncomfortably in my chest. Safely hidden behind a huge woven image of a squidspider—*who would want this hanging in their home?!*—I peeked around to see what he was doing. The elderly artisan slouched in an armchair behind me seemed to be in the middle of a very deep, snore-filled nap. They wouldn't mind me using their booth as a temporary hideout.

I didn't even know why I felt the need to hide. Maybe I wanted a chance to observe him, after the way he'd ruffled me in the square and then had the nerve to just walk away.

He looked distinctly uncomfortable, big shoulders hunched up to his ears as he muttered gruff apologies to passersby. When he came to Shree's table, his eyes lit up. Lifting a pair of long iron blacksmith tongs that looked, frankly, like a set of children's training chopsticks in his large hand, he cleared his throat and asked, "Excuse me, how much for these?"

Shree looked him over from head to toe, an appreciative glint in her eye. "For you, sugar, one silver and four coppers."

The man reached into the coin purse at his belt, not even trying to haggle. I snorted at his naivete, and he turned. In a flash, I ducked back behind the tapestry and held my breath, vision going wonky. A beat passed, and then another.

Shree, seeming to interpret his silence as a customer's hesitation, chirped, "But I could go down to one silver and a small favor."

"A favor?" he replied.

"Mm-hmm. Our guild here has been trying to reach that wee kitten up on the rafter all morning." She pointed to a high beam near the ceiling behind her, from where I now noticed the occasional plaintive meows through the din of the guildhall. Some wooden boxes were piled up on the ground below.

"Poor thing got stuck up there sometime in the night, and none of us can reach it. Always getting themselves into trouble, these stray cats," she said, shaking her head affectionately. "We were waiting for Farmer Ling to bring her ladder later today, but since you're here…"

Shree raised her eyebrows, tilting her head back toward the trapped kitten. After a few moments, in which the half-giant seemed frozen in place, he finally placed the tongs back on the table and moved wordlessly around it. Stepping close to the back wall, he reached one long arm up. From my perch behind the wall of tapestries, I could distantly hear him murmuring, "Come on now, you. Time to get down, love…We'll get you a nice chicken dinner, how about that, hmm?"

After some truly pitiful yowls and more gentle coaxing, the man finally scooped up a small gray ball of fur and held it to his broad chest. After doing a quick inspection, he passed it over into Shree's hands. A few of my fellow guild members nearby clapped at the rescue. I got a glimpse of his lavender cheeks tingeing mauve as he ducked his head.

Well. That was fucking adorable. Be still, my clit.

"Seems all right," he said quietly, eyeing the kitten. "Probably just needs water and some food." He reached into his coin purse, then placed some money on the table and picked up the tongs. Nodding a polite farewell to Shree, he turned to go, posture rigid.

"You forgot your discount, lad!" she trilled, pushing a few coppers back across the table to him with a smile.

He shook his head. "Keep it, ma'am. Just give that fluffball a good meal, all right? And try to keep it from climbing if you can." Cheeks still flushed, he hunched farther into his brown coat when a couple people tried to talk to him, seemingly trying to disappear despite looming a good two feet above folks. He moved toward the exit as quickly as he could without bumping into anyone.

I stood there awhile longer, eyes closed and back pressed against the squidspider tapestry's bulk as I replayed the image of that man cradling a tiny kitten in his palms. So gently.

The stall owner's snores ratcheted up to a choking crescendo, startling themselves awake and jolting me out of my reverie. We blinked at each other. Then I flashed them my most stunning smile, saluted, and pushed aside a heavy tapestry to reenter the fray of the guildhall. Stopping at other vendors to collect the rest of my supplies, I forced myself to put the lavender dreamboat out of my mind by focusing on charming my way into the best deals. It mostly worked. Sort of.

With my purchases safely tucked away, I hefted my rucksack and slipped back out onto the city streets, rumbling stomach leading me to find supper.

"This is HEAVENLY," I groaned, startling the server who had placed the heaping bowl of bread pudding in front of me. It steamed, soft and gooey with cream drizzled over it in swirling rivulets. I inhaled cinnamon and nutmeg. "Perfection."

After the day I'd had, I'd earned this. And to be fair, I had started with a respectable vegetable stew and one dry cider. Which turned into three ciders…

Now I was floating on a happy cloud of dessert, warm and cozy by the tavern's fire. This seemed to be the main gathering spot in the town. I'd been there for only four days, renting the smallest room upstairs while I sold off some of my jewelry in the market. I tended to never stay in one spot for longer than a week or two. Goddess, though, it was going to be a wrench to leave this bread pudding when the time came.

I groaned again, drawing an amused look from the server. I licked my spoon clean, then grinned wickedly at her. She giggled and tripped back over to the bar.

Looking around, I scanned the half-full tavern. Maybe that cute dwarf from this morning would show up after all. The barkeep lit a few candles as dusk settled. An old fiddler in the corner struck up a mild tune, and I bobbed my head along as I ate my squishy dessert.

In a corner booth, a young woman entertained a toddler by coaxing bubbles from his glass of milk with her magic. All it took was a simple gesture, her attention mostly fixed on his delight. The bubbles overflowed the glass, and the woman floated a few over to rest on his nose and chubby cheeks. Squealing, he popped them all, splattering milk on his face. They both dissolved into laughter, and I felt a sharp ache in my chest as I watched them. I should be able to do that. Have that. She made it look so easy—as effortless in her powers as the love in the child's eyes.

I wrenched my gaze away. Why would I need tricks like blowing silly bubbles? Look at what I *could* do when necessary—I easily defended myself against that creep today.

A little too easily...I probably broke his wrist, a small voice tried to pipe up, but I squashed it down and took another gulp of cider.

A heavy step in the tavern's doorway drew my eyes. Clad

all in brown, the half-giant from earlier had entered and was making his way to the bar. He carefully stepped around tables and stools—all looking like doll furniture next to him—and murmured an order to the barkeep.

Without a thought, I lurched out of my chair and sailed across the room. Suddenly, I was standing right behind him. Reaching out a hand—my, they serve some strong cider here—I tapped him once on the highest part of his arm that I could reach.

He flinched and whirled around. I put my hands up.

"Only me," I said lightly, ignoring the split-second thrill of fear I felt as he loomed over me.

"You again," he said.

"Yes, me! The dashing elf you tried to not-so-nobly save from a tiresome lecher this morning." I tried my signature sassy smile. No response—his lavender face was stern, a closed window.

Despite myself, I'd thought of him more than once since I left the guildhall. He hadn't, I finally acknowledged, deserved my prickliness earlier in the square. With a full belly and a few drinks now, I could admit that I'd been shaken by my unpleasant encounter with that creep, and I'd probably snapped at this man with a bit too much bite. He *had* been trying to help after all.

What better way to smooth things over than with some charm and a free drink? Or perhaps something more…diverting.

Reaching past him, I grabbed his tankard. Steadying it with both hands—this thing was practically a barrel!—I took a deep glug of his drink. And made a face.

"Is this…lemon water? You're drinking lemon water at a pub?" Plunking the tankard back down, I then poked him playfully. "Let me thank you with a proper pint."

He shifted on his feet. "Thank me?"

"Yes, thank you for your valiant, though needless, attempt to protect my honor from the mean wannabe jewelry thief." *What are you even saying right now, Elikki? Shut up!*

"That's kind, but...unnecessary." Amusement touched his face, and he relaxed slightly to lean against the bar. The low timbre of his voice rumbled through me. I felt a bit lightheaded. Leaning closer, I watched his eyes, wanting him to keep talking, and caught the faint scent of woodsmoke and mint. Like a fresh fire, it drew me in. Skin prickling pleasantly again, like it had in the market, I felt my pulse begin to race.

"Or...or I have a room upstairs...?" I heard myself say. He stiffened. His brown eyes sparked for a moment, burning into mine, and then shuttered closed. He shifted back again, putting space between us once more. The prickle turned into a burning sting, nettles brushed over my throat and chest.

My brain went into humiliated overdrive. *This is horrifying. One of the top-ten most uncomfortable moments in your stupid, idiotic life. Get. Out. Of. Here. Elikki. Now!*

He avoided my eyes. I laughed weakly, hiccuped. Then bolted toward the stairs as fast as my legs could take me and ran up. Safely hidden from view, I made it into my tiny room and plopped onto the bed.

No more cider, ever. No more cider and no more sexy half-giants. I buried my head under a pillow and moaned in embarrassment.

3

BARRA

Did that just happen? I glanced around me, but no one in the half-empty tavern seemed to notice anything amiss. Staring blankly into nothing, I tried to process the last few minutes.

I had walked up to the bar—yes.

Got my drink without drawing attention to myself—yes.

Was ambushed by the gorgeous, snappish elf from the market—yes.

Managed to not stare at her or make her uncomfortable—maybe?

Averted my eyes from her perfect face, delicate pointy ears, and lush curves—mostly?

Politely declined an invitation into her bed—wait.

No. No no no noooo.

Had I said anything back? My mind froze over when she'd leaned toward me, smelling of sugar and cinnamon.

She'd been hard to look away from even in the market, as I watched her chat so merrily with everyone who browsed the booth's wares, smile bright as the jewelry spread out in front of her. Even when she'd turned to me, cross and still fuming after her fight with that sleazy customer, I was only drawn in more. She was so *alive*—fierce and vivaciously herself. I'd just barely managed to turn and walk away then.

Finding her here, in the same tavern I frequented whenever visiting Povon on business, was a bit of a shock. I knew myself well enough to realize I should keep my distance from anyone that captivating. But then she invited me to her room…

There had been a moment, a split second, when I wanted to say yes. To hold her small hand and let her lead me upstairs. Follow her mischievous smile wherever it might take me.

But what then? Everyone in the tavern would watch us, knowing what we were doing. They'd whisper. Judging, maybe snickering. I began to sweat just picturing it. And what about when we got to the room? Standard tavern beds couldn't hold my large frame anyway. Would I even be able to please her? It had been so long…

It was better like this. She must have read something in my face—or my stupid awkward silence while my mind was racing through how things would play out—because she left quickly. She probably instantly regretted the offer anyway.

Or, oh goddess…what if it had just been one of her jokey flirtations? I'd watched her at the market for a long time this morning. Probably too long. The way she put everyone at ease with her smiles, her big kind laugh drawing people in, flattering and being flattered in return—it was like watching flowers perk up at the sun. She probably meant the invitation in jest, and I took her seriously like an idiot. I must be one of the most oblivious men in the entire realm of Kurriel.

But—there had been a moment when she was looking at me. Her gray eyes gazed into mine, and she seemed so sincere. Her focus entirely on me in a way I hadn't felt from another person in months. Years.

Enough. I mentally shook myself and took a long draught of water from my tankard. A small smile came to my lips at the memory of her trying to lift it. The drop of liquid left on her upper lip and the way she licked it away.

The tavern door slammed open, and two cross-looking fellows entered in a bluster. First, a town constable, wooden club hanging at his waist and a shiny badge with the queendom's insignia proudly pinned to his chest. Just behind him, I spotted that pig human from the marketplace. He wore an ugly glare, and his wrist was wrapped up with a makeshift sling.

They made their way to the bar. The tavern was starting to fill with folks dropping in for a pint or a meal after the day's work, and the constable banged his fist to get the barkeep's attention.

"We're looking for a woman," he blared. "An elf woman. Tall, reddish-brown hair, white, and…plump," he ended lamely.

"Aren't we all, mate," the half-orc barkeep replied with a chuckle. The customers around them guffawed, clinking their glasses.

"*Very* plump," the injured man sneered. "She's a dangerous criminal. Attacked me right in the square, she did. Almost swindled gold out of me and then broke my wrist with her evil magic when I tried to get away."

The constable put a calming hand on his shoulder. "We'll

find the elf, Felsith. Let me handle this." Turning back to the barkeep, he said, "Now, then. Have you seen this woman who accosted my cousin? She's a metal mage jeweler called Elikki. We were told she's a drifter who's been staying here recently. She's required to come in for questioning and subsequent sentencing immediately."

I tensed. The barkeep, who had been following this exchange as they wiped the damp counter, filled glasses, and collected coins, replied, "Haven't seen a lady like that, I'm afraid. We've only got two guests staying right now—an old gent and a pleasant little gnome. You've been misinformed."

They turned away, pouring a mug of mulled wine for a customer down the bar. The constable looked miffed. Felsith, who had entered with an irritated pink flush on his face, was now turning an alarming shade of red. "I *know* she is *here*!"

Suddenly spotting me down at the other end of the bar, he pointed wildly. "You! You were there today! Do you know the elf? Where is she?!"

Too many eyes were on me. They waited. Felsith tapped his fingers, staring me down. I swallowed.

"Don't know her. I was just passing by."

"I don't believe you."

"Well"—I took a slow drink—"that's how it is." I returned his stare. In my deepest, mildest voice, I said, "Think I saw her still near the square, though, at a pub a few blocks back."

"Probably at the Eagle," the barkeep added, shrugging.

I nodded. "The Eagle, that's the one."

Felsith looked back and forth between us skeptically. He opened his mouth to yell again, but the constable tugged his arm and began to maneuver him toward the door. He muttered,

"Come on now, let's at least check it out. Don't want to start something around these types of people."

The atmosphere in the area tensed further. Folks' attention in the room sharpened, staring daggers at the pair of them. Some hands strayed to their real daggers. The constable continued to nudge his cousin toward the exit as Felsith hurled insults over his shoulder.

Just then, I caught a flash of a familiar red corset coming down the stairs and into the fray of the main tavern room, also angling toward the exit. Elikki. Carrying a large pack on her back, she wore a long hooded cloak and a determined expression.

I saw the moment she noticed Felsith and the constable—her body halting, eyes searching for another exit.

And I saw Felsith spot her. Screaming his head off, he started to surge toward Elikki through the crowd.

Oh, fuck.

Her gray eyes met mine for a moment, wide in their alarm. Then she moved, darting toward escape with an elven grace, and shoving people out of the way when necessary. At the same time, I did the only thing I could think of. I grabbed Felsith's wrist, pulling him back, and dumped the contents of my massive, nearly full tankard over his head. I roared at Elikki, "RUN!"

He sputtered, shrieking. "What the fuck, is this *LEMON WATER*?! It's in my eyes, it burns!" And a second later, "Owwww, my *WRIST*! You broke my other wrist, you oaf!"

I saw Elikki make it to the doorway and run through. Breathing easier, I turned back to Felsith. He seemed to be trying to attack me by kicking my shins with his puny boots.

I stepped away from him toward the door, folks making room for my seven-foot-eight-inch frame. They parted around me and closed back in on Felsith and the constable, holding them off. I rushed outside, peering around for Elikki in the rapidly fading daylight.

Spotting her a couple blocks away—wow, she was fast—I raced after her.

Elikki

Hearing heavy footsteps behind me, I put on another burst of speed. Well, this did not go exactly according to plan. I cannot believe that worm sicced the law on me!

Earlier in my room, I'd paced the worn wooden floorboards, going over that brainless interaction with the unfairly hot man downstairs. The single candle in my tiny quarters flickered with the breeze my skirts kicked up as I moved around the room packing all my stuff into the large, trusty rucksack that held most of my worldly possessions. It was an annoyingly long process, since my things seemed to scatter of their own accord. But it gave me time to have a conversation with the imaginary, brown-cloaked man in my head.

After that was done, and I'd groaned and screamed into a pillow for a good while, I felt much better. Still couldn't quite shake that queasy feeling of rejection. I had nothing to be embarrassed about, obviously—I'd gone after what I wanted, and I refused to feel shame for that.

But it still...stung. A bit.

It's been years since someone I wanted didn't *jump* at the chance to be with me. Or around me. Or nearby, just on hand in case I needed a drink refill. I was charming as fuck, and everyone I encountered knew it. Still, I couldn't stay at this tavern anymore. Knowing it was probably his local spot, and having to run into him again and again while I was in town—not an option. So I decided to pack up my things and head to a different place for the night.

Now I was being chased out of town!

I snuck a glance over my shoulder to see who was still on my tail. Slowing to a stop, I turned and stared in disbelief. "Are you kidding me right now? Why in the goddess's name are you following me? I thought the constables were coming!"

The half-giant didn't stop, passing me. "They are. Keep running!"

"What?" From the direction we'd come, I heard voices. More than two. It seemed the copper had found some of his colleagues. I gulped and hightailed it after the half-giant.

"Where are we going?" I hissed.

"Just follow me! I have a plan."

We took a sharp right, racing along the quiet streets. Keeping to the shadows, we soon came near the town's main gate. He veered toward a stable nearby while I waited, hiding behind a stack of hay bales and straining my elven hearing to pinpoint where our pursuers were. We had one, maybe two minutes before they'd catch up.

He trotted out from the stable leading the largest animal I had ever seen in my life. A horse? My mind struggled to understand what I was seeing. This creature was a full two times the size of any horse I'd known.

He gestured at me hurriedly. "Get on."

"Get…on? Get on *that*?" I gawped. "This is the plan?!"

"Yes."

"No!"

In the quiet of the early evening, we heard shouts and running steps drawing closer. He tightened the saddle, large hands moving rapidly over the buckles and leather straps. As he worked he growled, "Your choice. You can stay and face the angry mob of constables. You can try to outrun them by yourself. Or you can get on the damn horse."

I was already heaving from the long chase, my pack weighing me down. I couldn't leave it behind. It had everything I owned—my jewelry, tools, coin purse, clothing—everything.

With one last look back—torches were coming around the corner—I approached the terrifying beast and tried scrabbling for purchase to pull myself up. The stirrups were at my chest.

He sighed. After lifting my pack off my shoulders and hooking it next to a saddlebag, he then lifted *me* up. Before I knew what was happening, he swung my right leg over the horse's back and placed me in front of the saddle. I squeaked, half in indignation at being abruptly lifted and half in shock. He just picked me up like I weighed no more than my pack. That was…a first.

Then he stepped into the stirrup and swung himself up behind me with ease. Reaching around me to grab the reins, he said, "Hold on."

"*To what?!*"

Our pursuers were a dozen feet away now. The coppers ordered us to halt, shaking their fiery torches. Felsith's twisted face screamed, "I'll TRACK YOU DOWN, you wretched elf!"

I blew him a kiss with an impish grin. The half-giant kicked, his horse lunged forward through the open gate, and I was pressed back into strong arms.

We were off.

4
BARRA

I was sweating. A disgusting amount, actually. Now that the adrenaline of the chase had faded, I realized how close Elikki was to me and how drenched I was from the run and the stress. She could probably smell me. Could she feel it on my chest, my arms, where they wrapped around her to steer? This was a nightmare.

I pulled back a bit on the reins, gently slowing Pebble down to a walk. With the sun nearly set, we couldn't keep up our pace on the forest road any longer. Anyway, we'd been cantering for at least fifteen minutes, with no sign of anyone following us. We were safe.

"Take the reins, please." I passed them to her and leaned back. She took them, surprisingly, letting go of her hold on Pebble's mane.

As far from her as I could get, I unlatched the thick cloak from my neck and tucked it behind me on the saddle. I surreptitiously pulled the damp linen of my shirt away from my chest. A cool breeze drifted across my skin. Its touch was blissful. Watching the back of Elikki's head with a wary eye, I slowly waved my arms around a bit, trying to get some air circulating through my sweaty shirt.

"What are you doing back there?" she asked, twisting on the horse.

I dropped my arms, lunging for my waterskin tucked into a saddlebag.

"Water," I said, thrusting it forward.

"...Thanks." She took a glug. "So. I guess I'll be going now." Judging by the way her fingers strayed to absently check a sheathed dagger at her waistbelt, she may have been second-guessing this mad dash with a large stranger into the forest.

"Going...where?"

"You know"—she gestured vaguely toward the dirt road in front of us—"off. On my way."

"It's nighttime."

"Ehh, not quite yet." She tugged the reins back, slowing Pebble to a stop. "Horse, can you kneel down or something? I'm a mile away from the ground here."

"Wait, you can't be serious."

Muttering to herself, Elikki started to inch to the side, foot searching around for the stirrup to dismount. When she started to slide off, I leaped down. With a shrieked curse, she half fell off the horse into my arms, hands hanging on to a saddlebag for dear life.

"You can let go. I've got you," I said, not quite able to keep the amusement out of my voice.

"No, you don't!"

Shifting for a better grip, I swung her legs up and then placed her carefully on her feet.

She leaned a palm against Pebble's flank, blinking.

"Right. Um. Well, thanks for nothing. I'll just be on my way." She snatched her pack, hefted it over her shoulders, and stomped off.

"Nothing? I got us out of there!"

"I never asked you to!" Elikki paused, swirling around with flushed cheeks. "Who even are you? Why did you come after me?"

"I didn't. They were chasing me too." I rubbed the back of my neck. "I may have…fanned the flames a bit with my diversion."

"Ahh, so *you* are to blame for me getting driven out of town."

What? She was truly blaming me *for our predicament?*

"You did that all by yourself!" I said, crossing my arms as I stared at her. "I was just giving you time to get away! I told you to run."

"I was already running, numbskull!" She fumed, pacing closer to me.

I couldn't remember the last time I felt this infuriated. And enthralled. She was beautiful and exasperating. Her eyes flashing at me like I'd kidnapped and dragged her to the woods, not helped her escape from an angry mob. And now she wanted to go off on her own in the dark. She might be fine—probably would be, judging from how she'd handled herself with Felsith at the market—but I'd worry myself sick.

I turned abruptly, leading Pebble off the road and into a small clearing on the edge of the forest.

"Where are you going now?" she yelled.

Elikki

He strode away. I could still see his outline near the trees, hear the horse's gentle snorts. Despite everything I'd just shouted, I felt a strange sense of disappointment as he got farther and farther away. And it was, frankly, rude that he didn't have the decency to let *me* walk away in a huff first.

"Is this fight over...? I'm leaving!"

No reply.

I turned, facing the dark path that led deeper into the woods. It was admittedly creepier now in the last thin light of sunset. I hugged myself. The early spring air was getting chillier by the minute.

You can do this, Elikki. You've been through worse than a little night walk in the forest. There probably aren't too *many bears. And snakes. And wild boars...*

Behind me, light flared up. I peeked back. The half-giant was starting a fire. He carefully fed it twigs and sticks, and it burned with tantalizing warmth. I let out a tiny groan.

Would it be so horrible to swallow my pride and stay? Just for the night. Now that the cider and the adrenaline had faded, I realized I was quite sleepy. How far would I get walking tonight anyway?

Yes, he'd rejected my sex invitation at the tavern. Yes, I'd made a fool of myself in front of him a couple of times. But he seemed...sweet. A sweet lavender tree of a man who had a fire and a sword. Very tempting. And if we did encounter a bear, at least he could be a useful distraction again while I ran off. He appeared to be a bit of a sucker for chivalry.

I looked back at the dark forest path. And then again at the fire. He had gotten something out of a pack now and was kneeling, toasting food on a skewer. A rich, comforting scent reached my nose. Was that…chocolate? And bread?

The bastard was making a chocolate toastie for himself. My stomach rumbled. I stepped closer to the fire.

He glanced up at me, expressionless. I glared back. He'd removed his cloak at some point, and his hair looked soft and slightly rumpled. It was lighter than I'd expected—a golden honey brown.

Holding the gooey bread out, he said, "This one's for you."

I eyed it, and him. "What's your name?"

"Barra."

"Elikki."

We watched each other for a moment. Then he began to bring the bread to his mouth—I lunged forward and snatched it back. I ate it in three quick bites, licked my lips, and grinned.

Barra

Thank the goddess that worked. When Elikki didn't return after I started the fire, I began to panic a bit. I thought I still saw her pale face in the distance but couldn't risk peering after her outright. Pulling out the chocolate that I'd been saving for my trip home had been a last-ditch attempt to draw her back.

Now we sat together by the crackling fire, toasting some of her cheese with my bread and chocolate. I listened to the sounds of the forest. Crickets chirped, birds rustled in the leaves overhead, and Pebble munched on grass nearby.

I didn't know what to say to her. My tongue felt thick in

my mouth. Tracing the past hours back in my mind, I wondered how I'd even gotten into this mess. I was just supposed to be doing a quick trip to Povon. Deliver a few custom-ordered swords, purchase some tools and bronze bars, and meet with a couple potential customers. Three days, tops—there and back home.

Now I'm heading in the completely wrong direction, about to sleep outside next to a total stranger. And I may have inadvertently gotten myself banned from one of the main towns my family does business with. Not good. All because I let myself be drawn over to Elikki in the market when I *should* have been focused on hunting down the replacement tongs we need.

On the other hand, I was watching a gorgeous woman lick melted chocolate off her fingertips with utter abandon.

I tried to look away. Impossible. Elikki seemed absorbed by the food, unaware I was even sitting there. She had made a mess of the chocolate. It was all over her left hand, and she was cleaning herself like a cat. She licked the side of her palm up to the top of the littlest finger, sucking the last speck off with a little *pop!*

My breeches tightened. I was so hard for her, so fast, that I felt dazed. I pulled my large brown cloak around my body and forced myself to look into the fire instead.

But—she had little breadcrumbs stuck on one corner of her rosebud mouth. I squeezed my hands around my toasting skewer to stop me from reaching out to brush them away.

Her pink tongue flicked up, catching the crumbs in a quick wet swipe.

Crack.

Elikki looked over, surprised. The wooden skewer was in bits in my hands.

"Old one," I grumbled, tossing it into the fire. "Broke."

She stood gracefully. "Oh, I should grab more firewood for us. Be right back." Without a backward glance, she sauntered away to the edge of the campfire's glow.

I stared after her, then hurried to get my bedroll laid out before she returned. After a moment's hesitation, I put my wool blanket on top of her pack. I rarely got cold, unlike other folk. Ma Reese said it was my giant blood that kept me warm in the frigid cold and cool in the hot summers. But Elikki was an elf, and she didn't have my thick skin. She needed the blanket more than I did.

I lay down on my bedroll, facing the fire and wrapped in my large cloak. "Good night, Pebble," I murmured.

A mischievous voice replied, "Night, boulder."

My face flushed. I propped myself up on an elbow and said, "No, I was saying good night to my horse. Pebble." I nodded in her direction. She whinnied back at us.

Elikki set down the branches she'd gathered and said in a faux serious voice, "And do you chat with your horse often, Barra?"

My pulse jumped the moment she spoke my name. "Sometimes," I said gruffly. "She's an excellent conversationalist."

"Ah! The mysterious monosyllabic man has jokes!" Elikki's eyes danced with laughter. "I think you need better banter than you can get from a horse. You have friends, a partner? Where do you live?"

I raised one eyebrow at her. She threw some wood on the fire, shrugging.

"Look, I'm sleeping out in a dark forest with someone I just met. I mean, sleeping *near* someone I just met," she clarified with a little smirk. "Not the most comfortable position for a woman to be in, alone. I need to know some more about you."

I instantly felt like a jackass. Too caught up in the notion of keeping her safe, I hadn't even thought about how she'd feel stranded here in the wilderness with me, a huge quiet man she barely knew. A stranger. No one even really knew she was out here. I'd gotten so used to her overconfidence that it never crossed my mind. She might be terrified under that smirk.

Granted, she didn't look terrified, as she yawned, adjusting the long, sharp metal pin in her auburn hair into a more comfortable spot for sleeping.

Nevertheless, my mas and sisters would be furious with me if they knew how oblivious I'd been. I was quiet by nature. As I grew up, surrounded by mostly humans, dwarves, halflings, and other similarly fragile creatures, I learned to move and speak carefully around others. My family and neighbors were used to me, of course. They never blinked twice at my size, strength, and deep voice. But despite how worldly and accepting most folks thought they were, it just took one slight mistake—letting irritation show on my face, say, or bumping into someone accidentally—before I got those inevitable looks of fear, discomfort, or distress shot at me. I hated those moments.

So, I was constantly on my guard. I had to be. Always aware of my body, and loath to draw attention to myself. In my experience, most people aren't too eager to get to know me either. It was for the best.

But that wasn't a good enough excuse here, with Elikki, when she was telling me she needed reassurance. I could practically see Ma Wren shaking her head at me, expression fond but stern.

"That's true. I should have realized." I met Elikki's eyes in the firelight, apologetic. "I'm from Nepu, a village west of here. A few friends, no partner." I coughed, then continued. "I spend most of my time with my sisters. There's three of them—Telen, Sassura, and Monty. Or my mas. Or I'm working." That's enough sharing, surely?

"Hmm. Interesting. And what do you do?"

"Bookkeeping, mostly. I handle the accounts for Ma Reese. One of my mothers. She's an armorer, runs a weapons repair and customization business. Specializes in swords and knives."

"That's really nice. You, working with your ma."

I snorted. "Sometimes. She can be a lot. Big personality." I lay back flat on the ground and crossed my arms behind my head, suddenly missing home. Which was ridiculous since it had been only two days.

Elikki drifted over to her bedroll and began spreading it out a few feet away from me. Reaching to her pack for something, she found the blanket.

"What...Is this yours?" she asked.

"You can borrow it," I said. "If you want. It'll get chillier in the night."

"Then won't you need it?"

"No. I don't feel the cold much," I said, meeting her eyes.

"Thanks," she said in a strange voice.

After placing a few more branches on our small fire, Elikki settled cross-legged onto her bedroll and spread my blanket over her legs. She held out her hands, letting the flames warm them, as she said, "So...know any good ghost stories?"

"Ghost stories?"

"Yeah, you know—tales about spooky spirits, murderous

monsters. Things that go bump in the night." Elikki wiggled her fingers in what I assume she thought was a menacing way. I couldn't help smiling a little, and she contorted her face into a creepy mask in return.

"Aren't things unsettling enough, sleeping out here in unknown woods, without intentionally trying to scare ourselves more?" I asked.

She dropped the face she was making and turned to me fully. In a mock-serious voice, she said, "Oh, Barra. Are you scared, sweetling? Don't worry. I'll protect you from any big baddies that come sniffing around in the night. Unless they sneak close and drag you away before I can wake up, of course…"

"Of course," I said dryly.

"Maybe I should scooch my bedroll a bit closer…just to be safe, you know?"

Elikki had a mischievous glint in her eyes that made the back of my neck prickle with heat. Before she could move nearer, I cleared my throat and threw out, "You're fine there. I mean, elves have the best hearing, right? And seem to have quick reflexes, judging by how you took care of that man today. I think we'll be fine."

At the mention of Felsith, Elikki's expression darkened a bit, and she shifted her gaze to the flickering campfire. Goddess damn it all. Why did I bring that up? The possibility of him or the constables tracking us down here suddenly seemed a bit too real, and I forced myself not to scan the dark tree line around us. Leaning closer to the fire's comforting warmth, I scrambled for something else to say. "Your magic seems so powerful. How did you learn to control it?"

Elikki let out a slightly hollow laugh. "I didn't. I've never been very good with my magic, actually." She threw a twig on the flames, making small sparks fly.

Somehow, I'd misstepped again. "But what you did at the market, with the bracelet…and all of the other jewelry…I'm no expert, but that sort of thing takes skill."

"If you think I'm being modest, I'm not. I don't think I have a humble bone in my body," she said with a light snort that I found oddly charming. "I've always had trouble controlling my power. It comes in these rushes when I get worked up. But otherwise, it just doesn't…obey me properly. It never has, even after lots of training. Though you saw what I can do when I get angry, so don't get any bright ideas." She shot me a quick smile so that I knew she was joking.

"Well, it was still quite impressive," I said tentatively.

"Thanks. Most of the time, I can only do small metal magic. Though it does come in handy in my jewelry making, I will say that." She glanced at me again, then said, "Would you like to see?"

"As long as I get to keep all of my limbs intact, absolutely."

Elikki rolled her eyes and tugged one of the thick metal bangles off her left arm. Then she bent forward to thrust it into the fire, hand and all. I yelped and threw myself toward her without thinking, grabbing her arm back from the flames. Flipping her small hand over and over frantically, I found only smooth, slightly warm skin. Elikki started laughing and I stared.

"I'm sorry! I'm not laughing at you! You just look so *worried*."

"I was! Shit, you could have warned me, Elikki!" I willed my heart to stop racing and took in a large gulp of air, trying to breathe normally. She was fine. The flames hadn't burned her.

And now that I realized this was part of her magic, a flush of embarrassment started to travel up my neck to my cheeks at the way I'd overreacted.

Her gray eyes flashed when I said her name. She put her other hand over mine where it still held hers. "You're right. It's just like second nature to me, and I forgot. It was very sweet of you to try and save me, though."

Her slanted mouth, half mocking and half sincere, drew me in, and I suddenly realized how close we were. I had lunged toward her from my bedroll in my haste and was kneeling, crouched so near that I could feel the heat of her, see the dance of flickering light in her irises.

Elikki began to brush the top of my hand with soft fingertips, featherlight strokes that stole my breath for the second time in the span of a minute. She didn't move closer, but I found that I couldn't move away. "So very sweet," she said quietly, with a contemplative breath that crossed the space between us.

I felt myself leaning forward toward Elikki, her eyes widening slightly in wicked delight before a loud *pop!* sounded from the fire next to us as a piece of wood cracked. Blinking, I moved backward quickly, retreating to my bedroll. After a few beats, she picked up the bangle from where it had fallen and waved it at me.

"Okay, fair warning this time. I'm going to put it in the fire again."

I nodded, avoiding her gaze, and she stuck her hand back into the dying flames. Once the bangle started to glow with heat, she pulled it back out and grabbed the sharp metal stick that held her waves of hair up. Focused intently on the bangle, she began to carve something into it as she said, "This handy—pun intended—trick saves me a lot of hassle when I'm working on pieces. I promise it doesn't hurt, just tickles a bit. I can also usually heat and cool metal without too much work, though some types are more temperamental than others. And most metal will sort of…let me know when it's hot enough. Or if it's displeased in its shape and wants to be, say, a cuff earring instead. It's a bit hard to explain. But see? Convenient to be impervious to fire when my livelihood revolves around working closely with it."

She finished carving and held the bangle up with a flourish. A bold little *B* was engraved into it, with a neat curlicue near the bottom. The metal cooled from burning red to gray pewter in her hand as I watched.

"*B* for Barra. Nice, right?" Elikki slipped it back onto her wrist, where it jangled musically against the others. "I can also do simple magical runes, but that takes much more work. And I'm still a bit tired from earlier. Guess I'll have to impress you with that another time."

"That's incredible. Just—so incredible. My ma and sister will be green-eyed with jealousy when I tell them. They'd love to have that kind of skill, working in the forge," I said. "But you should have done an *E*. It's your bracelet."

"Ahh, but then how would I remember this strange day and the equally strange and lovely man I met?" she said with a wink.

Tongue-tied, I felt a flush creeping up my neck yet again.

"We should get some sleep," I found myself saying. "You said you're tired. It's been a long day for both of us." I spread out fully on my bedroll again, trying to take deep breaths without her hearing them.

After a moment, she said, "I suppose you're right. Good night, Barra."

"Good night."

Elikki yawned, stretching hugely, arms reaching up to the dark sky. Her large breasts pressed against thin linen. At some point earlier she'd taken off the red corset and just wore her cream undershirt now; soft full curves filled my vision. I could see the hard nubs of her nipples through the fabric as she loosened up her arms and back. They looked chilly. I should hold them, warm them up. Tug that shirt down and take them into my hot mouth, one after the other…

I quickly rolled over, facing away from her. Closed my eyes. I heard her tamp down the fire and then whisper, "And good night, Pebble" as she settled onto her bedroll.

This was going to be a long evening.

5
Elikki

I was going to seduce the fuck out of this man.

Barra clearly wanted me, that much was obvious now. Despite how things went earlier at the tavern, he was definitely changing his mind. When I ate my chocolate toastie by the fire he practically drooled. And I *know* I saw him staring at my tits just now. I'd tested my theory with a casual little bedtime stretch. Success! I felt vindicated.

Snuggling into my bedroll—with the very comfy blanket he'd given me, much better than my tatty old one—I gazed at his broad back. I wonder why he wasn't just letting himself be into me. At the tavern, now here. We're practically outlaws on the run together. And for the goddess's sake, we were stranded in the woods with a cozy fire and no one around for miles! It was undeniably hot.

With anyone else, I bet I'd be rolling around on the ground by now, enjoying some lovely, mutually satisfying fucking in the crisp night air. Instead, Barra and I were apparently just going to...sleep? What an odd man.

Surely if there was someone in his life romantically, he would have told me when I asked. Or if he really wasn't attracted to me—hard to imagine—he would have just lied and *said* there was someone. That was his out. But he hadn't said anything. Just looked uncomfortable with the painful effort of sharing some minor personal facts about himself.

There was a moment by the fire when I almost thought Barra was going to do something. I could feel his eyes on me. Finishing the last bit of my bread, I pretended not to notice. Didn't want to spook him. But I saw him shift in my peripheral vision, sensed his focus. I got that pleasant prickle spreading across my chest and down through the belly. When we came together, I thought, would he grab my elbows and pull me to my feet? Kiss me hard and slap my ass harder? Stroke my skin softly, treat me like delicate glass? I couldn't wait to find out. Everyone was different.

But there was no way I was making the first move. He had turned me down earlier...abrupt and inelegant though my pickup attempt was. I wasn't taking the risk of being rejected again. So if Barra wanted me, he had to be the one to initiate.

Now. Now! Just say something. Or touch me. I had yelled at him in my head. But the moment passed. Frustrated, I'd swallowed my disappointment and went to gather some firewood. And then just minutes ago when he'd freaked out about my hand—that was...nice. Surprisingly nice. His expression, filling with fear and concern. For me. I still felt bad for accidentally scaring him so much, but to be honest, it was also kind of pleasant to see someone worry about me like that. I can't remember the last time a person showed that kind of care without wanting something in return. I turned in my bedroll, shifting to my back so I could watch the stars glinting above. Goddess, it was cold—but at least it was a beautiful, clear night.

Barra's unexpected concern was probably why I rambled all that about my magic—showing off in the small ways I safely could, but also telling him the truth about how I can't exactly control my power. I rarely shared my limitations with anyone. In my experience, it's a mistake to tell people what your weaknesses are. I'll probably regret it.

But for some reason, I found myself trusting Barra. Just a little. He was so damn sincere, really seeming to mean whatever he said. I loved how every feeling and thought flicked across his expressive face, and the way his words always seemed to match up with what I saw there. Most people—myself included, I could admit—wore some kind of mask, hiding or pretending what they wanted.

Not Barra. This man had such a complete lack of guile. It was…refreshing. Like the first crunchy bite of a carrot after days of eating soups and mushy porridge. Substantial. Real. A welcome change.

Above, the stars glimmered back at me. A despondent howl sounded from the forest—a wolf?—but I felt oddly safe. With one thumb, I rubbed the *B* that I'd hastily carved into my bangle earlier and thought about the way he'd looked as I'd ran my fingertips over his hand. Such a simple touch. But crouched over me, a torn look in his eyes, he'd seemed frozen in place by it. I had been so certain right then that he was going to kiss me.

Now, wrapped in his blanket that smelled of mint and horse, I forced myself to mentally shrug. Tomorrow's a new day. Another day, another sexual escapade! I watched Barra's chest rise and fall in slow deep breaths. He must be asleep now. After a few more minutes, I heard a low rumbling sound. The ground beneath me vibrated.

He was snoring. Gently, and in calming waves. I struggled to keep my eyes open. But moments later, I slipped off to sleep.

When I next woke, it was freezing. The fire's weak embers barely gave off any heat. A cold wind crept harshly across my face, reaching through my blanket and clothes with icy fingers.

I heard hoofbeats on the road nearby, loud in the night's quiet. That must have been what had woken me. That and the voices.

"...just figures he'd insist we set off in the middle of the goddess-damned night. So demanding, that one."

Two, maybe three, people. It sounded like they were close by—too close—but I knew the tree line of our clearing should cover any sign of us. I could see the brightness of their lanterns swinging, but no details of them, which boded well. Our own embers were barely visible. Barra's rumbling snores were steady and quiet enough that they blended into the sounds of the forest night. It was cloudy, the moon's light muted. We were safe.

Still, I slowly slipped one hand down to the comforting hilt of my belt dagger, tucked in its leather sheath. It didn't hurt to be prepared.

"Long as his coin is good, I don't care. We need an easy bounty, and I wasn't tired anyway."

The grumpy first voice replied, "Yeah, well, you have that insomnia, right? Doesn't make a difference to you."

"Hey, now. Let's not turn on each other already," a third bounty hunter piped up. "Keep your eyes peeled for any sign of them. Probably will be far ahead of us on their way to the inn, but the sooner we snatch her and get back to Felsith, the sooner we get our payment."

A chill that had nothing to do with the night's temperature slipped down my back. So. I guess Felsith had put a bounty on me after all.

Well, it wasn't the first time this had happened, and it likely wouldn't be the last. I thought back to that last view of his ugly face, shrieking that he'd find me. That stupid idiot. No one was going to put me behind bars—certainly not a weaselly weakling like him.

I stayed still on my bedroll, ears attuned to the sounds of the bounty hunters until they moved far enough along the road that even my elven hearing couldn't make them out anymore.

Mind still a bit fuzzy with sleep, I scooched my bedroll closer to Barra, trying to escape the wind and steal some of his warmth. He had turned over at some point in the night. I huddled back into my blankets, facing him but not crossing the divide over into his space.

He was so close now. In the moonlight, I watched the subtle flickers over his face, some dream playing behind those closed lids. Honey-brown hair brushed his broad forehead. I imagined running my hand through it, then tracing the large shell of his ear, down to his strong lilac jaw.

His bulk blocked the worst of the wind. I still shivered, but after a time the low rumble of his snores lulled me back to sleep.

Barra

I came out of sleep like a cork rising suddenly through water. One moment I was dreaming, adrift in fragmented memories and warped images. The next, I found myself thrown into the harsh light of morning—muscles aching with stiffness and a soft, warm body pressed against mine.

Oh no. Elikki was fast asleep, close beside me. She'd burrowed near sometime in the night.

My arm wrapped tightly around her soft waist; I couldn't move without the risk of waking her. After a minute of silent panicking, I forced myself to relax. Breathed deeply in and out. I could smell her spicy cinnamon scent more than ever before. I kept myself from burying my face in her neck, just barely.

Elikki looked so fierce in sleep, her face scrunched up in a scowl. I bet she was striking down assholes even in her dreams. I'd been drawn to her boldness yesterday. The way she confidently went for whatever she wanted—sales from the square's customers, respect from Felsith, even sex from me—she was unlike anyone I'd ever met. Brash and loud, yet charmingly cheeky. And here, tucked against me, she looked so peaceful. Vulnerable in sleep, and it made something in my chest ache slightly to see her so snug and safe. With my free hand, I moved a stray piece of auburn hair off her face. She murmured and snuggled closer.

This was...nice. Very nice. But what happened when she started to wake, found herself in my arms, and screamed? Or turned to me with a face full of unease or embarrassment or—the worst—alarm and fear?

It had happened before. It will certainly happen again. And I can't blame anyone, not really. I imagine it must be confusing in those moments between sleeping and waking, finding yourself being held by a muscled seven-and-a-half-foot-tall purple half-giant—no matter how intimate we had been the night before.

But I didn't think I could bear that right now, with Elikki. So I drew away, detaching myself from her grip as smoothly as I could. She stirred, face scrunching even more, and tried to hold on to me. I pulled back. Settled the blanket over her again, grabbed my water flask, and rushed out of the clearing into the woods.

I moved unthinkingly through the trees, half visible in the early dawn light, heading toward the stream I thought I'd heard last night while gathering firewood. Finding it, I dunked my large flask into the clear water to fill it up.

I glanced at my surroundings and tried to focus on something other than the thought of Elikki curled up alone, chilly without me to keep her warm. I should have at least built up the fire first—stupid. Stupid, stupid.

Negative thoughts swirled in my head, popping up one after another no matter how quickly I tried to force them down. I pulled my flask out of the stream. A deep draught of the icy water calmed me a little, and I focused on the sensation of the liquid cooling my mouth, my throat, down into my roiling stomach. I stripped off my jacket, then shirt, then all the rest of my clothes and stepped into the stream. Finding the deepest section, which came up to my hips, I took a breath and plunged my whole body underneath.

After a few moments, relief came. My racing heart slowed. My mind cleared a bit. My breath steadied. Stretching out face-up, I floated in the cold water. Clarity. I knew what to do.

I let the gurgling flow wash over me for another minute, eyes tracing the leafy tree crowns high above, then stepped up and out of the stream. I dried myself off with my shirt as best I could, then pulled it and the rest of my clothes back on. Shaking my sodden hair out and finger-combing it back from my face, I grabbed my water flask and turned to head back to the clearing.

"Morning." A sleepy-eyed Elikki stood in front of me by the tree line, looking me up and down.

I froze. "How—uh, how long have you been standing there?"

"Long enough," she said, that smirk creeping across her face. I felt a blush spreading across my own and coughed.

"Oh, I'm just teasing!" she said, rolling her eyes as she moved to the stream to fill her water flask. "I'm not *that* much of a perv. Just got here. And what have you been up to—taking a little ice-water dip?"

I let out my breath, relieved she hadn't seen me working through my anxiety attack. Though something about the idea of her watching me while I bathed was…interesting.

"Yes, just freshening up. If you want to do the same, I'll leave."

"Goddess, *no*, there is absolutely no way I am getting in there. It's freezing." She bent down, splashing some water on her face and quickly patted it dry with her skirt. "*Brrrrr…*There, that'll have to be good enough for now. Plus, you never know what's going to get you in these little streams and rivers. Once when I was a kid, I was swimming along and a HUGE toad jumped onto my head."

I couldn't help smiling. The disgruntled look on her face, and the way she grimaced at the water—I could so easily picture a young Elikki screaming with a toad perched on top of her head.

"Hey, are you amused by my pain?! It was horrible! Big as a loaf of bread, it was, and all gross and wet. Its legs got tangled in my hair, and the more I tried to get it off, the more stuck it became. Traumatizing!"

I was flat-out laughing now, and despite her protests she was giggling. Sitting down on a nearby stump, I said, "I actually hate toads too. Never have encountered one that big, thankfully—sounds like yours might have been a giant toad baby. But somehow one got into my bed once. It's hard to not be terrified of something when you've woken up with its creepy skin pressed against your face, croaking right at you."

"Ugh, that sounds *awful*," she groaned.

"It was! I'm still convinced one of my sisters put it there, but none of them ever fessed up. I've never been able to touch or be near a toad since. Why do they have to be so…bumpy?"

"And how they stare at you, with those beady little eyes?"

Elikki and I shuddered at the same time, then smiled at each other. Her eyelashes were wet, clumped together from when she'd washed her face, and I had the sudden urge to brush my finger across them. Feel the delicate lashes across the pad of my thumb. She looked happy, relaxed, though a bit cold. Her hands shook, and she tucked them against her body to warm them. I suddenly remembered the decision I'd come to earlier, before she'd shown up here.

"Should we head back?" she said, still smiling softly at me. "Get away from these treacherous waters?"

6
Elikki

I'd woken up shivering and extremely grumpy. The memory of the bounty hunters searching for me during the night just seemed like a bad dream in the fresh light of the morning. The unsettled feeling in my chest, however, reminded me that they were all too real. I could handle myself in a fight... but three against one weren't comforting odds. Best to stay on my guard today.

When I'd realized Barra was gone and the fire had died in the night, I'd grumbled around the campsite for a while. Loudly. My fingers felt like little icicles. I breathed on them until they thawed a bit, then grabbed one of the toasting sticks nearby and tried to poke the embers back to life. They stubbornly resisted, so I'd decided to warm up with a brisk walk to find some water.

I was grumpy all the way up until I'd stumbled upon a sopping Barra by the water, looking as surprised to see me as I was delighted to see him. Now, after filling up my flask with fresh, cold water and talking for a time—I couldn't believe I'd told him about my toad phobia—we were back at our campsite in the forest clearing.

He looked just delicious, all fresh-faced with his burnished gold hair pushed back. It seemed like this was the first time I could see his whole face properly, no hood or hair or shadows partially hiding him. Despite the disaster yesterday and the less-than-ideal sleeping arrangement, this was a nice perk—being greeted by a sexy, wet man soon after I woke up.

Barra patiently built the fire back up to a low blaze and placed more wood on top. Oh, two perks. I leaned forward, holding my cold hands near the warmth. He pulled a few things from the saddlebags and began to boil water. "Want some tea?"

Another perk! "Yes, I'd *love* some," I replied with a groan.

I'd never tell him, but this was one of the best mornings I'd had in a long time. Easy, simple companionship was hard for me to come by in my nomadic life. I was alone most of the time. And even when I wasn't, when I'd found someone I liked being with for a short while, I still had to stay on my guard.

For some reason, with Barra, it was different. I felt... comfortable. Safe. It was a bit unnerving, but I let myself enjoy it. We'd part soon enough anyway.

We chatted more while waiting for the water to boil, and before long Barra placed a steaming mug in my hands. His palm grazed my fingertips. I took a tentative sip. It was a strong black tea with a lightly roasted flavor. "Mmm, delicious. Thanks."

"You're welcome." He didn't move away. Just watched me take another sip, an intent look on his face. I smiled.

"No milk or sugar," he said, "but I have some honey."

I normally drink my tea black, but something about the way he offered made me want to keep taking whatever he was giving. "Sure, I'd love that. Just a little drizzle."

He went to his bags and came back with a small jar of honey and a spoon. It looked so comically delicate in his hand that I grinned.

"What is it?" he said with a wry smile. "You're always smiling or scowling about something."

"The little jar! You!" I waved my hands about, gesturing at the picture he made. "It's just so cute!"

Barra unlatched the lid, his smile deepening. He seemed different this morning—steadier, more present. In his low voice, he murmured, "You think I'm cute? That's new."

Laughing, I answered, "Very. But I mean, look at this. Possibly the cutest thing I've seen all week."

He had dipped the small tin spoon into the honey and was bent down, drizzling it carefully into my mug. I started to flush, watching him. He was so close. His big fingers moved gracefully, and I couldn't stop picturing what they could do to me.

His gaze flicked up, caught me staring. I had the strangest urge to look away—or run away—from his attention that I haven't felt in years. I pushed it down and kept eye contact, giving him my coyest smile.

I added, "And you're fucking gorgeous. Obviously."

Barra's eyes widened. He looked dazed, twirling the spoon between his fingers. A layer of honey clung to it, golden in the early morning sunlight. He saw me looking and lifted it up.

"You can lick it off, if you want," he offered. I could almost see the replay in his mind, of me cleaning chocolate off my hand last night.

I looked him dead in the eyes. "You lick it," I said, obeying the recklessness that surged through me.

His molten eyes flashed with desire and a touch of shyness. He brought the spoon to his mouth, and my stomach tightened. The tip rested on his violet lower lip. The air sharpened between us. Barra watched me with an intensity that I felt all over—it was as if every inch of my body was on alert, waiting for what he'd do next.

He slowly pushed the tip of the spoon between his lips, just a bit, a tentative taste.

"Again," I ordered.

He took a shuddering breath and pulled the golden-covered spoon out of his mouth, before licking the honey off one side in a steady swipe of his deep magenta tongue. I nodded appreciatively, and he swiped the other side clean. Running my gaze down the length of him, I took in the clenched fist held at his side and the truly massive boner straining at his tailored breeches. He held still, only trembling slightly, and waited.

"Missed some." I pointed at his lips. "Finish up."

"You," Barra ground out. "Please."

I paused. Stepped closer.

He bent down again. I went up on my tiptoes and lightly brushed my tongue up over the center of his lips. His breath caught.

I felt a swoop of happiness in my chest.

Reaching up farther, I caught his bottom lip between my own and sucked. Sweetness burst in my mouth. I heard one of us moan—whether him or me or both, I had no idea. I was lost in a rich, sticky pool of heat, my head spinning. I kissed him deeper, tongue swirling against his. Everything was honey golden, mint, bright and dazzling.

One thick arm came around my back, holding me close. I stretched up to touch him—his shoulders, neck, whatever I could reach—and distantly heard my mug fall to the grass. I pulled back, looking down to find tea splattered over the ground and our feet.

"Oops."

"I'll make you another," Barra rasped. "Later."

"What's happening now?" I quipped. I held the top of his forearms, squeezing the corded muscles distractedly.

"Now," he said, "I'm going to lay you down and lick something else until every animal in this forest hears you screaming my name."

My legs clenched tightly. My pulse ratcheted up. I leaned closer to him, pressing my hypersensitive nipples to his stomach through our shirts. His cock jerked against my stomach.

"If you want," he added.

"Yes. Yes, I most definitely want," I replied, digging my nails lightly into his forearms. He held my waist, hot hands warming me as they moved over my back, my large ass. I could feel him straining for me.

Suddenly, Barra swept his arms behind my back and knees, lifting me effortlessly. Three rapid steps and I was settled onto his bedroll. He knelt on all fours over me. I was caged in by his sturdy arms and legs. Brown quartz eyes met mine, and I wriggled with anticipation.

I loved getting what I wanted.

He dipped his head down, homing in on my right nipple and gently sucking through the linen. A light nip brought my head back flat against the ground, and I sighed in pleasure. He gave the same attention to my other breast and nuzzled between them. I ran my fingers through his damp hair and tugged, just enough to raise his face.

"Down," I half ordered, half begged. "Now."

Barra ignored me, continuing to lick and tease my nipples through the wet fabric. He pushed one of his thighs up between my legs, grinding with agonizing slowness. I already wanted to scream with how good it felt, and he hadn't even removed my clothes yet.

I kept running my hand through his soft hair, over his neck, his broad shoulders. He was focused on me completely. Barra reached up to kiss my neck, just under my jaw, palming my breasts firmly. I whimpered at the ache in my pussy.

Then he moved, shifting down my body—lingering at my stomach to nuzzle its soft squishiness—and pushed my long skirts up around my waist. I wore a pair of light wool trousers underneath for warmth. He untied the drawstring on them—slowly, too slowly—and I groaned, tried to reach down to do it myself. He pinned both wrists against my stomach with one of his massive hands, tsk-tsking at me.

"If we're going to do this, I'm taking my time. Understood, Elikki?"

I wiggled my hips and huffed. Barra's gaze met mine. Intense hunger and tightly wound control battled across his face. I playfully lifted one stockinged foot and ran it along the length of his cock where it bulged in his breeches. He closed his eyes, taking a sharp breath.

"Fine. As long as I get to play with you as much as *I* want afterward," I teased.

"No," he growled.

"But—"

"We can't do that. I can give you this. Now. If you want it. And that's all."

Confused, I dropped my foot back on the ground. He raised his eyes again, waiting. The lust and focus were still there—but hidden behind his careful control I could see a touch of something else.

He began to rub his palm against my entrance. The friction heightened my arousal again. If this was all Barra was comfortable doing, I wasn't going to push him. This was glorious.

"Yes," I gasped. "Yes, I'll take it."

He finished untying the drawstring and tugged my trousers down over my thick ass, underwear and all, and dragged them off completely. I shivered as the crisp morning air hit my bare skin.

Barra took in my exposed body, staring at me with undisguised lust. Rubbing up the length of me, he warmed up my skin with his wide hands and palmed every inch of my plump, dimpled legs. "So soft," he murmured against my thigh.

When he reached the inner curve of my hip, he bit gently. My breathing was ragged. I could feel how wet I already was, the moisture gathering, soaking my hair.

"Please," I whined. Knelt between my legs, he grabbed both thighs and hefted them up so that my hips were off the ground. He spread my pussy open and gave it a full slow lick from bottom to top.

"*Fuckkkkkkk*," I breathed. He did it again, covering the full length of my entrance with his hot tongue. "*Fuck,* Barra, yes, *yes* that feels amazing."

I heard him chuckle, the vibration tingling through my legs as he held them tight. I looked down again to see his big nose nudge gently against my clit. I keened. He circled around it with his tongue, glancing up at me with a roguish look. The more he circled my clit without touching it, the hotter and hotter I felt. My skin burned deliciously.

Flinging one of my legs over his broad shoulder, he sucked the index finger of his now free hand. I stared, transfixed, as it went in and came glistening wet out of his mouth.

Leaning down again, he poised that finger at my entrance and looked up at me again. "Is this okay?"

"Oh, fuck yes. *Please.*"

"Please what?" he urged, teasing me with just a centimeter of his fingertip. "Say my name, Elikki."

I growled in frustration. "Please, Barra! Barra, Barra, Barra. *I want it.*"

"Good girl." He smiled and plunged one large finger inside me.

He began to curl it toward him, over and over, slowly and relentlessly, while rubbing my clit with a gentle thumb. My head flopped back again, lost to sensation. I stared at the blue sky. Songbirds flew around us, trilling to each other in the trees. Puffy white clouds drifted. When Barra replaced his thumb with his tongue, licking me quickly as his finger built up a fire inside my cunt, I squeezed my eyes shut.

I heard myself whimpering, swearing, my arms covering my face as I held on through the agonizing bliss. Ten seconds or ten minutes, I don't know. Barra had full control of my orgasm, and I writhed as he brought me to the brink and took me over. I exploded into a fiery rainbow, screaming wordlessly into the sky. Flames traveled over my skin as he placed more gentle licks on my clit, drawing it out.

When the last fizzles faded and I was left melting into his bedroll, I laughed shakily and opened my eyes. I was a cloud in the sky—airy, free, and full. Everything around me glowed with a hazy golden light.

I smiled, reaching for Barra. He cleaned off his face with a handkerchief, then pulled my skirts down and moved up the bedroll to lay sideways against me. With his head propped up on one arm, he traced his fingers lightly over my body. Everywhere he touched tingled. I lay on my side to face him.

"You sure I can't do anything for you?" I asked, reaching out to brush his still-damp hair back from his face.

He leaned into my touch, but said, "I'm sure. You've already given me exactly what I wanted."

"I could rustle us up some breakfast?"

Barra returned my smile. "That would be wonderful. I'll be right back." He kissed my shoulder, then got up and strode out of the clearing.

I lay there a moment longer, limbs loose and a goofy grin on my face. What a way to start the morning! I had pegged Barra as more of a shy, awkward type in bed. Or quiet and serious as he pounded into me. Didn't expect he would be so…thoughtful. Though I should have, from the way he'd treated me so far. Making us dinner. Giving me his blanket. Worrying over the hand I'd stuck in the fire. Commiserating with me over our hatred of toads. Even the fact that he hadn't made a move last night. This man was as sweet as the honey he'd drizzled into my tea…and then licked at my command. I don't think I've ever been attracted to someone like this before. But I had to admit, Barra's adorable kindness was really working for me for some reason.

And he was undeniably sexy, in his careful, deliberate attention. I had gotten—and given—a lot of head in my life, and that was easily near the top three. And all the others in my top ten were women, so that's saying something.

Now if only I could figure out why he didn't want to share his other assets. I pondered this as I cleaned myself, pulled up my underclothes, righted my skirt, and went hunting in the saddlebags. I found a bag of oats and began to make some porridge over the fire. As it cooked, I grabbed a bag of walnuts and dried berries from my rucksack and stirred them in. Good enough.

I eyed the little pot of honey, abandoned on the ground, and grinned. We've probably used enough of that for one morning. I tucked it back into his bags and set about making us some more tea.

7
Barra

Goddess, what had I gotten myself into? I rubbed my hands over my face, trying to clear my head. This only made me smell Elikki more, the scent of her all over my hands, my mouth, my morning stubble. I stomped my way toward the stream again to clean off.

Part of me wanted to grab Pebble without a word and ride home—and away from that maddening woman—as quickly as possible. Another part wanted to run straight back to the clearing and bury my cock deep into her. Both were irrational.

The cool water refreshed me again. I splashed my face and hands, dried them on my shirt, and then headed slowly back to camp.

When she saw me, Elikki smiled and passed a bowl of porridge over. She had tamped down the fire and gathered most of her belongings back up into her large pack. A worn map was spread out on the grass. She sat cross-legged in front of it, tracing a path with her forefinger.

"So, it seems like the next town over is Old Orchard. That sounds nice! But hmm…looks kind of far." She frowned, heart-shaped face perched in her hands.

I said, "It's about a two-day walk east. But there's a small hamlet with an inn on the way. I've been there several times before, and it's very nice." My stomach swooped. I somehow hadn't realized that we'd be parting so soon. Of course I had to turn back and head west toward home, probably detouring around the town we'd escaped last night. And she'd continue on…wherever she was headed.

"Are you setting off, then?" I asked. The porridge stuck in my throat.

Elikki rolled up her map tightly and tucked it into a pocket of her bag. "Well, I guess I should. This was really lovely. You know, you and me. But, I mean, I can't go back there." She pointed back in the direction of Povon with a grimace. "And I don't want to get stuck sleeping in the woods again." She shrugged, avoiding my eyes. Fidgeting, she adjusted her laced corset—a butter yellow today—and moved to pick up her pack.

"We can go together, then," I heard myself say.

Elikki let go of the bag and turned to me. "We can?"

"Yes. I'm heading to Old Orchard too. Have a few orders to take care of there before I turn home."

What are you saying? You're due back home tonight. I squelched down those thoughts and watched Elikki's reaction carefully. If she showed annoyance or hesitancy or displeasure—any hint that my companionship was unwanted—I could just take it back. Say that I'd forgotten to pack the orders or that I actually felt like staying here and camping another night. Then I could be home by supper, no harm done. She would go her way, and I'd go mine. Probably for the best.

But Elikki beamed up at me, smile bright like I'd given her a present. With her yellow top, voluminous curves, and gold jewelry catching the light at her ears, neck, wrists, she looked like a sun. I was caught in her rays.

"Well, that's perfect, then!" she chirped. "We'll keep each other company on the road."

"All right. Good. Um. Let me just…finish this up and take care of Pebble, and we'll set off. If we make good time we should get to the inn before nightfall."

"I can handle Pebble. You eat and pack." She moved over to the big horse and warily patted her neck. "What do I do?"

"Just give her more water and mix some oats in," I replied. "If you're feeling brave, you could brush her a bit." I pointed toward the bag with her supplies.

Within ten minutes, the three of us were full, packed, and ready to hit the road. I saddled Pebble and led her out of the clearing with Elikki trailing behind us. I felt a bit dazed—this was becoming a regular feeling around her—and unsure of my plan. If I didn't return home tonight, my family probably wouldn't be too worried. They'd assume my business had taken longer than expected and I'd stayed an additional night. But if I went all the way to Old Orchard with Elikki, it'd take an extra four days to get back.

Maybe I'd just journey with her to the inn tonight, then turn around? I'd have one more day of sunshine, smiles—and maybe, more sex—and no one back home would have to know anything about it. I wouldn't have to deal with my mas' and sisters' pestering questions, all probing to know about Elikki. And the inevitable disappointment in their faces when nothing serious came of this dalliance, just like every other time before.

I knew they truly loved me and just wanted me to be happy. But they were all human—they couldn't understand why none of my romantic relationships worked out despite my best efforts. I'd long ago accepted that I was not what people were looking for in a partner. I'd heard every reason imaginable from the people I'd been involved with over the years. They didn't feel we were the "right fit for their future." They wanted someone who was more "on their level." They felt I wasn't "sociable" or "cultured" enough. All coded excuses for what I always knew was the real reason—I was too big, too much, too *different* for them to consider me a long-term partner. They liked me, and I was sure some even loved me a bit. They all certainly loved my body. But for most, I think I was more of a novelty. Something new to try out before they settled down for real.

And that was the hardest to come to terms with—that even if I connected intensely with someone in bed, if I gave them everything I had to give, they still didn't want me. I couldn't go to that place again. There had to be a line.

My last relationship had ended two years ago. It was the only time I'd dated another half-giant—there weren't many of us—and he'd broken it off just as I was falling for him. He told me he didn't want to play into such a stereotype, and he wanted to be with someone who would attract fewer stares in public with him, not more. It was the most honest breakup I'd ever had. I both appreciated and hated him for it.

After that, despite my family's urging, I decided to stop looking for someone. Ultimately, I already knew how every relationship was going to play out. It had happened dozens of times before. I could be spending that same energy doing positive, constructive things that made me happy. Yes, I used to want to find a partner. But we don't get everything we want in life. That's the reality. I had a loving, supportive family and work that I enjoyed. I got to travel as much as I wanted, and I was renovating my house in my spare time. It was enough. And, honestly, it hurt too much to keep having my heart broken.

Yet now I was willingly attaching myself to this gorgeous elf. Again. And I'd just eaten her out like I hadn't had a meal in years. Which…actually, I hadn't.

But this was only for one more day. Two, tops. Nothing else had to happen. I'd walk with her, enjoy her company, and then we'd part ways. We could be friends. Besides, Elikki hardly seemed like she was looking for anything serious. She had such a light, playful energy, and I've watched her flirt with almost everyone she met. And what had that scummy constable called her at the tavern—a drifter? If she was just traveling around the land, I'd probably never even see her again.

As I strolled along the road with Elikki humming at my side, shortening my pace to match hers, I ignored the uneasy feeling in my gut when I thought of us parting. It would be fine. Everything was under control.

8

Elikki

Well, this was an interesting turn of events.

I hadn't wanted to leave Barra just yet, and now I didn't have to. This was working out splendidly, all things considered! I'd have someone to keep me company—traveling could be awfully dull sometimes, all alone with no one to talk to—and we had a firm end in sight. Plus, I'd have some extra muscle around in case any of Felsith's bounty hunters managed to track me down. Once we got to Old Orchard, Barra would take care of his business there for a bit, then leave for home. I wouldn't have to wear a disguise or pretend I'd had an evil curse cast upon me or slip away in the dead of night and head to a different town to get away. No need for shenanigans to cut him loose, like previous times with other bed partners.

But unlike those other times, I didn't think I'd be able to brush off the sight of Barra's upset face when he discovered me missing. I doubted he'd get angry like some. He'd probably be worried and sad. Downtrodden. Miserable. Dejected. Concerned for me...

Oh dear.

Maybe he was *too* sweet for me to get involved with. Definitely had those partner-material vibes written all over him. I didn't feel amazing about leading him on if he was getting the wrong idea.

But no one could think a one-night-stand proposition or a little—albeit incredible—forest sex meant I had any kind of serious intentions. We were just two consenting adults who liked each other's company and who happened to be traveling in the same direction. Cut and dry. Simple and fun.

I watched Barra out of the corner of my eye as we walked along the dirt road. He seemed lost in thought. Loosely holding Pebble's reins in one hand, he gazed into the trees and silently strode along. In his fully brown outfit, he looked like a tree trunk. If it wasn't for his vivid lavender skin and golden hair, he'd blend right into the background. Thank the goddesses for his natural beauty because his dressing skills were seriously subpar.

"Sooo where'd you learn to give head like that? Former partner?"

Barra tripped on his own feet, catching himself on Pebble's saddle. When he finally righted himself, I saw a light rosy flush on his cheeks. Okay, that was adorable.

"Or current lover?" I waggled my eyebrows.

"No!" He coughed. "I mean, no, I wouldn't have done that...with you...if I was with someone. Obviously."

I shrugged. "If you say so."

"I wouldn't."

"Everybody cheats, Barra. At least a little bit."

He looked at me strangely. "Do you really believe that?"

"Yeah," I said lightly, pulling an apple from my skirt pocket. "In my experience, it's kind of inevitable."

"So, you have then? Cheated?" he asked, sounding flummoxed.

"Well, no. But I've never been involved with anyone seriously enough for it to even be an issue. It's not really my thing." I took a bite of the apple, munching contemplatively. "People have cheated *with* me though. I found out later. And it's happened to most folks I know. Just the way of the world." I shrugged again.

"I don't believe that." He frowned. "Sure, it happens sometimes, depending on the health of a couple's relationship. But it doesn't have to be inevitable. That's…that's kind of a depressing way to view things, Elikki."

I felt a flash of irritation toward him. "And I bet you've never been cheated on, huh?"

"Yes, I have. A couple times."

"That you know of," I muttered.

"That I know of," he acknowledged. "But we had other issues. I was hurt, of course, but over time it was clear that the cheating was a symptom of problems we hadn't dealt with. And couldn't deal with properly. Not the cause of the breakup." He peered at me. "Has that happened to you too?"

"Wow, I think that's the most I've heard you talk all at once!" I laughed and bopped ahead of him to feed my apple core to Pebble. I'd already said enough to this man. He didn't need to know about my abysmal relationship history. How the first person I'd trusted after I left home for good had serenaded me, spent weeks traveling with me, told me they loved me…

and then cheated with a tavern piper one night and robbed me blind. I'd never seen them again. That definitely wasn't the last mistake I'd made in the romance department—far from it—but it was the last time I let myself trust anyone else too much.

"Elikki..."

I hadn't even liked them all that much. *Certainly* didn't love them. But it had felt so nice to be wanted, adored, after so many years of being ignored. And all it got me was an empty coin purse, an empty stomach, and many horrible days before I could steal and scrape together enough money to get on the road again. Trust was overrated.

Damn, my family messed me up good, I thought, not for the first time, before shoving that back down with a sigh.

"Why are we even talking about this?" I said, flipping my long hair in Barra's direction.

"You brought it up!"

"Right, right. Why don't we discuss your abysmal fashion sense instead."

"Brown is the new brown."

I chuckled, shoving his arm playfully. My hand met solid muscle under his shirt, and he didn't budge an inch. *Whoa.*

Barra rubbed the back of his hair. "I like brown."

"I get that. But, I mean, you could pull your hood up and camouflage right into those trees."

"Kind of the point," he said under his breath.

"I'm just saying. You'd look amazing in some color. Or ohh—even black! Show off that hot body," I teased. "You're really denying the public a treat. That's just unfair."

He stayed silent. *Crap, had I taken the teasing too far? I wanted to open him up a bit, not make him self-conscious.*

I untied the ribbon that was pulling my hair back and held it up to his eye level. "Here," I offered, a touch too enthusiastically. "Start small. You can try this. If you want."

He stopped walking and lifted a hand to the ribbon. I let it fall into his palm. It was fairly thin, silky, and dark red.

"It matches the corset you were wearing yesterday," he said.

"That's…that's right. And it's basically the same as brown anyway. If you think about it. Just a bit more…reddish. It's red, but it could be brown if you squint at it." I was rambling again. *Shut up, shut UP!*

"Reddish brown," he said quietly, his gaze moving to my hair.

"Right…" I repeated, transfixed on his face.

He knelt slowly on one knee in the dirt in front of me, his face at my chest level. My eyes widened in surprise. What was he doing? Were we going to do something *here*, in the road? Even for me, that was a bit much.

I look in front and behind us. But I guess no one was around…

Barra held the ribbon out to me and bent his head forward. "Can you tie it in?"

I flushed, glad he couldn't see my face. "Oh—of course!"

Holding the ribbon in my teeth, I gathered his locks together with both hands. His hair was thicker than I expected, and very soft. I combed the golden-brown strands through my fingers. They caught the sun, bringing out a burnished glimmer that brought polished bronze to my mind. There was a slight curl to his hair, and it definitely could use a good brushing, but it was lovely. I could play with it for hours.

I scratched my nails experimentally along his scalp, moving

my way toward the base of his neck. Barra had been holding perfectly still through my initial combing, but at this he shivered. Reaching one hand back, he lightly grasped my wrist.

"Elikki."

His tone told me it was too much. I smiled evilly to myself and resumed pulling his hair into a low, simple ponytail. Tying it into a long, secure bow with a flourish, I announced, "There! Perfect."

"How does it look?" he asked, getting to his feet.

"Striking but understated. It works," I assured him.

"Thank you."

We resumed walking. Barra reached back to feel the ribbon, running it through his large fingers. I wound my locks up with a silver hairstick to keep it out of my face.

"My sisters are always telling me the same thing," he said.

"What?"

"To…try something new. Mix it up." He chuckled. "Once they even stole all of my shirts and replaced them with different styles they'd each picked out for me. Wouldn't give my own clothes back until I threatened to go to the market shirtless in protest. Our mas stepped in then."

"I don't think anyone at the market would have complained."

He gave me a sidelong look. "In any case…I was bluffing, of course. But it worked. Our compromise was that I'd keep their shirts in my closet 'for a special occasion.'" He rolled his eyes. "They've never seen the light of day."

"Wait, hold up. Are you telling me *all* of your clothes are brown? As in, *all of them?!*"

Barra said, "No, not all, exactly. Some are tan, some are a dark beige. I have a gray pair of breeches somewhere."

"Oh. My. Goddess." I stared. "No wonder your sisters took drastic measures! They should have burned them!"

"That would *not* have been funny. Besides, I would have just gotten more." He shrugged.

"Well, they clearly care about you a lot, even if you don't like their meddling. Tell me about them."

Barra lit up and launched into descriptions of each sister. Telen, the oldest—she was apprentice to Ma Reese, learning her mother's trade and helping with the business side of things when Barra was out of town. Sassura, the other middle child, after Barra—a dancer and the wild one of the family, apparently. She spent half of the year traveling with her troupe, performing in the surrounding towns and villages for the warm months. When the season turned, she returned to spend the winter at home and teach her craft. Monty, the youngest—was still figuring things out, and she was indisputably the best cook in the family. She and her partner had just moved in together, and they were expecting a half-human, half-fairy baby in a few months.

I listened to him talk on and on about each one, pride and affection clear in his voice. I loved hearing about all of them, loved seeing Barra so animated and fond. And I made all the right noises as he went on, building the picture of their lives. But I couldn't help the tiny flame of jealousy that ignited when I imagined it—the six of them together, cozy by the fire in their home. Or eating supper together around a big table. Or walking through the village market, laughing and happy.

What must it be like to have that? A warm blanket wrapped around your heart. Solid ground always under your feet. Safety. Home. I should have had that too. Why couldn't I have it now?

The envy flared brighter, and I wrapped my arms around my middle.

I hated myself for it, but suddenly I couldn't bear to hear any more.

"Wow, they sound amazing! Hey, maybe we should stop for a midday meal soon. See what we can pull together."

Barra looked up at the sun's placement in the sky. "We've only been walking for a couple of hours. It might be best to keep going if we want to arrive at the inn before it gets dark."

"Got it, got it. Very practical."

"Did I tell you about Ma Wren yet? She's a chatterbox, and she does the most intricate pottery you've ever—"

"Why aren't we riding on Pebble?" I interrupted. "We could make better time that way."

"Oh," Barra said, surprised. "I don't want to wear her out too much, carrying both of us and the packs all day. But she can definitely take one of us. Here, let me help you up."

"It's fine, I can walk," I said, suddenly feeling foolish. I was no stranger to walking. I spent much of my travels going alone on paths just like these, unless I got lucky and caught a ride on the back of someone's wagon.

"No, you're right—we'll make better time this way. I can walk at my full stride. I should have thought of this earlier."

Barra stopped, halting Pebble. She dropped her gray head and began munching at the grass off the path. He bent, lacing his fingers together into a step.

"Let me boost you up."

"She won't like me riding her without you."

"I promise you she won't mind."

"What if she bolts?"

"She will not bolt. She never has."

"But what if she *does*?"

"Elikki, even if she did—which she won't—I'm sure you're more than capable of holding on until I catch up. You're strong, you have elven reflexes, and I know you're not really as frightened of this horse as you think you are."

I harrumphed. Eyeing Pebble as she grazed nonchalantly, looking the perfect picture of innocence, I finally sighed and placed a foot in Barra's waiting hands.

"One, two…" and on three he lifted as I jumped. I swung my other leg over Pebble's gigantic back and landed solidly into the leather saddle.

"Well done." He placed the reins in my hands. I gripped them. "Not too tightly," he said, prying my fingers looser so I wouldn't pull at Pebble's mouth. "You all right?" he said, and I nodded.

I was way too far from the ground. But it also felt a bit… thrilling? I'd ridden horses before, though not since I was young. And even then, they were about half the size of this one. I was even a little taller than Barra now!

It was strange seeing him from this angle. He was patting his horse's neck, talking quietly. The way he murmured reassuringly to her, taking time to make sure I felt comfortable, was thoughtful and so achingly cute. I smiled when he slipped a sugar cube from his pocket and offered it to Pebble. She sniffed, then lipped it up.

"Bribing her for good behavior?" I joked.

"Just a little incentive. We've agreed she gets three more if you arrive at the inn in one piece."

"HA. HA. You're hilarious."

"I'm sorry." But his eyes glinted with laughter. "You'll be

fine, I swear. Here." He pulled something from a saddlebag near my leg and held it out.

"What, a sugar cube for me too? I promise I'll be good." I fluttered my eyelashes. He snorted.

"A snack," he said, and I took the dried jerky he held out.

"Yummm, thanks."

Barra started walking along the path again, and Pebble followed without my prompting. I took advantage of my added height and watched him. He moved with grace, comfortable on this quiet forest path in a way he hadn't been in the tavern.

"So, what about you?" he said.

I started. "What about me?"

He threw a glance over his shoulder at me. "You grilled me about my whole life, my family, everything—tell me more about yourself."

"Oh, right," I said. "Well. There isn't that much to tell."

Barra stayed silent. He was right. I'd convinced him to open up to me. I could share a bit. Even if everything in me wanted to distract him with a joke or well-timed flirtation. Turn the conversation back to him. Or maybe just bolt into the forest…

Come on, girl. Sharing time. You can do this. I swallowed hard. "My mother is a sun elf. My father is a moon elf. I… happened. Accidentally. They didn't get along, and I didn't quite… fit. With either of them. Neither of them really wanted a child."

"I'm sorry, Elikki. That sounds very difficult."

I took a large bite of jerky. Deliciously smoky, it tasted of citrus and maple. When I'd finished chewing, I took a long swig of water. Barra kept walking silently by my side.

"I left home when I was pretty young. And I've been on the road, for the most part, ever since. After learning my jewelry craft from a master many years ago, I became a member of the Artisans Guild, so there are workshops for me to use in most towns and cities across Kurriel."

I took another ferocious bite, chewing and avoiding Barra's gaze.

"How young?" he asked after a few moments of silence.

"Fifteen."

He didn't reply, and I shifted uncomfortably in the saddle.

"You don't need to feel sorry for me. I'm happy with my life now," I said.

"I don't feel sorry for you," he said. "I'm just sorry that happened to you. Every child deserves to be raised with love and security."

My stomach twisted. It was probably the jerky. "Maybe I didn't have it easy growing up, but who does? At least I found a craft that I love, and I'm good at it. The metal calls to me. It's enough that I found my own way, in my own time."

Barra looked at me. "Is it?"

"Yes."

Silence again, and this time I couldn't stand it. He pitied me. I should never have shared so much. I felt that familiar rush of anger course through me. It washed over my chest, down my arms, and through my stomach. It burned in the tips of my toes.

I reached for metal around me—the gold bands on my fingers and the silver of my hairstick flowed to my grasp, liquid and pliant. I held one in each hand, reins forgotten in my lap. When I held them in the full grip of my mind, I wrapped silver and gold around my fists in thin loops. Spinning rapidly, shining in the sun. I opened my palms and sent the metal skyward in streaking drips of upward rain.

They fell back to the earth and I scooped them up before they landed, pulling them close to me again. I sent them soaring—silver and gold, gold and silver—through the air around Barra, spinning in an ever-tightening spiral. I almost couldn't see him through the blurring movement of a hundred tiny shards.

When he began to look alarmed, I tried calling them back to my hands. Shards ricocheted around us. Suddenly, I could feel them slipping from my magical grasp and scrambled to maintain control. Sweat dripped down the back of my neck. Metal pieces began to fling from the spiral into the air, lightly pinging into trees, the grass, far into the distance. *No no no.*

Desperately, I tried tightening my hold. The fiery anger inside turned to panic as more and more of the metal escaped. In a last-ditch effort, I called the remaining pieces toward me, slowing and soothing them into simple mounds of metal once again. I barely had half left. The others were gone, lost. Scattered across the forest floor. Frustration bit bitterly at me, and I cursed my powers for the thousandth time in my life.

Barra watched me steadily. We had stopped on the path. I was breathing hard, power tingling through my fingers.

My long hair, now let loose, fell around me in waves. Barra stepped closer. He gently pried open each hand where they clutched the small clumps of metal. Gold. Silver. They were warm in my palms.

I closed my eyes. Tears prickled at the backs of my eyelids, and I suddenly felt drained. I was empty, alone, with these stupid lumps of metal. Childish toys. Party tricks and shiny baubles.

Barra's palm brushed my cheek, light and cool. He slid his hand through my hair and cupped the back of my neck. I sighed into his grip, leaning down in the saddle toward him.

"It's okay. It's okay. I've got you," he said. Rubbing my neck with his fingers in a slow rhythm, Barra brought his forehead to mine. I focused on the contact, letting him ground me. My head spun. "You're all right, Elikki. Just breathe."

We stayed there together as the minutes passed, until I came back to myself. His solid forehead, cool against my hot skin, and his steady breath slowing down my rapid inhales.

Breathe.

Just breathe.

When I could think clearly again, I realized how close we were. Barra still gently stroked the back of my neck.

Our faces were hidden together under the thick curtain of my hair. All my awareness had narrowed down on him—the firm press of his forehead on mine, his mint and woodsmoke scent, his broad chest.

I could sense his lips just a few inches away. This somehow felt a hundred times more intimate than in the morning, when I licked honey off those lips and begged him to let me come. This felt new, strange. I couldn't remember the last time someone had comforted me.

I should kiss him. Did he want me to kiss him?

And then a second later—*Oh goddess, I probably have horrible jerky breath.*

Pebble, bless her, saved me at that moment by shifting forward to reach a fresh patch of grass. Barra and I were broken apart.

I blinked at the sudden sunlight. Barra took a couple steps away, giving me space. I looked at the small chunks of metal still in my hands.

Holding the silver one out to him, I said, "Thank you."

"You don't need to give me anything, Elikki."

"I want you to have it."

He hesitated, then reached out. I passed him the silver. Picking up Pebble's reins, I nudged her forward on the path.

"It's almost like a river stone," Barra said, inspecting the lumpy metal as we began to walk again. "Can't you turn it back into your hairstick?"

"Even if I wanted to—which I don't, particularly—I probably couldn't. Not without a proper fire and some time with my metalsmithing tools. I can only magically manipulate metal using strong emotion, and it typically only works if I have a bond with the metal itself. I'm a bit…tapped out right now."

Not to mention, I tried to avoid doing it at all costs. Using my magic like that always felt amazing in the moment. But the emotions that seemed to power my gift—fury, anger, frustration—created an edge of unpredictability that often scared me. That wasn't who I was. And once the rage faded away, I was usually left with a deep sense of loss and regret.

There was a time when I'd thought I could be a powerful mage. I'd thought my destiny was to become an official Mage of the Realm, certified and everything, and rise to the top of our ranks in the Artisan Guild across all Kurriel. "Grand Mage Elikki Sunstorm"—the sound of it had rung so perfectly in my imagination. I felt the ghost of a bitter smile return as I remembered that foolhardy time.

When I was young, about twenty, I'd sought out a master metal mage renowned across Kurriel for her skill as a sculptor and convinced her to train me. But no matter how hard I tried, or how patient she was with me, my magic refused to submit to my will. "Too wild, too little control," my mentor would chide, clicking her tongue at my latest failure. "You must master your anger and pain, child, or you can never hope to master your magic."

After a year of little improvement, and increasing frustration on both ends, we parted ways. I went back on the road, resigned to tucking my powers away and just focusing on my skills as a jeweler. As my work has improved over the years, I've built a bit of a reputation for myself. And I could still *feel* the metal, connect with it, even if I usually couldn't risk drawing on my magic. It was fulfilling enough work. That's what I told myself, anyway.

I could tell Barra wanted to ask me more. He was going to bring up what just happened. Me, losing it. Freaking out on him. I had too many thoughts running around in my mind—too much of the past dredged up. I needed silence.

"Would you mind if we didn't talk for a little while?" I asked. "It's not that I don't want to talk with you—I do! I just… have to think."

"I don't mind at all," Barra said.

"Are you sure? Because I—"

"I'm sure." He gave me a small, reassuring smile.

I tried to smile back. "Thanks."

9
Barra

This was bad. This was very, very bad.

I was pretty sure I wouldn't be going home tonight. Or any night for the foreseeable future. Because I was fairly certain that I had feelings for Elikki. Strong, mushy, unbearable feelings for this elf with her artistic and magical talent, boundless flirtations, fiery temper, and bubbly light that contained hidden depths.

As we continued on the path, me striding beside Pebble's plodding steps, I thought back over the last few hours. The things she'd shared with me. Everything I'd shared with her—I couldn't believe how long I'd rambled about the girls! Ma Wren usually teased me for being such a closed book with strangers.

My fingers found the red ribbon that Elikki had used to tie back my hair. I hoped it didn't look ridiculous. But I trusted her when she said it looked nice. *Striking but understated.* I warmed at the memory.

Usually, I aimed for more of a bland and forgettable style—all the better to blend into the background. Elikki called me out on that within a day of knowing me. This seemed to be one of her signature skills. Even more than that, she somehow made me break out of my comfort zone a little in a way that didn't make me feel judged or pressured. I still wasn't even quite sure how it'd happened.

But I knew that I liked it. And I wanted more.

I wanted her to keep nudging me, in her teasing way, and for her to let me nudge her a bit more too. There was so much locked up in her about her past, her family, her childhood. Maybe it would be a release for Elikki to let it out. I had experience with that. I could help if she wanted me to. Hopefully in a way that didn't cause more balls of ricocheting metal to storm around me and my horse.

But I hadn't lied. The sight had been incredible. Beautiful. *She* was.

And a little terrifying, in a sexy way. I could only imagine what else she was capable of. The image of Elikki commanding her power for those moments, gray eyes blazing and auburn hair tumbling over her shoulders, would be burned into my memory for a very long time. It was like when I first met her in the market. The way she took control of the situation with that sleazeball Felsith was one of the hottest things I've ever seen in my life. Probably second only to what had happened just now.

When I steadied her, held her neck as she came back to herself—it had been a long time since I connected with anyone like that. I knew what she needed, and I reached for her without a second thought. I would have stood with her there for hours in the road if that's what it took.

I would have kissed her back if she had moved toward me. I had almost thought she was about to.

I would, I realized suddenly, have done anything to stop her from hurting.

At some point during our short time together, my walls had started to come down for Elikki. My carefully constructed, two-years-in-the-making walls that I fancied were made of thick, solid steel. It had taken so little for her to disintegrate them.

Was it because of Elikki specifically and how amazing she made me feel? Or was this just my old patterns emerging again, urging me to give and give and give to convince people to love me?

Either way, what should I do now? I abhorred the thought of leaving her, but could I trust myself to not lose my sense of self this time, with someone new?

As my mind was churning over these frustrating questions, I began to hear a strange noise in the distance. It sounded like a manic, slightly off-key fiddle. Or...a few fiddles?

"Do you hear that?" Elikki asked.

"Yes. I think it might be music?"

"Or it's trying to be."

The sounds got louder as we walked on. After a couple of minutes, an unusual group of people appeared around a bend.

There were six of them. Musicians, apparently. Or perhaps more accurately, enthusiastic instrument players.

Leading the group were the fiddlers I'd heard—two fauns and a gnome carrying instruments of varied sizes. Incongruously, the gnome held the largest one, its hefty bulk held up with a shoulder strap and her sturdy shoulders.

Behind the fiddlers followed a plump, sky-blue caravan wagon pulled by a large brown-and-white spotted horse. A dwarf and a fairy sat driving the wagon. Well, neither of them seemed quite to be driving, as they were engaged in an intense make-out session, but the horse calmly followed the fiddlers down the road. Trailing behind the motley crew was a dazed-looking centaur who weaved along as he conducted to the clouds above, singing happily to himself.

One of the fauns, a tall tawny-skinned fellow wearing voluminous pink pantaloons cropped above his hooves, caught sight of Elikki and me as his group approached. He stopped playing and cried, "Fellow travelers! What a delight!"

The other faun perked up, bow pausing in the air above her fiddle. Her curvy body was wrapped entirely in intricately tied colorful scarves, with only the tawny skin of her head, neck, and shoulders visible.

"Greetings and good wishes!" she said.

My ears were relieved to have a slight reprieve from the noise. Unfortunately, though, the gnome seemed to be the loudest—and most erratic—among the fiddlers. She carried on unbothered, dancing in place as she played.

"Hello!" Elikki called back with a laugh. "What a treat to get a free performance on our long walk. But maybe your companion could take a break from fiddling for a moment?"

At that, the gnome's music stopped with a screech. She swung her head around and peered at Elikki with disdain.

"This ain't a fiddle, lady, it's a *lute*. Are ya *blind*?"

Holding in giggles, Elikki said, "Right you are. Deepest apologies." The little gnome scowled, her russet-brown face pinched under a mop of stark white hair.

"Oh, chill out, Mavis," Pink Pantaloons said. "Don't insult our charming audience!"

"Audience?" I said, slightly alarmed.

"Yes! How fortuitous! We can try out some new material for you!" Pink Pantaloons seemed to speak only in excited exclamations. He and Scarf Girl jumped forward, corralling Elikki and me to sit on a large fallen log at the side of the road.

"Those nincompoops at the inn had no taste," Scarf Girl said. "We had to…er…move on after just a couple songs. Uncultured twats."

"But you two look like just the kind of folk who would appreciate ingenious melodies when you hear them! I'm Vin, and this is my sister, Niv! Just rest here a few moments while our world-renowned troupe prepares to WOW you!"

Vin bowed. Niv winked. They were off in a flash, a whirlwind of color shouting excitedly at their companions and pulling instruments from the wagon.

I was about to protest, but Elikki was clearly loving this. Her eyes sparkled with amusement. I sighed. If this was what brushed away the shadows from earlier and brought a smile back to her face, then I could endure an ear-grating song or two. We had to stop for lunch soon anyway.

I tied Pebble loosely to a tree near a small creek. After grabbing a few items from my saddlebags, I settled onto the log beside Elikki. I laid a napkin on the log between us and spooned some preserved fig spread over two slightly stale flatbreads and added walnuts, honey, and cheese on top. I cut a few thin slices of cured meat and added that. Folding them in half, I passed one to Elikki. She raised an eyebrow.

"It's good. Trust me," I said. She took a bite. Chewing, her eyes widened.

"Okay, that is *amazing*. The spicy kick in the meat is genius."

She took a bigger bite, eventually swallowed, then said, "Wow, I'm obsessed with this."

"One of my sister Monty's creations. A favorite of mine." Pleased, I started on my own meal as we watched the performers setting up.

The dwarf and fairy had finally untangled their limbs and climbed down from the driver's bench. The fairy, a willowy young man with deep black skin, helped Vin unlatch the wagon's door. They placed the thick piece of wood on the ground to create a small stage of sorts. The fairy stood in the center and cleared his throat, then began running through a series of warm-up vocal exercises.

Niv raced around, scarves flying, positioning the rest of the group in the road. The ruddy-faced dwarf man helped her pull the centaur's attention away from the clouds and got him next to the fairy.

Mavis the gnome began to do her little hopping dance around the centaur as she tuned her lute. It was hard to tell whether her goal was to keep him in place, entertain him, or bother him. But the muscular centaur laughed good-naturedly, his two golden arms and four oak-colored hairy legs moving in time with Mavis's wild tune.

Spotting Elikki and me on our log, he waved and let out a "WOOOOOOO! Hotties in the house!"

"That man is as high as a kite." Elikki giggled, nodding toward the blissed-out centaur.

"Seems to be enjoying himself though," I said, laughing with her.

We waved back at him, and I did a high, appreciative whistle. Delighted, the centaur flexed his pecs and made an elaborate kicking turn, nearly trampling Mavis. She shook her tiny fist at him and huffed off to the other side of the makeshift stage. The dwarf came over and passed a tambourine up to him. The centaur looped it on one wrist like a bracelet and resumed his flexing.

"He must be their eye candy backup dancer," she said. "Look at that body!"

"Mm-hmm. Guess it wouldn't hurt to stay for a song or two. Since he's so excited we're here," I said. Elikki and I grinned at each other.

We ate our meal and watched the troupe prepare. I savored the sweet spiciness of my flatbread sandwich, chewing slowly. It reminded me of home. Elikki went to her pack and brought back two small cloudmelons, perfectly sky blue and ripe, passing one to me with a lingering touch. We enjoyed our dessert in content silence, watching as the flurry of activity gradually slowed into some semblance of order.

Finally, Vin stepped up to the front of the group, clapping his hands loudly once. "Good afternoon, dear friends! My companions and I are ready to display our prodigious musical talents for your enjoyment!"

Elikki cheered. Encouraged, Vin went on, "Let me introduce your fine performers! Niv, my fellow fiddler! Mavis, on the lute! Kramdor, our dwarvish piper! Mulberry, with the most ethereal voice in all the lands! And Gethos, our hunky tambourinist!" The centaur shook his jangly instrument flirtatiously, winking at the audience.

Vin shushed him and shouted, "We are...the Warbling Wanderers!"

"Hang on," Niv said, "I thought we agreed on the Wandering Weevils."

"No no—it was the Wistful Wailers," said Kramdor.

Mavis piped up, "I still like the Winsome Wonders."

"The Wiggling Waffles!" Elikki threw out before dissolving into giggles again.

"All right, everyone, all right," Mulberry soothed. "Let's table the name discussion again for now. We'll take another group vote after the show."

The rest of the musicians assented. Gethos sighed. "You're so smart, Mulberry." Kramdor shot the centaur an exasperated look and poked his flank with the pan flute.

Vin cheerfully shouted, "Right then! Name TBD, but we persevere! We will now play a new song we're working on! Count yourselves lucky, my friends, for you're the first audience we're gracing with this tune!"

He stepped off to the side where Niv was standing. Fiddles perched at the ready, they waited. Kramdor piped a few long pitchy notes, which seemed to be their cue. With gusto, Niv and Vin launched into a jaunty song that *almost* made up in enthusiasm what it lacked in rhythm and skill.

Mulberry stood poised on his door-stage and began to sing. I tensed at first, preparing myself for the worst. But he was clearly the talent of the group, with a voice as clear and refreshing as a crystal goblet of spring water.

He spun a melodic tale about a glum jester who trades places with a wily princess and the love affair that ensues. Kramdor continued to blow low strange notes on his pan flute, his already ruddy face getting redder and redder. Mavis leaped into the song with her truly awful lute playing.

I resisted the urge to cover my ears and focused on Mulberry's rich voice. And Gethos was dreamily swinging to the discordant sounds of his fellows, toned golden arms conducting the clouds above once more. At a nudge from Kramdor, he grabbed the tambourine. He shimmied his whole body along with the instrument, a glad smile on his handsome face.

They were mostly terrible. It was a mess of sounds and notes. But they were all having so much fun that it was impossible for me to really care. Elikki bounced next to me on the log, still grinning hugely and tapping a foot along with them.

With a crashing of lute strings and a final tambourine rattle, the song ended. Kramdor heaved over, hands on knees, gasping in air. Elikki and I clapped hard. I whistled again for good measure. The troupe seemed pleased, all smiles as they bowed and curtsied.

"Marvelous, just marvelous!" Elikki cried.

Niv swiped her forehead with a handkerchief and curtsied again. "Thank you, dear friends. And now our next tune."

"One of our most popular!" Vin added.

"A most popular, vivacious tune," Niv said. "'The Elvish Darling of Drallomere.'"

As the fiddles began a gentle beat, Elikki turned to me. "Wait, I know this one! Heard it in a pub once, and a friend of mine swore that it was written about him."

Kramdor, his face a less alarming shade of red now, produced slow, long notes from his pan flute and focused on breathing. Mavis strummed a surprisingly melodious harmony as Mulberry began to sing again.

He sang of first love and sunshine, of hope and incomparable beauty. Years of playing this tune must have worn away the rough edges of the troupe's musical skills—I had to admit that it was quite enchanting. Even Gethos, swaying his chiseled body in the background, tambourine forgotten on the ground, added to the magic of the moment.

As Mulberry crooned about the elvish darling's many suitors and the one who'd finally won their heart, I held my hand out to Elikki. She looked up at me, confused.

"Dance with me?" I asked.

I didn't know what I was doing, or why. I felt like I was going to choke or vomit or possibly turn into a puddle and sink into the dirt.

But it also felt right—here, with this silly troupe, in the middle of the road in a forest, I wanted to let myself dance with her. Wanted to let myself jump off that cliff again and be all right with the possibility I might fall crashing to the rocks.

Elikki's eyes gleamed. She put a hand in mine. I stood, pulling her to her feet.

Our palms clasped together, and I wrapped my other arm lightly around her back. Grazing her free fingertips up the side of my rib cage, she placed her hand against my chest. We began to move, turning and swaying more than proper dancing, letting the song carry us.

The music drifted around. Mulberry's clear voice twined through the air, weaving magic into the golden afternoon light.

Elikki's gray eyes were on mine. I couldn't look away. I didn't want to.

She filled my arms, my awareness, and everything—the tall trees surrounding us, the troupe nearby, the feeling of my body, and the ground beneath my feet—everything narrowed down to her, only her.

Pressing closer, she turned her cheek against my shirt. I tightened my grip, holding her gently as we swayed together. My eyes closed. Resting my chin on top of her head, I let myself stop thinking and worrying, and instead just focused on the feeling of Elikki's closeness and the burning warmth in my chest.

This was right. This felt *right*.

And in the uncertainty of everything, I wanted that to be enough. What is more important, in the search for love, than that feeling of connection? However imperfect, however fleeting—it's what we all long for.

I reminded myself that I wasn't searching for love anymore. I had given that up.

But here and now, it felt like a pointless lie.

10
Elikki

Wow. Way to make a girl swoon.

Barra held me in that firm way that would give anyone jelly legs. The music, the soft light, the dancing, the centaur writhing in the background—incredibly romantic. Barra was giving me serious puppy eyes, and I could feel his strong heartbeat against my cheek. And his half-hard cock against my hip.

I wondered how long it would take to get to the inn from here if we galloped. Or maybe we could just sneak into the woods again after the troupe moves on…

Mulberry had reached the end of "The Elvish Darling of Drallomere." His beautiful voice spun the lovers' ending. Happily ever after, of course, they lived in peace and harmony until their dying days. Forever and ever.

Bullshit.

But the kind of very pretty bullshit I liked to hear about

in songs sometimes. I closed my eyes against Barra's chest and enjoyed the calm and happiness of this moment. Mulberry stopped singing, and the strings stopped playing. Kramdor's pan flute closed out the song, his final lone high notes floating in the air.

And then silence. The song was over.

I reluctantly broke away from Barra and cheered, clapping hard for the troupe. Barra joined me. The musicians soaked up the praise, blushing and chattering.

"Well, we really ought to be getting on now," I said. "Thank you all so SO much for playing for us! You're fantastic."

I elbowed Barra.

"Oh, right—fantastic! I will certainly remember this for a very long time," he said.

Vin jumped forward, tipping horns toward us and curtsying once more with his pink pantaloons. "The pleasure was all ours! Thank you for giving us your ears and your praise!"

"And your dancing skills! You make an adorable couple," Niv said.

"Oh, no no no, we're not a couple," I said. "Just a couple of people. Walking. Together. To the inn, you see."

"Sorry, my mistake," Niv said.

"Give it time!" Gethos yelled. Kramdor shushed him. Gethos stage-whispered to Barra and me, "*You two look hot together!*" The dwarf rolled his eyes.

"You are all magnificent," I said, true affection in my voice. "I hope our paths cross again."

"Can we give you anything in return for the performance?" Barra said.

Niv said, "No need, no need. We just wanted to enjoy

playing for a while. Wash the bad taste of that dreadful show at the inn out of our mouths."

"You two clearly have superior taste to the folk we encountered there!" Vin said.

"Just promise to tell everyone you meet about the magnificent troupe who dazzled you senseless—the Willful Wheels!" Mulberry said.

The others jumped in, all talking at once, arguing for their preferred name choices. As they gathered, jabbering together, Barra and I packed away our food. He boosted me into the saddle again—I gave a half-hearted protest, but I obviously wasn't going to turn down a free ride—and we headed out with a final wave to the troupe.

As we set off down the road, Mavis's lute plinked discordantly and Gethos waved his tambourine back at us with a cheery "Goodbyyyye, hotties!"

We turned the bend, and they fell out of sight and earshot. Barra caught my eye. We both burst out laughing.

"I liked them!" I said finally, trying to catch my breath. "Maybe they're not the most naturally gifted, but what sweethearts."

"You're right. I'm surprised to say it, but I'm glad they cornered us into an impromptu performance," Barra said.

"Me too. I hope they find a better reception at the taverns in Povon."

"Maybe they will. Although we didn't have the most pleasant experience there, *they* have a great deal of charisma. With luck, they'll charm the townspeople out of their coin."

"What are you saying?! I have charisma for days."

"You absolutely do. You're brimming with charisma. But—"

"BUT! You have a but!" I yelled.

"But," Barra continued, "you are also very…passionate. And maybe that passion shows up a bit, um, forcefully?"

I snorted. "You've known me for one day, Barra. Let's not pretend you're an expert on my *passions*."

He flushed and didn't respond. Just inclined his head in acknowledgment. We walked along in silence for a while.

My indignation faded a bit, and I said, "Well. You might not be entirely wrong. I suppose."

"You did break a man's wrist for speaking rudely and touching your arm. Not that it was unwarranted. He was a creepy bastard. I'm just saying."

"In my experience," I said carefully, trying to keep my temper in check, "it's better to shut someone like that down as soon as possible—as completely as possible—rather than play it nice and risk them trying again."

"I can understand that. But—"

"No. No, you don't understand." I fumed. "You don't have any idea what it's like, living the way I do. You're this huge, seven-foot-something giant, and a man besides. How do you think I survive, as a woman traveling alone? Do you think I haven't tried the kind approach? The gentle but firm, 'thanks but no thanks' response?

"I meet everyone with friendliness and an open heart. A smile and a compliment. That's the way I am. And most folks match me kindness for kindness. But certain people—they've always been men—seek to take advantage of someone the moment they perceive a weakness. I've encountered enough of them on the road, been *hurt* by enough of them, to know that type when I see them.

"So yeah. Maybe I lost my temper a little. Maybe I shouldn't have broken his wrist. A finger might have been enough. Or a very tight five-second squeeze around his sweaty neck. But I don't regret it. And I don't need you trying to reprimand me when you have *no idea* what my life is like or what I've been through."

I broke off my tirade, breathing hard. I concentrated on reining in my irritation. Pebble was solid underneath me, and I stroked her neck, focusing on the rough gray hair against my fingers and the feeling of her steady steps along the road.

After a while, Barra said solemnly, "I'm sorry, Elikki. I didn't mean that to sound like a reprimand, or a judgment. I do think it was a bit more violence than the situation called for. I'm not going to lie about that. But I also didn't think through what your reasons might have been. Or how your life experiences informed that decision. You're right." He swallowed hard. "I don't know at all what it's like to grow up the way you have, rely on only yourself for so long. I can't imagine. Of course you do what you feel you must in order to be safe."

His soft voice stopped. It felt like a relief, to be heard and properly listened to. I let out a long sigh.

"To be honest, I don't even know if it was a conscious decision," I admitted slowly. "My magic…sometimes it's difficult to control. In that moment, there in the market, I felt so powerful and—and *furious*. Part of me wanted to wrap his entire arm, his whole body, in metal and crush it. It was nothing to snap just a wrist. My anger just kind of…takes over sometimes."

I took a breath and tried to look at Barra. "I just want you to know. Even though I don't regret doing things like that, I don't feel good about it either. I'm not sure it was even a fully conscious decision. Afterward, I always feel a bit crappy. So I tend to push down any misgivings I have later with things that feel good. A tasty meal, some drinks. A fun night, and everything looks better again."

"A one-night stand with the first person you see?" Barra looked at me, realizing something.

"Maybe," I said, watching him. "Is that so horrible? Sex is one of the few fun, free things we get in life. Why not enjoy it when we can?"

"It's not horrible. It's just not me. I don't want to be used in that way."

"Used?" I laughed. "Used how? If two consenting adults want to bone, neither is taking advantage of the other."

Barra shrugged. Gruffly, he said, "I just can't do that. I've never been able to have sex with someone without feeling… attached."

I gaped. "So you've never just slept with someone for the fun of it? Had a one-night stand? Is that why you didn't come upstairs with me?"

"I have, but it hasn't ended well for me," Barra said, ignoring my last question. "I've been told that I can get a bit clingy. I suppose I…misinterpret peoples' actions."

"Hmm. What a complicated way to live. Probably hard to have a good sex life, then, especially in a small place like Nepu."

Barra coughed, flushing a deeper violet.

"Well, wait. How do you feel now, after what we did in the woods this morning? Are you all right?"

Barra looked equal parts embarrassed and gratified that I asked. It took him a while to gather his thoughts. I was getting used to that about him.

We walked along. I felt a light breeze play with my hair, and I admired the way the late afternoon sun fell through the trees' leafy branches. Dappled light spotted the dirt road in a playful pattern.

"I do feel all right. I think. I care about you—probably more than you care about me—but I deeply enjoyed our time together. And I'd...I'd like to repeat it. If you want to," Barra said.

My pulse raced at his words, but I tried to stay calm and not spook him. "First of all," I said, "I don't think it's good practice to assume others care less about you than you do about them. You don't know how I feel! I like you very much. Second, I absolutely would like a repeat of this morning. Yes, yes, yes. No question. And third, I have a proposition. Why don't you use our time together to try again at simple sex for sex's sake. Maybe it didn't work with those other people because you were always envisioning a future with them and overromanticizing it. But with me, that won't be an issue since we'll be parting ways soon. Too soon to develop real feelings for me. It could just be fun."

At Barra's long silence, my stomach clenched. Had I pushed him too much? A better person than I would probably suggest that we take sex off the table permanently now, knowing that he gets too easily attached. But...Barra *had* said he wanted to repeat things. And he was a grown man—if he wanted to risk it, who was I to deny him?

Trying to lighten the mood, I batted my eyelashes dramatically and winked a few times. He smiled distractedly at my antics.

"I don't quite know what to say to that, Elikki. But I'll think about it," he said.

"This is obviously my blatant attempt to get into your pants. Just to be clear. But I also really think you'd enjoy it," I said.

"I know," he said. "...Thank you?"

"You're very welcome."

We carried on in silence for a while again. Suddenly, Barra said, "Did I tell you that I actually think I broke Felsith's other wrist?"

"What?!" I screeched. "Wait, you're giving me a hard time, and you did *the same thing*?"

"It was when you were trying to get away from him and the constable at the tavern. He tried to bolt after you, so I grabbed him. Breaking his wrist was an accident! I just meant to hold him back. Although I must admit, it was pretty funny." Barra chuckled.

I sputtered, indignation and amusement warring. Picturing Felsith, amusement won out.

"I wish I had seen that." I broke out laughing. Barra joined me, and we cackled together. "Both wrists!" I howled, wiping tears from my eyes.

"That poor fool," Barra said, chest heaving. I loved seeing him laugh so wholeheartedly. "Bad luck crossing the two of us."

"He better hope he doesn't again."

"From what you've said, Elikki, it sounds like you hurt him by accident too. Your power and your anger are hard to control. Just like my physical strength. I need to be on constant guard, watching myself when I'm around others, and I still make mistakes like yesterday."

I murmured something noncommittal, thinking about everything he'd said. He wasn't wrong. But I'd rather just laugh at stupid Felsith's misfortune and put him in the past. He was on the road behind me. I was moving forward and leaving all that.

"How much farther do you think the inn is?" I asked.

"Not far. We should arrive within the hour," Barra said.

11

Barra

By the time we got to the stables of the Painted Dragon, I was about ready to fall asleep. This was much more excitement than I was used to. I had my routines, my rituals at home. And while I did travel sometimes for my work with our family business, it had never been this unpredictable. Or exhilarating. Being with Elikki nonstop for over a day was the most fun I'd had in...well, years.

But I was also exhausted. I needed a bath, a hot meal, and a large bed. I helped Elikki down from the saddle and grabbed the packs we'd want for the evening. After checking Pebble's hooves quickly and giving the stablehand a few instructions on her care, we entered the inn.

It was as warm and cozy as always. A crackling fire burning in the large hearth filled the room with a comforting, smoky scent. Just a handful of patrons occupied the main room. Most folks in Kurriel kept their evenings quite tame in the week leading up to a Rising Night, and there was one coming up in just a few days. Held every month as one ended and another began, it paid homage to the two facets of the Dual Goddess: sun and moon. Day and night. Beginning and end. That was the symbolic meaning, at least. In reality, across most of the lands, apart from the priories, the monthly tradition was more an excuse to let off some steam with the indulgent merriment of Rising Night. And then, of course, have a lazy, post-revelry lie-in the next morning of Resting Day.

To the left of the main room was a sturdy wooden bar, handled by Saho, one of the innkeepers and someone whom I considered a friend. A half-elf with green-copper skin, they had a restless energy and an insatiable thirst for gossip.

I led Elikki up to the bar and hailed Saho from one end.

"Good to see you again, Barra!" they said. "And who is this incandescent vision you've brought tonight?"

Elikki preened. After setting down her pack, she extended a hand. "Elikki Sunstorm. Jeweler. Elf mage. Bewitcher of hearts." She threw Saho one of her enticing smiles as they swooned melodramatically.

"Okay, okay. Saho, Elikki. Elikki, Saho. Now you've met," I said. "Saho, is Legus here? Your *partner*? We'd like to arrange for rooms tonight."

"Rooms? As in plural?" they said, chewing on a hangnail and looking us over skeptically.

"Yes, two rooms," I said. I refused to look at Elikki.

"Okayyy," they said. "I suppose that can be arranged. I'll go find him."

They called a barmaid over and then disappeared into the kitchens. I ordered a pot of peppermint tea, and Elikki got a large mug of mulled wine. We both asked for the day's soup. I also got a chicken pot pie and urged her to do the same.

"Trust me—Saho is an incredible cook. Their pot pie is half of the reason I ever even travel this far on business."

"You don't have to tell me twice. I'm so ready for this hot meal, I'll eat anything that's put in front of me. Two pot pies, please!" she chirped to the barmaid with a wink. The woman smiled back and went into the kitchens behind the bar to put in their order.

Elikki took a glug of her steaming wine. "Goddesses, that's delicious," she said with a groan.

I watched her throat move, captivated by the soft skin there. Her neck, her collarbone—I wanted to run my fingers over it all. Pull her close to me like when we danced in the road and kiss her.

Eyes closed in contentment, Elikki did a full body wiggle as the hot liquid traveled through her, drawing my gaze down to her full chest. The tops of her breasts peeking out from the yellow corset moved enticingly as she did her happy dance.

I shook myself and turned away, back to the bar where my tea now sat. I focused on pouring it out. The comforting smell of peppermint cleared my head a bit, and I took a careful sip.

Elikki

"Two soups for the sir and his lady."

Saho reappeared carrying two deep wooden bowls filled to the brim with a creamy mushroom soup sprinkled with herbs. A tall red-scaled dragonborn who I assumed was Legus trailed behind them with utensils, cloth napkins, and a basket of rolls. He had a delicate tattoo on his right pinky finger, encircled with runes for stability, faith, love. A common tradition for dedicated partners in Kurriel, and I spotted a matching runic tattoo on Saho.

In a deep voice, Legus said, "Barra Draos. Welcome back to the Painted Dragon. Let's get you both settled at a table."

He led the way to a well-worn table with four large and sturdy chairs. I didn't always trust a wood chair. If they were old or shoddily made, they might not hold my weight. It was safest to test them out a little at a time, sitting on it halfway at first. But these looked so stable, and both Legus and Barra sat their even larger frames heavily onto them. I plopped onto mine and took another happy swig of my mulled wine.

I was beginning to realize another reason besides the food why Barra came here regularly. With his size as a half-giant, it was probably difficult to find places that could accommodate him. But at an inn owned by a dragonborn, who looked to be almost seven feet tall himself, everything would already be tailored to fit guests of varying sizes.

Even the utensils Legus had brought out for us were different. My spoon was a normal size—what I thought of as "normal" anyway—but the handle of Barra's was almost twice as big as mine. Seeing me observing him, he raised one eyebrow.

Saho placed the soup in front of us, and I inhaled the savory steam.

"Mmm, thank you," I said, ripping apart a warm roll and dunking half into the soup.

Saho waited until we'd taken our first bites and heaped praise on them before they hopped back to the kitchen. The earthy garlicky mushroom flavor was delicious, with just the right amount of salt and creamy richness. It warmed up my insides, and the blazing hearth fire nearby chased the chill away from my fingers and toes.

A halfling sat in an armchair in one corner, strumming prettily on a small harp. There were a few patrons scattered around the room, and the atmosphere was peaceful. People ate and talked, dice hit a nearby table where two dwarves played, and the fire crackled and popped merrily. The halfling's gentle music floated around the room.

It felt good to be indoors again. Safe and warm. Before I'd learned my metalsmithing trade and figured out how to live on my own, I'd spent many of my days and nights outside. More than I cared to remember.

Now though, I made enough coin that I could always afford to stay at inns or taverns on the road, even if not all were as nice as this lovely place. Or I'd barter with a kind family, trading jewelry or metalwork tasks in exchange for staying in a spare room of their house for a week. Sometimes—the most fun times—I'd find an attractive local and have a fling at their place.

Barra and Legus had been chatting quietly as I'd been lost in my soup and my thoughts. When I set my spoon down in the now-empty bowl and let out a contented sigh, they both looked over.

"I see you are as taken with my Saho's cooking as Barra is," Legus said, his voice an alluring rumble.

"That," I said, "was the *best soup* I've ever had in my life."

He inclined his horned head at the compliment, baring sharp teeth in a smile. "Be sure to tell the chef. Saho lives for praise about their craft," he said.

"I will." I grinned back. "It's nice to meet you. I'm Elikki."

"A pleasure to host you at our humble inn, dear," Legus said.

He pulled two iron keys from his pocket.

"Your favorite room is available, friend," he said, placing one in front of Barra. He laid the other down near me, saying, "And the Yellow Room for you, my dear. Saho thought it fitting." He gestured one clawed hand toward my butter-yellow corset.

"Oh, thank you. Um…what are your rates?" I said, taking out my coin purse.

"For friends, one silver each," he said.

"Are you sure? That hardly seems like enough," I said, skeptical.

"I am sure," Legus said without budging.

I laid down the paltry amount and added one more silver. "For the outstanding food and drink," I explained, firmly ignoring his protests. Barra also laid down two silvers.

The dragonborn inclined his head again. "I will have Saho bring out dessert as well. Will you both be wanting baths upstairs?"

With our enthusiastic yesses, he swept the coins into a large pocket and left to prepare our rooms, lifting our heavy packs with ease. Saho trotted out from the kitchen soon after with our steaming pot pies, the barmaid following with drink refills. I persuaded Saho to join us for a while since it was a slow night. They grabbed a pint of cider and sat down with a dramatic groan.

"Agghhh, my achy bones. I'm getting old," they said, clutching their back.

Barra chuckled. "Saho, you're still in your thirties, same as me. And you're a half-elf. You're not allowed to complain like that until you're at least eighty."

"Tell that to my bad back, know-it-all," they said. "All that hunching over the stove, chopping vegetables—I'm aging prematurely!" They twisted their torso, face a mask of pain. "Don't you hear my creaky bones crying out? Ahhh, this arduous life!"

The barmaid, who was dropping off a bowl of nibbles for Saho, rolled her eyes and raced to clean up a spill a few tables over while she balanced a leaning tower of dirty pint glasses with the other hand.

"Well, I'm sure everyone deeply appreciates your efforts. This is certainly some of the best food I've eaten." I was already halfway through my chicken pot pie. I almost didn't want to finish because I knew I'd be sad when it was gone.

"Just *some* of the best? Not *the* best?" Saho cried. They stared at me, wringing their apron in their hands.

Barra nudged my leg with his knee under the table. His eyes widened in warning, and he shook his head slightly. I felt a sharp frisson of desire at the contact of his leg on mine but tried to focus on the conversation.

"Oh no—the best, hands down," I said, grabbing Saho's hand and giving them my most earnest face. "What is the seasoning in here? Thyme?" I poked my fork into my pot pie again.

Barra also made a show of taking another big bite. "Rosemary maybe?"

"Sage," Saho said smugly. "A variety I cultivated myself. It's probably a bit zestier and more peppery than you're used to."

"Delicious," Barra said as he chewed.

I nodded in agreement and took another bite. "It's like my taste buds are dancing a jig in my mouth!"

Placated, Saho trilled with laughter. "Your taste buds are dancing a jig! I love that. You are delightful, aren't you?" We clinked our glasses together. They said, "I'm so glad you two stopped in tonight. Livened up a dull evening for me."

"Me too! You have a wonderful inn." I downed the rest of my wine. Barra sipped at his peppermint tea and smiled at me. I could still feel the heat of his knee against my leg. He hadn't quite pulled it away.

Saho looked back and forth between us. They stood, saying, "Well, your baths should be ready by now. Better get up there while the water's hot. I'll bring dessert up to your room in a bit."

"Rooms, Saho. Our rooms, plural," Barra said.

"Oh, right. Silly me. Two separate desserts for your two *separate* rooms." With a sly look, they bounced back to the kitchen.

Barra and I finished up our pot pies, eating every last crumb of that perfect flaky, buttery crust. He led the way upstairs, slowly weaving around tables and chairs toward the far corner of the main room. We climbed a stairwell lit with only a few candles. It opened into a hallway with six doors.

"That's the bathroom," he said, pointing at the first door on the left. We walked down the hallway together. The next one had THE BLUE ROOM painted on it in flowy letters. The last door on the left read THE YELLOW ROOM.

"This is me," I said.

"And I'm just across the hall here," Barra said, pointing over his shoulder at the door that read THE GREEN ROOM.

"Hmm not 'the Brown Room'? I'm shocked," I teased.

"If only that was an option. What a dream," Barra said.

We stood there near each other for another moment before it suddenly grew awkward. I should go. I had to respect that he got us separate rooms. That was intentional, and I knew what it meant. He wasn't taking me up on my sex proposal. Disappointing, but not altogether surprising.

Unlike me, Barra was sensible, rational, and controlled.

He'd probably weighed all the pros and cons. This situation with the two of us, however exciting it started, didn't work long term. And he was clearly a long-term kind of man.

We'd sleep in separate beds, have a pleasant breakfast downstairs together tomorrow morning, and by nightfall we'd reach Old Orchard and part ways. *No more mind-blowing orgasms or cuddles from him, greedy,* I told myself.

But if I wanted to, I could always go downstairs after my bath and see who was around. I was surprised to realize I hadn't done my usual scan of the room for potential bedmates. Huh.

Barra was grimacing a bit and squeezing his metal room key in one hand, looking like he wanted to get out of this uncomfortable moment as soon as possible. I swallowed down my disappointment and mustered a sunny smile. "Well, good night! Sleep well." I turned and unlocked my door.

As it closed behind me, I heard him quietly say, "Sleep well, Elikki."

I stepped into a warm, cozy room with beechwood furniture and—surprise, surprise—pale, yellow-painted walls. Brass candlesticks were scattered around, holding beeswax candles that burned cheerily. A cut-glass vase held a small bouquet of daffodils, probably the first of the season. Despite the dark night outside, the room felt bright and filled with light. I saw my pack leaning in one corner. Fluffy white and yellow pillows filled half of the plush bed, on which a robe and towel were laid out. And best of all, a metal bathtub sat at the foot of the bed, radiating a gentle heat.

I groaned. I pulled the curtains closed, then shed my clothes—all covered with a fine layer of road dust and horsehair from our travels—and practically leaped into the tub. Splashed some water over the edge, of course.

Goddess, it felt amazing. The perfect temperature, just hot enough. This tub was wide and deep, and I ducked under to douse my hair. It smelled like Legus had scented the bathwater with something. Was that lavender and…jasmine? Fancy, for a little country inn.

Finding a round cake of soap sitting in a dish nearby, I did a full wash. After that, I rinsed my hair and rested back against the curved metal. I lost track of time. It was so soothing to just sit in this hot tub and drift blissfully. I was full, warm, clean, and I smelled incredible. A nagging feeling in my chest was the only thing that stopped this night from being perfect. My mind kept going to Barra, probably sitting in his own tub just like me right now. Naked. And very wet.

He was probably only what, twenty feet away? Two wood walls and two slabs of metal were all that was between our bodies. That, and some distance.

I imagined the water dripping over Barra's lavender-skinned forehead, down his large nose. It sluiced over those huge shoulders and across a broad, muscled chest that I hadn't seen—I wish I could have seen!—but had already imagined often in the short time I'd known him.

Picturing him dripping in his bathtub—maybe scrubbing with a tiny washcloth and spreading bubbles all over himself—I reached down into the water to touch myself. Surely it wouldn't be bad to just think about him while I did this? I slipped two fingers into the folds of my pussy, rubbing slowly and firmly.

I let out a deep sigh. Sinking lower into the water, I saw Barra behind my closed eyelids. He was standing in his tub now and stroking his huge cock firmly in one hand. Breathing heavily, he gripped one side of the high tub, muscles straining as he built toward climax. He clenched—

Knock, knock.

My eyes flew open, fingers freezing on my clit. Someone was at the door. Not Barra's door in my wankdream, but my real door, here in this room.

Oh shit. Was it him? Did he sense me in here thinking about him and come over?

"Elikki, I have your dessert. And I've come to clear away the tub." Legus's kind, deep rasp sounded through the door.

I hadn't realized the water had cooled around me. I must have been in here for ages. "Sorry, just a minute!" I called.

Getting out quickly—and splashing a small wave on the floor again—I grabbed a towel and dried off as best I could. I threw it on the ground to soak up the puddle, then wrapped the soft robe around me before flinging the door open.

The dragonborn innkeeper filled the doorway. He held a covered woven basket in one scaly hand. Holding it out to me, he said, "Saho sent me up with this. Make sure to compliment them tomorrow or I won't hear the end of it."

I took it with a smile. "Thanks! Dessert is the perfect way to top off the most relaxing evening I've had in weeks."

"May I?" Legus gestured to the bathtub.

"Of course, of course," I said. "Do you need help?" I moved as if to grab one handle on the tub.

He chuckled, tucking the damp floor towel under his arm. "No, small one." Grabbing both ends, he lifted the tub like it was as light as the dessert basket. "But you are sweet to offer. A kind heart. I'm glad Barra has you."

I blinked. He was gone before my brain could catch up enough to say that Barra didn't have me. We were just traveling together. He hardly knew me.

I put the basket on my bed and lifted the cloth off. Two large slices of lemon cake were nestled inside, drizzled chaotically with white icing. Wow. I knew I gave off big "two desserts" energy, but that was going to be a lot for even me after the dinner we'd had.

Then I saw the small bottle of mead tucked next to the plate. And two glasses.

Saho, you wily busybody.

They had intentionally given me both desserts. So that I'd have to bring Barra's over to him. I groaned for the second time in an hour, this time in annoyance.

Good try. I'll just eat both desserts. *And* drink the mead. That'd serve Saho right. And Barra, for turning me down. Again. I couldn't face him right now. I just wanted to have my cake in bed and then pass out in this pile of pillows.

I took a bite of one slice. Sweet lemon burst onto my tongue, the light sponge almost melting in my mouth. It was quite possibly the most delicious cake I'd ever tasted.

"Fuck you, Saho," I grumbled to myself. I don't think my conscience would leave me alone if I deprived Barra of trying this too. And, to be fair, I got to ride Pebble most of the day while he walked. Maybe he deserved it. I pictured him enjoying the cake—maybe still covered in bath bubbles—and made up my mind.

I took one more bite and then sighed, covering the dessert up with the cloth again. I tiptoed out my door, crossed the dim hallway, and placed the basket in front of Barra's room. Chewing my lip, I hesitated. He wouldn't know it was out here for him unless I knocked.

Steeling myself, I rapped two quick knocks on the wood

and bolted back to my open door. Just as I reached it, I heard a low voice.

"Elikki?"

I paused, then swiveled, plastering a smile on my face. Barra stood leaning in the doorway. He'd changed into a pair of loose drawstring pants and a knit sweater. His hair was wet, combed and hanging around his face. Damn, he looked good.

"Did you need something?" Spotting the basket, he reached down. "What's this?"

"Saho sent up some dessert," I said.

"This one has a bite missing," he said, frowning.

"Two bites," I said, inching backward. "Well, good night! Again!" I moved to close the door.

"Do you want to join me?"

I hesitated. "Do you want me to?" I asked, confused.

Barra slowly padded toward me across the hall. The closer he got, the faster my pulse raced.

"Yes," he said.

"But…I thought that you—" My mouth snapped shut as he leaned in, reaching one arm behind me. He grabbed the doorknob and tugged it closed, trapping me outside.

Barra's arms bracketed me against the door. I could smell his minty, woodsmoke scent, and I had to stop myself from tucking into him and inhaling. It was too dark in the hallway to see his face properly. But I could sense him. Tensed. Breathing too rapidly, like me. He was going to kiss me. *Please let him kiss me.*

And then suddenly he was gone, striding back across the hall. He scooped up the basket. Not looking back, he entered his well-lit room and disappeared to the right.

I followed him without thinking. It wasn't until I was inside and had closed the door behind us that I realized I was still in my robe. Feet bare, and my hair a wet, tangled mess since I hadn't combed it out yet after my bath.

Looking around, I took in Barra's bed, his tidy belongings, and the burning fireplace he stood next to. His room was easily twice the size of mine. With dark, polished wood furniture and sage green walls, the decor almost made me feel like we were back in the woods. There was a large window, closed tightly against the cold night, and I could see the moon shining through. It was nearly full.

With my back to him, I held in a smile and loosened the neck of my robe a bit so that my cleavage would show.

What an interesting turn of events.

12

BARRA

What was I thinking? This was exactly the kind of situation I hadn't wanted to find myself in tonight.

For the past hour, all I could think about was Elikki. She was just across the hall. Maybe still in her bath, dripping wet. Or already stretched out on her bed, yawning and sleepy. It was driving me mad. I'd felt myself nearing the edge of my self-control, and all I wanted to do was rush across the hall and be near her.

So I threw on some clothes and decided to go downstairs for a distraction. Saho at least would be awake; I knew from past trips that they were a complete night owl. Even if they'd talk my ear off and probably pry about "my lady," at least I'd put distance between myself and her until I could be sure she was asleep.

As I was about to leave, two knocks sounded on my door.

Swinging it open, I found Elikki hurrying to her room and the basket she'd left behind. When she turned, uncertain but still her confident self, my resolve started to crumble. And when I saw she was wrapped in only a robe, damp skin flushed, I think I blacked out for a minute.

Now she was here. In my room. Wandering around. Looking extremely sexy.

I coughed nervously, clearing my throat. Arranging the plate of lemon cake on a small table in front of the fire, I laid forks next to it and set the mead bottle and glasses out. Elikki joined me. We settled into the two armchairs that were tucked close to the table.

"This seems very unfair. Why do you get this massive room, with a full *fireplace*?" Her eyes sparkled with mischief.

"Well, I'm much bigger than you. I need more space to move around," I said.

"Mine is half the size of yours, and we paid the same amount!"

"Ah. You see, I received the friend discount. You got the friend of a friend discount. Big difference," I said, moving the plate toward her.

Elikki ate a big bite and pushed it back to me. "You need to try this. It's incredible."

I took a forkful, and it was like summer in my mouth. Bright, citrusy, both sweet and sharp—even Monty would be impressed with Saho's creation, and she had notoriously high standards for any fellow chef's cooking. I ate another large bite and tried to memorize the flavor. Maybe Saho would let me steal the recipe for my sister.

"Want some?" Elikki had uncorked the mead and was

pouring a bit into a squat glass. It caught the fire's light, a dark golden slosh.

"I don't drink much," I said. "But I'd take a dram."

She poured a second small glass and handed it to me. Our fingers brushed, and I quickly sipped the mead.

"What do you think?" she asked.

"Lightly sweet." My mouth was somehow dry, and I took another gulp. "Rich flavor." She was watching me steadily, her silver eyes tracking my movements. "Smooth."

"Very smooth," Elikki agreed, sipping. A smile played at the edge of her lips.

I set my glass down on the table, suddenly afraid of having any more. "Maybe we should call it a night."

"Already?"

"Maybe."

She ate another bite of cake. I watched a couple of crumbs clinging to her full bottom lip, again. Stopped myself from brushing them away, again.

"Why did you invite me in here, Barra?"

"I…I couldn't finish all of this on my own," I said, gesturing to the dessert. "And Saho would be devastated if they thought we didn't like it." That sounded reasonably plausible.

Elikki ate another forkful. And another. And another. When the cake was gone, she washed it down with a long drink of mead.

"Well," she said. "We finished it. Should I go now?"

I was frozen. Muscles tensed, I clenched the arms of the chair, eyes locked on the dancing flames of the fire. I didn't know what to do. If she stayed, I felt like I'd be gone for her. I'd lose myself again. Need her too much. But if she left…

After a long silence, I heard her sigh. She stood and began moving toward the door.

"Wait."

Elikki paused, turning.

"What do you want from me?" I asked, frustrated, wary. "What is this?"

She walked closer. "I want to make you feel good." Her voice was sweet as the mead, warm like the fire burning next to us. "Like you did for me."

I drew in a ragged breath. "What if I just do that for you again? Would that be enough?"

Elikki stepped in between my legs, her thighs nudging them farther apart.

"I can make myself feel good," she whispered.

She moved her left leg until she was straddling my thigh. Lowering her weight onto it, she began to grind, slowly, against my leg.

She kept eye contact with me. Bold, daring me to do something, to grab hold of her. I didn't want to. I didn't want this to end. Had I ever met anyone this confident, this brash, this utterly sexy?

She moved against me, firm and intent. Pupils dilated, a pink flush crept over her neck and cheeks. Her breathing grew shallow.

"Elikki. Do you have any panties on?" I said, my voice low.

She shook her head, rubbing herself harder on my leg. I wrapped my arms around her waist, steadying her. I moved one hand down her curves to her ass, palming her through the fabric of the robe. She whimpered and grabbed my arms.

"Touch yourself," I said quietly, straining to control myself.

She moved one hand down to her pussy at my command. Shifting her weight back, she dipped her fingers in a rhythmic circle over her clit. Her robe slipped off a bit, exposing a perfect, soft shoulder. Eyes closed, she dug her nails into my arm that gripped her close.

I forgot what I was worried about. I forgot about all my past relationships, the hurt, the loneliness, and my fears about future pain. All I could see was Elikki, shamelessly riding my thigh to orgasm, and everything else I wanted her to do. There must be something wrong with me that a deep part of my heart cries out "Use me, use me!" to every person I'm attracted to who shows half an ounce of interest.

But right now I didn't care. She could have me. I'd deal with the consequences in the morning, damn them all.

I swung Elikki's legs around my waist and held her tight against me, firm on my lap. She ground against the length of my cock, hard through my pants. Pulling the robe down fully off her shoulders, I revealed her full breasts. She wiggled out of the sleeves and lifted her chest to me.

Nearly lightheaded from the sensation of her grinding on top of me, I bent my head and sucked at one of her rosy-pink nipples. She whimpered again. Her hand moved between us, and I licked and nipped the rigid points of her breasts, loving the sound of her losing control.

Elikki went taut against me for a moment, and then gulped for breath. Clenching my shirt between her fists, she gasped, "Oh fuck, fuck! Yes, yes, yes, *fuckkkk*."

I held her through her orgasm, moving from her nipple to her neck. I kissed her there, lingering, blowing cool air on her sweaty skin.

Hands came up to my jaw, and Elikki pulled my face to

her eyeline. She gleamed with satisfaction. Stroking the sides of my face, she watched for my reaction, her eyes unguarded and waiting.

I didn't think. I closed the short distance between us and kissed her. Her hot lips met mine, hungry. She tasted as delicious as I remembered.

Honey and sunshine. Warmth and desire.

She hummed happily against my lips and deepened the kiss, wrapping her arms around my neck. I rubbed my hands along her back, feeling the soft curves and dips. I wanted to touch her everywhere, all at once. And this damned robe was in the way. It still hung around her waist, covering the lower half of her body. That wouldn't do.

I planted my feet and stood, lifting Elikki up with me. She laughed and locked her legs around my waist at the ankle.

"Are we going somewhere?" she said. "I was just getting comfortable."

"My bed," I growled.

"Oh, good," she said, wriggling happily. She kissed the small patch of my chest that was visible at the top of my sweater. My cock jumped, and I focused on walking steadily toward my large bed on the other side of the room. Lowering her onto the green coverlet, I nuzzled Elikki's soft tits.

"Can I get you out of this robe?" I said, kissing her rib cage.

She stretched at my touch. "You first," she said, propping herself up on her elbows.

I hesitated, then pulled my sweater and undershirt off. Elikki raised an eyebrow. She looked pointedly at my pants.

"I'd rather...leave them on. For now," I said. Maybe it was silly, but the pants felt like my last line of defense.

Elikki looked like she wanted to protest. But she held herself back. Instead, she shrugged and focused on untying the tightly knotted sash at her waist. Gently pushing her hands away, I undid the knot in seconds. I was going to wash that disappointment off her face.

She lay sideways on the bed, legs dangling partway off. I moved close, leaning to unwrap the robe from her body. I took in her plump, soft stomach, hips flaring wide and solid beneath my hands.

"You're so beautiful, El," I said in awe.

She smirked. "I know."

My palms roved over her strong, thick thighs, squeezing them reflexively. I kissed her belly.

"Goddess, that feels amazing," she said with a groan.

"This?" I said, planting another kiss on the soft skin of her stomach.

"No, your hands," she said. "My muscles are so sore from riding."

"From riding my leg? You were going at it quite intensely," I murmured with a smile. Shifting my hands to better massage her tight thigh muscles, I focused on the task, trying to ignore her bare pussy a few inches away.

She snorted. "No, from the horse. I haven't ridden in a while. Beginning to think it was a mistake."

Elikki groaned again, flopping back on the bed as I found a particularly tender spot. Working it away, I then moved slowly down her legs, massaging as I went. I kissed every thigh dimple I found. Her calf muscles were sculpted and firm from walking. My thumbs rubbed away knots and loosened the tight muscles.

When I got to her feet, Elikki's blissed-out groans and mumbles reached a new level.

"Ohhhh, fuckkkk. Barra, yes, yes, that spot."

After who knows how long, she quieted. I continued massaging, more gently now. It made me so happy to see her like this, cared for and calm. I would do this for hours, every day, if that's what she wanted.

Propping herself up again, she grinned lazily at me. "That. Was. Incredible. I can't remember the last time someone did that for me."

She paused, thinking. "Well, a couple months ago. At a winter festival up north for the moon goddess. But that guy just did the feet. Think he had a bit of a fetish."

"I can't blame him," I said, kissing the arch of her left foot. She shivered, smiling.

Elikki sat up and reached for me. I let her pull me in, and she hooked her legs around the backs of my thighs. Skating her palms lightly over my bare chest, my shoulders, my arms, she explored me in a way I hadn't let her before. She brushed her lips across the ridges of my muscles. I felt her tits press against me, and I filled my hands with their weight.

One of her small hands found my cock and began to caress me through my pants. I was already hard, and her touch made me rigid.

"Is this okay?" she whispered. Our heads were bowed together. I rested my forehead against hers.

"I don't want you to stop," I said. "But…"

Her hand stilled. "But what? You can tell me."

I didn't know how to explain. How do you say *don't hurt me*? *Don't disappear*? *Don't make me love you*? Everything sounded so melodramatic in my head.

"El, what do you want from me?" I just said.

She pulled back a little, her eyes searching mine. Moving her hands away, she said, "I don't want anything from you. I just want to give you pleasure. Like you've done for me, a few times now. You deserve to feel that too. You—you know that, right?"

Did I? In most—maybe all—my relationships, my pleasure had come second.

Was that because of me, wanting to make my partners happy? Or was it really them, and their selfishness? I didn't know anymore.

And here was Elikki, such a force of nature in all things, trying gently to give me something. To return care with care.

I wanted the press of her hand against me. I wanted her full laugh and her flippant smile. I wanted the pleasure that her eyes promised when she looked at me, full of excitement and affection.

Letting out a shaky breath, I cupped the back of her neck with one hand and kissed her again, long and slow. She followed my lead, meeting my lips eagerly but letting me set the pace. With my other hand, I pulled loose the drawstring tie of my pants. Pulling back from Elikki's mouth, dizzy with lust, I let my pants fall and gripped the hard length of my cock. Her eyes widened.

I took one of her hands in mine and guided it to my shaft. She wrapped around me with a firm hold at the base and slowly moved up and down. I found myself relaxing bit by bit.

"Okay?" she asked in a low voice. Her other hand stroked my cheek, my neck. I leaned into her again, focusing on her herbal-sweet scent and the feel of her.

"Yes. Very okay. Better than okay," I said.

"Just tell me if you need a breather. Barra?" she prompted when I didn't answer.

"I will. I will," I assured her.

Elikki scooted back a bit on the bed and bent at the waist, bringing her mouth close to my cock. She licked up one side of my shaft, then swiped around the ridge of my tip. She did it again and again, circling around, before covering my whole tip with her hot, wet mouth.

I was lost to the sensation, completely at her mercy. But I knew she'd stop if I asked.

I didn't want her to stop.

Weaving my fingers through her tangled hair, I gripped it loosely and held on. Elikki was sucking and still stroking most of my length with her small, strong hands. It felt too wonderful. My blood sang, and I squeezed my fingers and toes tight. I was going to—

I was going to—

I jerked away from Elikki suddenly, my cock popping out of her mouth. She sat up, surprised, and I came, hard and fast. I saw stars for a second, my orgasm exploding against my will.

When my vision refocused, I went stock-still.

My cum was splattered across Elikki's chest and collarbone. It dripped down the slope of one breast, a drop wavering dangerously on her nipple.

We were both frozen, watching each other and the mess on her naked body. I was mortified. In one part of my brain, this was incredibly hot. In the other, bigger part, I couldn't believe I'd let that happen.

This was bad. So, so bad. She was going to hate me. I was disgusting. How could I let this hap—

Elikki burst out laughing.

I stared at her as she crowed, body jiggling with the force of her laughter. She pressed one hand on her chest as she tried to catch her breath. Finding the cum there, she looked at her hand and started laughing again.

"Elikki—I am so sorry. So *so* sorry," I said, still frozen in front of her.

"Ohhh goddesses!" she said. She wiped tears of mirth from the corners of her eyes with her non-cummy hand. "Well. I count that as a success."

I yanked up my pants and raced around the room looking for my damp bath towel. I found it, then rushed back to her and began to clean off her chest. I dabbed gently, on my knees in front of her, wiping up every drop. It was shockingly erotic, even though I still felt horrible.

One of her hands came over mine. She stopped my cleaning.

"It's okay, Barra. I'm fine," she said. "It was an accident."

I couldn't look her in the eyes.

"Really. I understand," she said, massaging my neck. "If it was anyone else, I'd be pissed. But I could tell you didn't mean to."

"I didn't," I said.

"It was even weirdly…adorable? And your face—hilarious." She chuckled again. "So shocked!"

"I'm really sorry," I repeated. I could feel that my face was flushed.

"And I say that it's really okay." She gathered me close and hugged, wrapping her arms around me. "Let's just make a better plan for next time," she said, a smile in her voice.

Next time.

She wasn't mad at me. I hadn't screwed everything up.

I sank into her warmth, running my palms up and down

her back. Ducking into the nape of her neck, I kissed her there. I found her ear, tracing the pointy elven tip with my tongue. She shifted against me, and the heat between us charged again.

Moving my lips down, I kissed across her chest. I tasted the faint hint of cum. Her breathing quickened. I looked deep into her stone-gray eyes and then ran my tongue from between her breasts all the way up to her throat.

"Fuck, Barra," she breathed.

Finding my way to her nipple—the one that had been dripping with my cum a minute ago—I circled it with my tongue and then sucked. When it was a hard bud, I ran my teeth against it as I palmed her other breast. Looking up into her eyes again, I bit lightly. Elikki's gaze was dark, her laughter gone as suddenly as it had come. I bit down harder. Her eyes flashed, desire burning through her.

I moved my attentions to her other nipple, giving it the same treatment. Dipping my fingers down to her pussy, I murmured, "You're so wet for me."

"I have been since I was in my bath," she said. "Thinking of you. And touching myself."

I started growing hard again at the image. "You were thinking about me?"

"Yes," she panted.

"I thought about you too," I said, nipping gently at the sides of her breasts, her belly. She lifted her pussy up to me, a pleading look on her face. I held her down with one arm. Moving ever so slowly down her body, I took my time as she squirmed. "I thought about the way you screamed my name last time. How much I wanted to hear that again. And what else I wanted to do to you."

I spread Elikki's thighs apart, burying my face in the

sweaty musk of her bush. Licking her the way she seemed to like, I focused on the small twitches and movements she made. Exploring, I adjusted my tempo and pressure to meet her need.

When she finally came on my mouth, I felt the same deep sense of satisfaction that I'd experienced last time. She ran her fingers through my hair, mindlessly swearing as the orgasm rolled through her. I drew it out with light, sensitive licks until she settled, sighing into the mattress.

Then I picked her up, repositioning her correctly on the bed so that her head could rest against the pillows. I grabbed a throw blanket and covered her up.

When I hesitated over her, unsure if I should lay down, she grabbed my arm and tugged. I let myself slide down into the bed beside her. She threw the blanket over me too and snuggled into my chest. Suddenly exhausted, as if my mind had finally caught up and remembered how tired I was, I found myself sinking into the mattress. Elikki smelled so delicious. I felt boneless and happy, and she looked much the same.

"Mmmm," she said, sleepily. "Good night."

Was she sleeping here?

I guess she was. Her breathing slowed. Eyelids closed. A peaceful little smile touched the corner of her mouth. Tentatively, I wrapped one arm around her and lightly stroked her back. She made a contented sound and shifted closer to me.

The candles burned down and went out. The fire crackled to embers. I lay there, holding her and soaking up this moment, until sleep overtook me too.

13

Elikki

I woke up slowly, morning sun seeping through the wide window. As I came to, I took stock of my surroundings.

Naked under the covers—not unusual.

Cuddled up next to someone else who's mostly naked—also not super unusual.

Feeling blissfully serene after a deep, peaceful night's sleep—very strange. Almost alarming.

I sat up slowly, blinking at the bright sunlight. I almost never slept through the whole night. The early years of being on my own, when I often had to sleep outdoors or in dodgy places, had forced me to adapt to more of a cat-nap style. I usually slept lightly, waking to the smallest noises, often needing hours to fall asleep for even a short time. It was a habit I mostly hadn't been able to shake all these years later.

Sex helped. A few drinks. A good solid lock on my bedroom door. But I could barely remember falling asleep last night. Just a calm warmth overtaking me, and Barra tenderly wrapping me with his blanket and his body.

It must have been the head. It was incredible, just as good as the first time, and it probably relaxed me so much I just drifted off. I'd also had a big meal. And a long day of travel. It definitely wasn't because of Barra specifically. Even if he did make me feel safe and cared for. Secure...

I looked down at him, still sound asleep. Shirtless, his lavender body sprawled over half of the bed, and I admired the muscles and curves of his thick torso, the slight paunch at his stomach. Last night I'd run my hands all over them, and my fingers itched to do it again now.

He looked so serene in his sleep. All those worries and anxieties that often flit over his face when he was awake were swept away.

I bet he slept like a baby every night. His mas probably read him and his sisters bedtime stories and sang lullabies when they were growing up. Tucked into his bed with gentle hands, a kiss on the forehead. I pushed down my jealousy at the thought.

It had been the circumstances that overrode my sleep survival instincts, I told myself. Not him. He was just a person that was here for now. Soon he wouldn't be. And that was fine.

I stretched hugely, enjoying the sensation of being well-rested and warm, comfortably swimming in this sea of a bed. Part of me wanted to lie back down and tuck into Barra's arms again. Maybe watch him while he slept. Enjoy the drowsy look in his eyes when he woke up and saw me.

But I desperately had to pee. Slipping down from the bed as quietly as possible, I put on my robe and padded out to the hallway bathroom. After I'd done my business and washed up, I glanced in the mirror.

Oh, shit.

With everything that had happened last night, I never got around to combing my hair. It had dried tangled, and now there was a huge, knotted mess blooming around my head. This was going to take forever to fix.

Still—worth it. I pinched my cheeks and smiled at my reflection. *Looking good, girl. Ravishing, as always.*

Grumbling only slightly at the state of my hair, I stopped in my own room to throw some clothes on and grab a comb before heading back across the hall. Forgetting that Barra was sleeping, I banged the door open.

"Oops! Shit. Sorry!"

But he was sitting up in bed, propped against a couple of gigantic pillows and glaring out the window.

"Oh, you're awake! Never mind, then," I said, jumping onto the bed.

"You're back," he said.

"Yeah, I had to pee. And freshen up a bit." I winked at him. He blinked back at me.

I started attacking my hair with the comb. Pulling one section apart, I worked it through in bits, painfully.

"Ow, ow, owwww. Stupid long hair," I said. "I'm chopping it all off!"

"I love your hair," Barra said.

I ignored the warm buzzing his words sparked in my chest and focused on hacking my way through the tangled strands. "Well, right now I hate it. I'd rather cut it than deal with this mess."

"Come here. I'll do it for you." Barra opened his legs to make space and patted the coverlet.

"Really?"

"Yes. I used to do it for my sisters all the time. Let me."

I wasn't going to ask twice. Scooching my ass backward on the bed, I kept going until I was pressed against his crotch. Leaning back, I laid myself against his solid, bare chest and wriggled happily.

Barra chuckled. "El, you have to move forward a little for me to do this." He tugged the comb out of my hand.

Sighing, I scooted away a bit. "Fine. But be gentle. I'm not above biting if you hurt my scalp."

"I've been warned," he said, starting to carefully move the comb through a piece of my hair.

I needn't have bothered. He worked through each knot methodically, making sure to hold the strands so it didn't tug painfully on my head. Whenever we got to a particularly nasty section, he distracted me with stories about all the mischief his younger sisters got up to when they were little.

"And I suppose I'm to believe that you were perfectly well-behaved?" I said, grimacing as he reached a tough tangle at the back of my head where I'd thrashed against the coverlet last night.

"I was, for the most part," he said. "I was afraid not to be."

"Right. Because your mas sound *so* strict."

"I know, I know. But it took me a while to realize they're such softies." He cleared his throat, hesitating. "I grew up with my da for the first years. With the giant folk, in the mountains not far from Nepu. It was…difficult. Half-giants aren't easily accepted among their own kind—giants or humans. My birth mother had run off when I was small. She wasn't happy with my da. Or me."

My chest tightened painfully, imagining this young, unhappy version of Barra. He continued, "My da cared for me, but he couldn't be everywhere. I was much smaller than the other giants my age, and children can be cruel. When I was about six or seven, he decided that it wasn't a healthy environment for me. I was bullied, I didn't have any real friends, and although overall the adults treated me with kindness, I could always sense the edge of pity and distaste that most of them felt toward me."

I touched Barra's knee, stroking it with my thumb. He worked the comb through my hair, gentle as ever, even as he spoke about this.

"So he arranged for me to live in Nepu. Get a fresh start. Ma Reese is technically my aunt—my birth mother's sister. She and her partner, Ma Wren, welcomed me with open arms. They'd already adopted Telen at that point, and they say that they'd always wanted a big family. Sassura and Monty came along soon after."

"Do you still see your father at all?" I asked.

"Oh yes, of course," Barra said. "We do a camping trip twice a year. And I try to get up to visit him at least once every month or so. It's too hard for him to be accommodated in Nepu. He's about seventeen feet tall," he said, affection in his voice.

"Damn! And I thought *you* were tall," I said. "Well, that's wonderful. That you and he still have a solid relationship, despite everything."

"It was difficult for him to let me go. But he wanted to do what was best for me. And even though I couldn't understand it when I was little—part of me just thought he didn't want me, like my birth mother—I realized later how untrue that was. And my mas made sure I knew how loved I was."

He had three parents and three sisters. I barely had one, even if you counted my mother and father together.

As if he was reading my silence, Barra said, "You told me before that your ma and da didn't get along. Were they together or did you grow up with one of them?"

I barked a laugh. "Neither. They lived far apart. Both found me to be too 'difficult,' so they were constantly shuttling me back and forth. I don't think I ever went longer than a year at a time with either one of them."

"Assholes," he said.

That surprised another laugh out of me. "They *were* assholes. They really were." The familiar hurt was there, that soreness on my heart whenever I thought of my childhood. But for once it felt good to talk about this, like lancing a wound I'd been ignoring for too long.

"I can't imagine anyone not wanting to be around you," Barra said, still running the comb through my hair.

"I don't know. I could be a lot when I was young," I said.

"Or maybe they just weren't enough."

Tears pricked the corners of my eyes. I blinked furiously, glad he couldn't see my face. I swallowed hard, then said, "Thank you. For saying that."

The comb stilled. Barra leaned in, resting his chin on my shoulder. "I meant it."

"I think—I think I was unhappy. For a very long time." *I think I'm still unhappy a lot of the time*, I thought to myself.

His arms looped around me, holding close. He didn't say anything. Didn't try to make it better or prod for more details. Just held me, somehow knowing what I needed in that moment. After a while, my body relaxed and he resumed his slow combing. The rhythm soothed me, though my skin felt stretched too tight.

"There," Barra said eventually. "All done." He gathered up the weight of my hair and smoothed it out, throwing it over one shoulder. Bending, he pressed a kiss to my bare neck. I shivered at the touch.

This all suddenly felt too intimate. I had to get moving.

Scooching from between his legs and off the bed, I said, "Thanks! I'm starving. Want to get some breakfast before we set off?"

"Oh. Sure." Barra stood. "Is everything okay?"

"Yeah, of course. All good." I took my comb from him and slipped out into the hall. "See you downstairs in a few!"

I could breathe easier once I was in my own room, the solid door closed behind me.

Where were my shoes? Focusing on hunting them down distracted me from the scramble of thoughts storming around in my head. Thoughts I couldn't quite look at straight yet.

The boots were strewn underneath a chair where I'd apparently tossed them last night. I put them on, then gathered everything else into my hefty pack. I looked myself over in the mirror.

Gorgeous. There was a small tinge of sunburn on the bridge of my nose, but otherwise my skin was just lightly tanned from the journey yesterday. I really needed to get a new hat. My familiar face reassured me like it always did. Heart shaped, with my snub nose set below slate gray eyes. Full, plump cheeks. I particularly loved my big rosebud lips—everyone always said I had a beautiful smile. I bit them softly to bring some color out.

Forcing a smile now, I said to my reflection, "Everything is fine. You're fine. You just need some breakfast and a good walk in the fresh air."

Braiding a strand of auburn hair on either side of my face, I kept talking to myself. I complimented my outfit—my third and last corset, a pale lilac. It was even lighter than Barra's skin.

I found myself thinking about the way his firm lavender muscles felt under my hands last night. He was almost shy at first, holding himself back from me. Most people I'd been with couldn't get out of their clothes fast enough.

But he'd taken his time, slowed everything down to a pace that should have frustrated me but honestly just made it that much hotter. I was used to instant gratification—if I wanted something, I got it. If wanted *someone*, I got them.

But Barra only gave me small pieces of himself, bit by bit. Even his cock—usually the first thing a man wanted to get out when we were together—he'd been so hesitant that I almost thought there'd be something wrong with it. But no, he was thick, curved, and *huge*. Goddess, he was huge. I wondered what he would feel like inside me, pushing deep. I wanted to feel his bare chest against mine, have him cover my body with his as he slid that long cock into me.

I closed my eyes, imagining it. Maybe he was still in his room. I could go over there, see what might happen…

I shook myself. Enough. We needed to pause. I could feel myself growing attached to him. The way he looked at me, combed my hair, kissed me so sincerely, somehow got me to open up about my past—it was all too much. Too much.

Staring again at my reflection, I refocused on checking over my clothes, pushing thoughts of Barra away again. Under my corset I wore a simple ivory short-sleeve linen blouse, along with a boot-length, dark gray walking skirt and black belt. When I finished weaving the two thin braids, I pulled the long strands behind my head and tied them together with a blue ribbon.

I kept my jewelry simple, thick silver earrings that hugged my lobes and wound delicately up to the pointy tips of my ears. At the last minute I threw a few weighty silver bangles on one wrist—I always felt more secure when I had some metal to hand. Just in case. I always had a couple of daggers tucked into my boot and belt, but there was something about the solid weight of simple metal against my skin that calmed me.

I pulled on my rucksack and headed downstairs. The main room was mostly empty, with just a few sleepy folks sipping at steaming mugs. I joined Barra at his table. He pulled an Elikki-sized chair over for me, and I smiled my thanks.

"Good morning! Again," he said, returning my smile. I didn't reply.

His deep voice unsure, he said, "I ordered breakfast for us. Hope that's all right."

"Oh. Okay," I said, plopping my pack on the ground.

"Well, more like Saho told me what we were getting," he clarified. "But it sounded like something you'd like, so I didn't protest."

"I'll eat anything right now," I said. I grabbed a mug, then reached across the table for the teapot. Barra moved at the same time I did, and our hands banged together.

"Sorry, sorry," he said.

"Nothing to be sorry about," I said, holding out my cup. He poured the fragrant black tea to the brim.

After a strained pause, he said, "You look very lovely this morning."

"Thank you, Barra."

"And those earrings are beautiful—your work?"

"They are, yes," I said, touching the metal tips of my ears. I gazed around the room, drinking my tea and avoiding his eyes.

There was an awkwardness between us that I hated. I could tell it was coming from me, but I couldn't seem to stop it. I just wanted to go back to when we bickered with each other, or when we'd chatted easily about things. Barra seemed so uncomfortable now, his brow furrowed and arm muscles clenched.

"El, is there something—" he started to say, just as Saho descended with two massive plates. They placed them in front of us with a flourish. Each was overflowing with big fluffy pancakes, covered in a cheerful yellow compote and whipped cream.

"Morning, beautiful!" they sang to me. "Chocolate chip and sunberry pancakes today. House special. Tell me how much you love them."

I cut a bite and chewed. "Mmm, so delicious, Saho, thank you. Oh—and the lemon cake last night was wonderful too," I said, remembering what Legus had warned. "We enjoyed it very much."

"I bet you did," they said mischievously, eyes twinkling. "I heard you *enjoying* it when I came up to collect the plates later."

"Scheming trickster. Menace," I reprimanded fondly. Barra was blushing, that dark pink shade making my heart squeeze. He was so cute.

Saho returned to the kitchen. I dug into my stack of pancakes. In the corner of my eye, I could see Barra doing the same, keeping his head down.

We demolished our breakfasts. When he was done, every neat bite tucked away and crumbs wiped from his mouth, Barra excused himself to go ready Pebble. I lingered with another pot of tea.

Maybe I should stay here for a little while. Just a week or two. Saho and Legus were so kind, and I felt sure I could convince them to give me a bit of short-term work for room and board. This was one of the nicest, friendliest places I'd ever stayed, and I could easily see myself cleaning rooms with Legus and chatting with guests. Gossiping with Saho in the kitchens or weeding the garden and learning more about their strange plants.

I'd been intending to stick around Povon for longer, before Felsith and my temper hastened me back on the road. So I found myself wanting to rest somewhere for a bit more. The new plan had been to do that in Old Orchard, but if I stayed here, Barra would have to continue without me. We could say our goodbyes now.

I wouldn't have to deal with the sudden discomfort between us or the jumbled mess of feelings I had around him now. He wouldn't fall for me, and I wouldn't have to disappoint him. He'd take Pebble to Old Orchard, finish his business there, and maybe I'd see him briefly again on his journey back home. It would be a clean break.

Ignoring the sharp twinge in my chest, I nodded to myself, knocking the last gulp of tea back and slamming down the cup. This was the right decision. Time to find Legus or Saho and see what they thought. I rose, making my way toward the kitchen.

"All saddled and packed up," Barra called. He ducked in the doorway, coming to me. "We can set off whenever you're ready, Elikki."

I considered him, suddenly exasperated. How dare he look at me like that, with such warmth and affection. And the way he says my name—*El-eee-key*—softly wrapping the syllables around his tongue with that deep bell of a voice. It was unfair.

He waited, expression growing worried again as I stood there watching him. I wanted to close the space between us and pull him down by the neck, smooth those anxious lines away from his forehead. He couldn't leave. My chest squeezed again at the thought, painfully this time.

That was a bad sign. Time to end this. "I was thinking..." I said, fiddling with my bracelets.

Barra came closer. "Yes?" he said.

I cleared my throat, scrambling to put the right words together.

Just then, Saho bustled up, arms straining to hold a large covered basket. "Provisions! Travelers need snacks for the road."

Barra lifted the heavy basket up for them. "Saho, it's barely a day's journey. This is too much." He pulled some coins from his purse, which the half-elf waved off.

"Pshhh, I've seen the way you two eat. You need all of this to keep up your strength," they said breezily. "It's just a bit of this, a bit of that. You can have a little picnic luncheon. And I packed a couple extra slices of lemon cake since you liked it so much."

They winked at me. I gave a shaky smile back.

And then we were being hustled out the front door, Saho's skinny hands prodding us along. Legus came up behind us and wrapped his arms around Saho, his tail curling tenderly over one leg.

"Come and visit us again anytime, my dears," Legus said, his red scales glinting in the morning sunlight.

"Thank you, friends. I should be back this way soon." Barra waved and went to get Pebble from the stables.

I hesitated, trying to muster up the courage to turn this fond farewell scene into an awkward request for a week's worth of work instead. They were both waving, smiling. Sighing internally, I just waved back. "Thanks again for everything!" Then I turned, following Barra.

Well, I'd tried. I guess we'll have one more day together. Resolving to keep my distance and cool things off with Barra, I pushed down the glee that squirmed around my stomach.

This was idiotic. I knew better.

But damn if I wasn't relieved.

14

Barra

Something was bothering Elikki. I must have done something to upset her without realizing it. Did I pull too much while I was combing? Or maybe it was the spunk disaster from last night? I wouldn't blame her for being annoyed about that today.

Whatever it was, I had to fix it. For a moment back at the inn, it had almost seemed like she didn't want to continue traveling with me. What I did must have been bad.

We'd been walking along the road for twenty minutes now—Elikki had opted to walk rather than ride Pebble, which somehow seemed like another sign—and neither of us has said a word. For me, that wasn't unusual. For her, that was definitely cause for alarm. She was always such a chatterbox.

I snuck a few quick glances down at her face as we walked. She looked lost in thought, a slight frown tugging at her mouth.

Say something, you idiot, say something! I took a few long, slow breaths, trying to calm down without her noticing.

"El—I mean, Elikki," I said. "Is everything all right?"

"Of course!" she said brightly. "Why wouldn't it be?"

Okay, this was really, really bad. I knew that tone all too well from my sisters.

"You can tell me. If anything's bothering you, you know?" I said, starting to sweat through my linen shirt.

"Mm-hmm," she said, not looking at me.

I reached for the waterskin hooked onto Pebble's back. "Do you need any water? Food? Or maybe you're too hot? It's quite sunny today."

"I'm not a plant you need to tend to, Barra," she said with a slight bite to her words. "I can take care of myself, and I'm *fine*. Just let me be, please."

I felt as if she'd slapped me.

I couldn't believe this was happening again. Not that I thought we'd ride into the sunset together—though I may have imagined it once or twice—but I'd let my guard down with her. Against my better judgment. After two years of keeping up my defenses. We'd laughed together, eaten meals, gone on the run. I'd *tasted* her. A flurry of moments from last night flashed through my mind.

We'd said that we would keep this casual. That was what she wanted, at least, and I was trying my best. I hadn't made any of my usual mistakes, going too fast too soon. Had I? I'd just been focusing on her and our time together. Having fun, like she'd said.

But I'd still managed to mess up somehow. Elikki was pulling away. She didn't even want to talk to me now. I was so stupid for thinking it could be different with her. I mean, for goddess's sake—she spent her life on the road! Constantly traveling, never putting down roots or being with one person for too long. She'd told me so herself.

And I still, somewhere in the back of my mind, thought I could be the exception. Despite all my past failed relationships. Despite all evidence to the contrary.

Stupid.

I slipped behind Pebble and walked on her other side. It helped to have the horse's broad body between us, blocking my view of Elikki. I could only see her dusty walking boots through Pebble's legs, and the swish of her gray skirt around her ankles. I took a long drink from the waterskin, forcing my eyes away from her feet and focusing on how the cold water moved down my throat.

Time went by, and we walked in silence. I counted my breaths and tried to relax my mind. We walked through a large prairie field, the road cutting straight through the middle. The sun beat down, and I resisted the urge to ask Elikki again if she wanted any water.

After a while, we entered another green forest of the Willow-isp Woods. Trees grew larger around us, some trunks triple the size of my torso. The road was smaller here, and it meandered in curves around the trees, up and down hilly inclines. Tiny birds chittered above our heads. They flew from branch to branch, dancing around each other and singing noisily. I spotted a few rabbits hopping around in the undergrowth. Encountering a small green turtle, I carefully picked it up before Pebble's hooves trampled it, moving it off the road and back onto the forest floor.

Elikki caught me doing this. She had a strange look on her

face, her mouth scrunched up tight. When her gray eyes met mine, I saw the woman I'd kissed just this morning. Then she shifted, darting her eyes away to look anywhere but at me.

"I—I'll catch up with you in a minute," she said. "Have to pee." She moved off the trail, slipping between large ferns and tree trunks until I couldn't see her anymore.

I should keep moving. This was probably creepy, waiting for her to pee over there, right?

Or—what if she was so uncomfortable with me now that she was actually leaving? For good. My heart seized up at the thought, but I took a breath. If that's what she wanted, it was up to her. I wouldn't make things worse and run after her.

Wait—her pack was still here, on Pebble. She'd never leave without that. It had all her earthly possessions. *Where is your brain today, Barra?*

Reluctantly, I tugged Pebble's reins a bit and started walking again. If the way she ran from the constables was any indication, Elikki could easily catch up with us when she was finished.

And when she was back, we were going to have an honest conversation about this weirdness between us. I would apologize for whatever I'd done, and we'd figure out a plan. If she wanted to journey separately, I could give her Saho's packed lunch and hold back to give her a head start to Old Orchard.

…And then return home instead. Where I belonged. That might be for the best. My family might be getting worried, and if Elikki didn't even want me here—what the fuck was I doing?

Lost in my thoughts, I ambled along the road. A sudden scream pierced the forest.

Elikki!

My mind froze for a split second in terror.

Then I dropped Pebble's reins and tore back up the road and into the woods, guessing at where she'd entered. The scream came again, more muffled this time, along with some loud, angry cursing.

"Elikki! ELIKKI!"

Panicked, I ran, swinging around for a glimpse of her. There!—a flash of lilac through the trees. I dashed toward her as quickly as I could, stomping plants and twigs beneath my feet.

"Gerroff! Agh!!"

A stout cloaked figure was wrestling with Elikki and trying to carry her off. They had one arm clenched around her neck, the other gripping her wrists tightly.

"GET. THE. FUCK. OFF. ME," she managed to grind out from the chokehold her attacker had on her. She thrashed back and forth, trying to throw them.

"Let her go!" I yelled desperately, still fighting through the undergrowth toward them. I reached for the sword at my waist and—*fuck*, I'd left my sword hitched to Pebble's saddlebags.

Elikki lifted one foot and kicked back, hard, ramming her boot heel into their knee. The attacker's leg buckled, and they loosened their grip on her. She wasted no time. Yanking one arm free, she called her power to her with a few abrupt movements.

Faster than a blink, a dagger flew into her hand, and she stabbed the arm that was clamped around her throat. The attacker yelped, releasing her. Elikki spun, slashing out again with the knife. They backed away, clutching their shoulder.

Their hood had fallen back, revealing a dwarf woman with light sandy-colored skin and an irritated face. No—she must be a half-dwarf because she was nearly as tall as Elikki. Full cheeks and a strong jaw led down to her sharply pointed chin, with the equally sharp slashes of her brows set above fierce and *very* vexed eyes. She radiated desperation. This was not someone I'd want to encounter in a dark alley, never mind that she was at least two feet shorter than me.

"All right, damn! Calm down," she shouted. "I wasn't going to hurt you!"

"*Calm. Down.* Really? CALM DOWN?!" Elikki advanced on the woman. Her face was beet red from being choked. Hair in disarray, fierce anger pouring out of every inch of her.

"I'm a bounty hunter! I'm supposed to bring you to Povon on the lord's orders."

Elikki shook out one wrist, thick silver bangles jangling, wincing at the pain from how tightly they'd grabbed her. "Good luck with that," she said ferociously, taking another stride toward her prey.

The bounty hunter stepped back. She'd pulled two long knives from somewhere and settled into an attack stance, seemingly resolved to settling this with weapons instead.

With a wicked smile, Elikki flung her arm toward the half-dwarf. The bangles flew off her wrist, zipping to her attacker. She curved her hand outward, whispering something. The metal expanded, widening.

Two clamped onto the bounty hunter's own wrists, jerking her back roughly against a tree. They pulled around the trunk and hooked together, forcing a pained shout from their prisoner. Two more held her ankles. The final bangle had stretched wide around the woman's head and settled on her neck.

"Drop your weapons," Elikki hissed.

"Let me go!" The bounty hunter writhed, but she was held fast against the tree. I watched, gaping. I think they both had forgotten I was there—if they'd ever noticed to begin with. They seemed quite absorbed in their fight.

Elikki's smile widened at the words. I did not like that smile. She looked like a cat who'd caught a mouse. And was going to eat it for dinner.

She lifted one hand and slowly made a fist. The metal circle around the half-dwarf's neck tightened as she moved. Tighter, tighter—until it was pressing against her windpipe.

"Wait!" the other woman tried to say, panic setting in when she realized what was happening. Her weapons fell to the forest floor.

Elikki's eyes gleamed.

"Wait? But why?" she asked softly, clenching her fist tighter. "This is what you were willing to do to me, just a moment ago. Remember? Wrapping your arm around my throat?"

The sharp metal cut into skin. The half-dwarf struggled to breathe.

I jumped forward and said, "Elikki, stop! That's enough!"

Startled, Elikki flung her other hand up. One of the bounty hunter's knives leaped from the ground and darted straight at me. I lunged out of the way, just barely avoiding it. It clattered against a tree and fell to the dirt.

I stared at Elikki.

She stared at me.

"Barra—I...I'm so sorry." Her eyes were wide, shocked. She blinked rapidly, hate fading from her face as if she was coming back to herself from a trance.

The gurgled sound of the half-dwarf's choked breaths drew our attention. Elikki immediately opened her fist, loosening the metal band's hold.

Her attacker-turned-prisoner sucked in ragged breaths.

"You nearly killed me!" she croaked, trying to wriggle out of her bonds. The metal remained tight around her ankles and wrists, still pinning her to the tree trunk.

Elikki had the grace to look a bit uncomfortable. "Don't be so dramatic. Besides, what do you call what *you* were doing to *me* before I got the upper hand?"

"*I* was doing my job and catching a dangerous criminal," she said, trying again to jostle her handcuffs. "You're wanted for maiming Lord Renalo's brother."

I groaned. A laugh bubbled out of Elikki.

"*Of course* he's a noble. The brother of some powerful lord. Of fucking course. That pompous, slimy, idiotic *asshole* had to be connected to someone in power. It's not enough that his cousin is a fucking *copper*," she said, half to herself.

"And two counts of disorderly conduct. And you started a brawl. And you disobeyed the orders of a town constable. There are witnesses," the bounty hunter said.

Looking hard at her, Elikki said, "Listen, I didn't maim anyone…intentionally. Okay? He was trying to make off with one of my most expensive wares. And he got all touchy-feely with me. It was self-defense."

"Just like *this* was?" She stretched her head back slightly, showing the bright red line where Elikki's metal had nearly sliced into her skin.

"Well…yes," Elikki said, slightly abashed.

"Look," said the half-dwarf, "it's not my job to judge who's right and who's wrong. They put a bounty on bringing you in. Kind of a cheap one, and I'm maybe regretting stooping this low…" She sighed. "Don't make this harder than it needs to be.

Just come with me back to Povon. I get my money, and I'm sure you can sort out this misunderstanding with the bigwigs there."

Elikki snorted. "Well, that's obviously not happening. But good try."

"She's not going anywhere with you," I said.

The half-dwarf looked up at me, skeptical. "Oh, really, big man? What are you going to do, flex your muscles at me? Frown harder?"

I scowled and crossed my arms across my chest.

"That's it. Be more intimidatingly purple at me. I'm shaking in my boots."

"Hey, leave him alone," Elikki said. "This is ridiculous. What's your name?"

She hesitated, and then grumbled, "Maerryl."

"Okay. Maerryl. I'm Elikki, as you know. This is my… friend, Barra."

Rolling her eyes, Maerryl said, "Pleasure."

Elikki took a calming breath and said, "If we let you go, do you promise to leave us alone?"

Maerryl paused for a beat too long. "Um. Yes?"

"Well, I'm convinced," I said dryly.

Elikki let out a frustrated screech. "Goddess dammit, dwarf! Right. Fine. We can't trust you. Option two."

She lifted both hands toward her prisoner. Grabbing them before she could do anything, I said under my breath, "Wait—you're not going to…" I trailed off, raising my eyebrows meaningfully.

"Not going to what?"

"…Kill her? Right?"

"DON'T KILL ME!" the half-dwarf shrilled.

"Oh, for fuck's sake!" Elikki cried. "Why does everyone suddenly think I'm a raging murderer?"

Yanking her hands from my grasp, she glared at me and then Maerryl.

"No, I'm not going to kill you. *Obviously*. But I am getting rid of you." She raised her hands again.

Sweeping her arms out, Elikki used her magic to move the bangle-cuffs on Maerryl's hands and feet again at her command. The wrists unhooked from behind the tree. Maerryl let out a relieved groan and swiveled her shoulders and arms to loosen them up.

With a jerk of Elikki's arms, Maerryl's ankles moved, propelling her forward across the forest floor. Her wrists moved in time with her feet, keeping her at a steady march around the trees and back toward the road.

"Elikkiiiii! Let gooooo!"

I stared after her, and then at Elikki. She was looking very smug with herself.

"How does this solve our problems?" I said.

"You'll see," she said and began walking after the baffled woman. She called over her shoulder, "Grab those knives, would you?"

I rustled around until I found Maerryl's knives where they'd fallen in the forest undergrowth. They were shoddy quality—the kind of pieces Ma Reese would melt down for scrap metal. I tucked them into my belt and followed Elikki out of the forest. When we all reached the road, Pebble was right near where I'd left her, munching on some grass. I went over and patted her neck, pouring some water into a large bowl for her to drink.

The two women stood glowering at each other. Without taking her eyes off Maerryl, Elikki said to me, "Write a note to Legus explaining the situation. It's not a horribly far walk to the inn. And if anyone could deal with this properly, I bet it's him."

She was probably right. We couldn't trust Maerryl not to follow us, and we couldn't take her with us. What else were we going to do, leave her tied to a tree? Someone might not journey this way for hours or days. Knock her out? I didn't want to hurt her, and I knew that deep down Elikki didn't either. Just because she'd lost her temper—understandable, considering she'd been jumped and put in a sleeper hold—didn't mean she wanted any real harm to come to the other woman. Probably.

So bringing her to the Painted Dragon might be our best option at this point. Legus could be intimidating and persuasive when he needed to be. He always knew how to deal with troublemakers. I'd once seen him firmly sit down a pickpocket who'd been bothering the inn's guests. Two hours and many cups of tea later, the thief was sobbing into the dragonborn's handkerchief as they worked through his abandonment issues together.

And after Legus sorted things out, Saho was usually able to win folks over even further with delicious baked goods. That pickpocket worked in the kitchens part-time now, last I'd heard. Watching Maerryl as she not-so-subtly tried straining against the metal cuffs' magical hold, a dark look on her face, I thought that even my charismatic friends might have their work cut out for them.

"But what is the note for? We can explain everything when we get there," I asked Elikki.

"I'm going to try to charm my bangles to take her there for us. Like they did just now," she said.

"I...didn't know you could do that."

She huffed a bewildered laugh and said, "I don't know if I can for sure. But my magic feels...good right now. Strong, and calm. I'm not sure how, but it's worth a try." Shrugging, she tried to act nonchalant, but I could feel the excitement rolling off her.

It seemed like something that would take a tremendous amount of her power. Maybe I should bring Maerryl to the inn instead. But I hated the idea of losing the remaining time I had with Elikki. If we left things so unresolved, I'd always wonder what had happened. What I did wrong.

More importantly, there might be more bounty hunters out to capture her. She shouldn't be alone right now. And she wasn't asking me to take Maerryl—surely if she wanted to get rid of me, that would have been an easy way to do it.

If she wanted to try trusting her volatile magic, that's what we were going to do.

After some discussion about the knives, we decided not to give them back to Maerryl. If things worked out at the inn, I could always return them later, on my way back. *After a good cleaning and sharpening*, I thought privately.

And if things didn't work out...well, it's probably best if she doesn't have weapons on her.

With that in mind, Elikki patted the half-dwarf down quickly. She found a few small daggers, which she pocketed, ignoring Maerryl's outraged squawk. She also lifted the thin, stretched bangle from around her prisoner's neck and sized it back down to fit on her own wrist. I caught sight of a runic tattoo tucked along the back of Maerryl's left ear, a thick scrawl that I didn't recognize as any standard runes in the realm. Unusual. Ancient runes were potent when etched into the body. There were only a handful that folks commonly used in the realm—those safe enough for a practiced mage to inscribe—protection against illness, warding off pregnancy, solidifying a partner bond, and so on. I'd never seen a runic tattoo so strange, the dark twisting symbols curving ominously along the shape of her ear. What could it mean?

Maerryl flexed her neck back and forth, clearly relieved to have the neck restraint removed. Her thick, bluntly cut hair fell back and covered the tattoo. "Listen, I think we got off on the wrong foot. It's clear now that I must have been…misinformed."

Elikki snorted, not deigning to reply, and closed her eyes to focus. The bangle-cuffs still held the other woman fast.

"But if you let me go know, I promise to leave you and His Royal Purpleness alone for good. I swear it," Maerryl tried, cajoling.

Ignoring her, Elikki stayed very still and intensely focused. Breathing deeply, slowly, she sank into her task of enchanting the bangles.

I found my paper and quill and, using Pebble's saddle as a writing surface, scratched out a note to Legus explaining our predicament and requesting his help. He was no doubt still going to be confused, but I could clear up the rest of the story when I saw him next. I signed my name neatly and blew on the ink to dry it.

After some time, Elikki came over to me. She scanned the letter and added a couple of lines. Looking over her shoulder, I read:

> *My bangles are charmed to bring her to you.*
> *They'll fall off when you say the release phrase—*
> *the name of the sweet dessert you served us last*
> *night. Thanks for your help. I owe you!—E*

After a moment's thought, she added:

Please keep the bangles as a token of my appreciation. ☺

"All right, let's finish this up," she said. She folded the letter, and then pinned it to the front of Maerryl's shirt.

"Look, I think we're all on the same page now," the other woman said. "I choked you; you choked me. We're even." She tried to shrug, but the bangle-cuffs limited her movements.

"Listen, lady. Be grateful I'm not knocking you out and leaving you tied up in the forest. That was my plan B if this didn't work," Elikki snapped.

The half-dwarf looked at me, wide nose wrinkling. "I have information about your boy toy, you know. Someone's not happy with him either."

Elikki paused. After a long beat, she said, "Fine. Tell us what you know, and I may release you."

"Release me first and I'll tell you everything."

"Counteroffer—if you don't tell me right now, I'll have these bangles make you run the entire way to the inn. It's what, an hour away?" she asked me lightly.

"More like two," I said.

"All right, fine, fine. You win." Maerryl huffed. "Word is Felsith was set on putting a bounty on you too, giant. Lord Renalo wouldn't let him for some reason. But from what I hear, he might try to go through...less official means to track you down. Better watch your back."

Elikki and I exchanged a worried glance. I did not like the sound of that.

Maerryl wiggled her arms and legs. "Now come on," she said, "get these stupid things off me."

"Sorry!" Elikki chirped. "Can't do that. But thanks for the warning."

She made a few abrupt motions with her hands. The bangle-cuffs twirled Maerryl's body around and sent her on a quick march back down the road. Her arms swung stiffly at her sides and her legs jerked like a marionette.

"Gahhh!" Maerryl shouted. Furiously, she yelled over her shoulder, "You'll pay for this, Elikki!"

"Bye! Hope we never see you again!" Elikki waved cheerily at the woman as she disappeared around a bend in the path, trees swallowing her up, the last of her spitting curses fading away.

"Well, that's done," she said, slapping her palms together. "The charm should last at least until she gets to Legus. Should we have a snack?"

I stared at her. She looked tired, weariness pulling down her shoulders and gathering in the tightness of her mouth.

"How did you even do that? It seemed so…easy. But I've seen magic worked before. There's lots of spells and…and runes. And it takes ages to do something that powerful."

Elikki reached for the waterskin, taking a long swill. Thinking carefully for a while, she then said, "I've had those bangles for a long time. Years. I made them myself from a block of silver I won in a card game. It was more about convincing them I need their help with this than anything. And pouring my will in to make it stick. But it definitely wasn't easy," she said with a long sigh, stretching out her neck muscles.

"Incredible. Did you ever have formal training? Try to become certified?"

I caught a flash of irritation, but I could tell it wasn't directed at me. "When I was younger, yes. Found a master through the Artisans Guild after I joined. She's a metal mage like me, working with bronze sculptures, but it quickly became apparent that my magic is strange. Difficult to control." She reached to fidget with a bracelet that was no longer there. "I've never really been able to use my power in the proper way—my mentor basically wrote me off as a lost cause after a year of failing to improve beyond simple spells—but friendly metal has always felt more malleable. Alive. It's hard to explain."

"El, I'm definitely no expert, but the magic I've seen you do while we've been together…it's not nothing. It's strong. Confident and self-assured. I think you have more control over your power than you realize." I paused, trying to find the right way to say this. "It just seems to go a bit, um, violent at times. Have you thought that maybe it's not your magical will that's the problem, but…but your anger?"

Elikki blinked at me, seeming to consider my words. Then she wobbled over to a large rock by the side of the road and sank down with a groan.

"Goddess, but I'm tired," she said. "Do we have time for a quick nap?"

I shook my head. Leading Pebble over to her, I held out my hand. She took it.

I wanted to ask her more about her magic, her time training with this mentor, everything. But Elikki seemed like she was about to pass out from exhaustion. Holding the stirrup steady, I waited as she clambered up from the rock into the saddle. I grabbed a few things from Saho's basket and then patted Pebble's neck, leading her forward on the road.

"Listen," she said. "I'm really sorry about earlier. Throwing the knife."

I swallowed, remembering the way the blade had whistled past me.

"I know," I said.

"It was just instinct. Reflexes. I didn't mean anything by it."

Her voice was strung tight. She gripped the reins with white fingers. I placed one hand over hers as we walked together through the quiet wood.

"I know. It's okay. We're okay." I slipped my hand away and passed her a buttery nut muffin.

We were going to be okay.

15

Elikki

I was not fucking okay.

Was this some kind of twisted cosmic payback for past crimes? I haven't even done anything that bad! Yes, stolen a few goods here and there. When necessary. Broke a few hearts. *Maybe* some light arson and breaking of bones.

But enough to deserve this kind of punishment from the gods?

No!

Yet now I was a wanted woman with a bounty on her head. Running from the law. Who had also gotten a sweet, innocent bookkeeper mixed up in her mess. And now, I guess, also a couple of new friends were involved in this disastrous shit pile of stupidity.

Truly, it's a shock no one sticks around me for long.

Over and over, I replayed that horrible moment when I'd almost stabbed Barra. The way he'd looked at me, so shocked.

Almost frightened of me. Self-defense instincts were all well and good, but I could have really hurt him. Killed him, even. And Maerryl too...I could see now that I'd gone too far. They were both right.

I'd just been so terrified in those seconds when she'd had me in a choke hold. And then anger soon followed, as it always did, once I got the upper hand. It unleashed something in me. And when that happened, sometimes it's hard to tell where the lines are.

My power—my own body—had betrayed me. I never wanted to slip up like that again. Especially with Barra, for the little time we had left together. I need to be more careful. Stop relying on my fight-or-flight instinct and just take a second to *think*. It shouldn't have taken accidentally throttling a stranger and almost maiming someone I liked to make me realize just how firmly I'd let my anger take hold of my magic over the years. But now that I could see clearly, I wasn't going to let myself hurt anyone like that again. Not even weaselly assholes like Felsith or his ilk...unless they *really* deserved it, of course.

I was taking control of my magic back.

The way I'd managed to charm those cuffs with Maerryl showed me I could do it. The sense of calm confidence I'd felt, a soothing wave that washed over me as I'd forced the fury and frustration aside and focused on the task at hand—it was astounding. It was like the perfect feeling I got when I managed a simple magical working or created something beautiful while jewelry making, but multiplied a hundredfold. Dare I say, it might have been even better than sex.

It had taken a hell of a lot out of me. I was wrung out, thoroughly exhausted. Like the chewed grass in Pebble's mouth, actually, is how I felt right now. And yes, it will probably be hard to get back into that calm, focused mental state next time I wanted to work some magic. But somehow, I knew I could do it.

Putting two people in mortal danger forced me to confront myself. I had so much anger simmering for so long, even when I didn't fully realize it—toward the communities that were supposed to raise me and instead turned up their noses. Toward the people who harassed me, attacked me, tricked me when I was young and naive, just learning how to survive by myself on the road. Most of all, toward my parents—their dismissal, their disinterest, their utter lack of love for me driving a wedge through my heart from childhood…driving me away from home, just like they wanted.

How had it taken me so long to see the depths of all this anger, how it had grown roots and taken hold of my emotions and my powers? I dashed the back of my hand against my cheeks, quickly wiping away the wetness there.

I wouldn't let my past define my future any longer. *I* had control over *my* magic. Not those ghosts. It was mine alone, and I intend to make the very most of it from now on.

We walked in silence along the road for a long time. Seated on Pebble, I tried to ignore my aching thighs and just relax into the rhythm of her gait. My drooping eyes drifted closed. So, so tired.

Pebble stopped. Barra swung up into the saddle behind me. Despite myself, I let my body relax back against him. He was solid and warm, a reassuring presence, and I felt the tension leaving me as I listened to his steady heartbeat.

"Wha' 'bout Pebble?" I mumbled. "Too heavy."

"She's fine for a bit. Strong horse. Just nap, El. You need rest," Barra said. "I'll wake you up for lunch."

Drowsy, I hummed my assent and let my mind drift. "Sweet. You're so sweet."

As everything faded and I slipped off to sleep, I felt Barra wrap his arms around me with a sigh. He held me tight and said, "So are you, love."

When I woke, we were slowing to a stop near the edge of a small lake. Barra brushed my hair out of my face with gentle fingers.

"Good morning. Or—early afternoon, I suppose. Sleep well?" His deep voice rumbled against my back. He still had me tucked against him, strong arms keeping me from tilting to either side of the horse.

I yawned hugely. Though I was reluctant to leave the cozy embrace, my limbs were aching with stiffness. I wiggled my way out, Barra releasing me quickly, and stretched my arms over my head. Rolling my neck and shoulders to loosen up the muscles, I took in the serene scene around us.

"Where are we?"

"About two hours along the road. Still have a few more until we reach Old Orchard. But I thought we should stop here and eat."

The water sparkled with sunlight. Next to the lake, the grass looked soft and inviting. A few early bumblebees buzzed around, and some bright splashes of color signaled the start of spring's blooms. I was tempted to drop down into the grass and slip back to sleep. But food also sounded wonderful.

My growling stomach decided the matter for me.

Barra braced himself and swung out of the saddle. He

reached up for me, waiting. Attempting a more graceful dismount this time, I twisted my left leg over the front of the saddle and turned so that I was sideways and facing him.

"I've got you," he said.

I slid off Pebble's back without hesitation. Barra caught me, his arms firm around my upper thighs, just under my ass. We were almost face-to-face like this, me just a little above him.

Barra's gaze searched mine. So serious and worried all the time. I traced one fingertip down the bridge of his large nose. His eyes closed. Touching his chin, eyebrows, cheeks, I committed his face to memory.

Gently, I leaned in and kissed him. He drew in a small, surprised breath and then kissed me back, his arms pressing me tight against him. I tangled my fingers in his hair and deepened it, twining my tongue around his. He'd worn my red ribbon again today, tied carefully in a bow, and it had been driving me mad all morning.

Barra followed my lead, kissing me hungrily as I captured his mouth. We were frenzied, lost in each other's lips. I hugged myself tight to his body and relished the way he squeezed me back, as if he wanted me as close to him as possible. When I nipped his full lower lip, he groaned so deeply I could feel the rumble through his chest.

But then suddenly he was pulling away. Just slightly, enough that it broke off our kiss and made me *hmphh* in protest.

"El, we should talk," he said.

I stiffened.

"I'd rather not," I said, trying to lean in for another kiss.

Barra evaded and reluctantly lowered me to the ground. "I know. But we still should."

"Why, exactly?" I stepped into his space again and ran one hand up his thigh. Flashing my wickedest grin, I trailed my fingers up up up and over to the laces of his breeches. Before I could even start to untie them, though, he firmly took me by the shoulders and stepped away.

With a pained expression, he said, "You may not want to, but I—I need to discuss some things. With you."

"Okay, okay." I raised my hands in a show of innocence. "But couldn't we just…continue this and talk *after*?"

Barra shook his head slowly. "No."

Apprehension, annoyance, and guilt rolled around in my empty stomach, making me queasy. This did not sound good. If we had to have a Talk, I should at least eat something.

"Fine," I huffed. After unhooking Saho's lunch basket from the saddlebags, I stomped over to the lake. Barra sighed and followed me, unfurling his blanket out over a soft-looking patch of grass before leading Pebble to the water for a drink.

I plopped down and pulled item after item from the large basket. Two stoppered bottles, a few large golden pasties, plums, nut cake, a watercress salad, a wedge of hard cheese, tiny apples, and a mysterious round breaded object that I couldn't identify. It was the size of Barra's fist and heavy. I left that in the basket and grabbed a pasty, taking a huge bite. Delicious. Chicken, potato, carrots, and something spicy that added a bit of a kick to each bite.

Barra joined me on the blanket. He laid out napkins and utensils for us. Oops. I always forgot about stuff like that. I offered him a pasty, and he accepted with a nervous smile. I popped one of the jugs open and took a long swill. A light, refreshing pear juice—perfect.

"Thank the goddesses for Saho, right?" I said, passing Barra the bottle. He grabbed a tin cup from the basket—*oops again, Elikki*—and poured himself some with a murmured thanks. I held out the other cup and he filled it up for me.

"They certainly found their calling as a cook," he said.

I nudged the big round thing wrapped in a napkin. "What do we think this is?"

"I know, actually. They packed one for me last time, but the recipe wasn't quite…perfected yet. They've been attempting to create a scotch egg egg."

Seeing my confusion, he went on, "So their idea was instead of just small individual scotch egg snacks, it would be one massive scotch egg. More filling and satisfying, especially for people like Legus and me. At least that was the concept."

He took a knife to the center of the breaded ball and began to saw into it. "In the one they gave me last time, the sausage meat wasn't exactly cooked all the way. But they said they've been experimenting more since then."

The ball finally split open into two halves. Each half showed four eggs—yellow yolks surrounded by their white rings. They were all packed in together with a light green mixture studded with brown bits. I dipped a fork into the mystery mixture to try a tiny nibble. "Mmm! It's some kind of potato mash! With bacon and…chives, maybe?"

Around all this was the traditional sausage-meat shell—this time it appeared to be cooked to completion—and finally the outer layer of crispy, golden breadcrumbs. "Holy shit." I gaped at the glorious vision in front of me. Picking up one half, I took an enthusiastic bite. "I think Saho is a genius."

Barra broke off a piece from the other half with his fork and tentatively tried it. His eyes widened. "Wow, they really did it. This is delicious."

"I want to write a love poem about this divine creation. An Ode to the Scotch Egg Egg!"

"The Master of All Eggs?"

"The Eggy Extraordinaire!"

"The One True Egg!"

I gulped more pear juice and sighed happily. "Now I just need a little dessert, and another nap, and then I'll be fully revived."

"Elikki…" Barra's voice lost its playfulness. Oh no. He hadn't forgotten about the Talking.

I chewed more of the egg egg and swallowed. "All right, what's on your mind?"

Sitting cross-legged next to me, he watched the rippling lake.

"I think we should discuss…everything. What's going on between us." He spoke carefully, eyes flicking to check my reaction. "I clearly did something to upset you this morning. And whatever it is, I'm so sorry. But—but I need you to talk to me instead of just shutting down. Can you tell me what you're feeling? What's going on?"

He paused, waiting for me to respond. Several minutes went by. In my mind, there was a storm of thoughts—a dozen things I should say—but I also felt terribly blank. Numb.

He tried again, saying, "Everything that happened in the woods—that must have been terrifying for you. I understand why you reacted the way you did. Really, I do. It's just…you can't kiss someone like that, here, after ignoring them for hours and then almost stabbing them. Me. You can't use me like that, as—I don't know, as a release for your fear and anger and frustration."

Barra wanted to catch my eye, but I avoided him. I rolled a plum in my palms and tracked a hawk swooping over the lake. We sat in silence.

"If you want me to just go, I can," he finally said. "I can head out now and ride Pebble so you have the road to yourself. Or hang back here for a while and give you a head start. It's fine."

He waited again, the long moment stretching out into minutes. My tongue felt numb. For once, I had no idea what to say. I was frozen on the blanket, staring down at the dark plum in my hands like it held an answer for this stupid, ridiculous problem I'd somehow stumbled into. There *was* no right answer. What do I do?

He should go. I should let him go. Everything would be easier.

Everything would go back to the way it had been. The past days wouldn't matter anymore. I could have the road to myself, like he said. Complete freedom, beholden to no one, the whole world open to me. That's what I wanted.

Is it *all* I wanted though? Barra wasn't trying to take any of that away. Maybe there was a way I could have all that—everything I cared about—and still have someone like him in my life. Someone to share laughter, dancing, music, silliness, amazing sex, and long conversations over tasty meals. All of it.

Or him, specifically.

And this ache that I felt when I pictured it—us together, never parting—it was so good. Like when I jumped off the cliffs of Morfya into the sapphire-blue ocean for the first time after

I'd finally left home. Exhilarating. Terrifying. And more powerfully satiating to my soul than anything I had let myself imagine before. I just needed the courage to jump.

But Barra was clambering to his feet. I caught a glimpse of his shuttered face, and something stabbed sharply in my chest. He walked away from me, clicking to Pebble as he swung her around. Dropping my pack on the ground, he led the horse back toward the road.

He couldn't just *go*. He wouldn't.

"Wait!"

Barra turned.

"You—you forgot your blanket," I said.

His face fell even further somehow.

"Keep it," he said as he turned away.

I watched as his large form became smaller and smaller, until he disappeared in the tree line. He didn't look back.

I was alone again.

16

Barra

ell, that was it then. I'd left. Elikki will go her way. I'll go mine. It was the right thing to do.

Wasn't it?

Yes, absolutely, I told myself bitterly. *She wouldn't talk to you. Didn't even look at you.*

Whether she refused to communicate or just plain wanted you gone—that silence was pretty damn clear. I swung up into Pebble's saddle.

This wasn't doing me any good. She'd made her decision, and I'd made mine. I'd done what I'd always told myself I would, for the past two years. I needed to stand up for myself, make my feelings and thoughts known. Letting someone walk all over me—no matter how magnificent they were—wasn't healthy for either of us.

If she didn't want me, I had to move on. I shook myself and tried to focus on what I was doing. Not think about Elikki alone, all by herself, sitting by the lake looking like she'd always known I would leave.

Squeezing my eyes shut, I wiped away the wetness that threatened to spill over my cheeks. Pebble kept moving down the road back west. We moved closer and closer to my family—my normal life—with every minute. And farther and farther away from her. I settled in my seat and tried to relax. Distract my thoughts from where they naturally wanted to go.

Time trudged along in a gray fog. I attempted to focus on the trees and the birdsong, with little luck. My mind kept drifting back to her.

Her heart-shaped face, so sad as she avoided my gaze. Distance in her eyes. She looked out at the lake, world-weary, as if she was calmly waiting for the next inevitable disappointment.

"Is that him?"

A low, hissed voice pulled me out of my reverie. Two grimy-looking men were approaching me on the road. They rode bony plodding horses whose flanks were caked with even more dirt than the humans were.

One of them stared hard at me, utterly unselfconscious. A slow grin stole over his face.

I didn't say a word.

They passed by. When they thought they were out of earshot, they bent their heads together. "Yeah, I reckon that must've been him. She's probably close by."

My back stiffened. No. No no no.

They were after Elikki.

What was I supposed to do? Turn back and play the valiant rescuer? She would hate that. However much I knew she could handle herself though, I kept seeing Elikki as I'd left her. By the lake, still tired even after her nap. She might have tapped out her magic during the last encounter. I didn't know exactly how it worked. *She* barely seemed to understand how her magic worked.

I reasoned with myself. Even if that was true, and she couldn't use her metal magic, she certainly wasn't helpless. Elikki had daggers hidden all over her body. I'd seen them.

But—I couldn't help thinking of buts—what if she'd fallen back asleep again? What if she'd decided to take a dip in the lake? What if those thugs took her by surprise, pouncing like Maerryl had in the woods?

There was nothing for it. I had to turn back.

I swung Pebble around by the reins, forcing myself not to go galloping after the men immediately. It wouldn't help to draw attention to myself. And though I knew I had an advantage—my massive size, sword, and Pebble's bulk usually dissuaded anyone from attacking—I didn't love the odds of two against one on an empty road in the woods. Better to track them at a distance and see if they made a move against Elikki.

Up the road, I could see the pair approaching the point where a path split off to the lake. They were snickering over something, one of them reaching out to punch the other in the arm with a guffaw. Spotting the side trail, they looked at each other and shrugged.

I held my breath.

They turned their horses to the right and headed down to the lake.

My stomach dropped. If she had resumed her nap, Elikki was in real danger. They'd find her, catch her by surprise, and tie up her hands so she couldn't magic her way out. And then what? She'd be dragged back to Felsith for his revenge?

I couldn't let that happen. I wouldn't.

Drawing my sword—I remembered, this time—I urged Pebble faster. We reached the side trail and turned. There—they were just about to exit the last wooded area of the path before it opened out into a grassy field that led down to the little lake. I couldn't see Elikki from my viewpoint. Maybe she'd already left and was farther down the main road. Or maybe she was lying down among the tall grass, asleep and unaware.

Taking a big huff of air into my chest, I channeled Ma Reese and attempted an intimidating tone. "You two! What is your business here?"

The bounty hunters swung around. They eyed me up and down, taking in my height and bulk. Pebble, though she was gentle at heart, made quite an alarming first impression. Paired with a fierce half-giant wielding a massive sword, we could cut quite a figure together. Wariness crept into their faces, and they stiffened.

Good. Now I just needed to keep up the act.

Gripping my sword firmly, I pointed it straight toward the one on the right, who was string-bean thin and hungry-looking. He froze.

"I said—" I shifted my sword arm toward the other man. He was trying to play it cool, but I saw his eyes widen. "What is your business here?"

"We're on a stroll for some fresh air, en't we? Is that a crime?" he said.

I rested my blade on my shoulder. Thinking about the look Ma Reese would give someone when she caught them making trouble, I fixed him with a stern stare. His eyes wavered, shifting away from mine.

"Get out of here before I run you both through," I said in my lowest, deepest rumble.

"Why?" Shifty Eyes shot back. "Got something you don't want us to see? Some*one*?"

"Look," String Bean cut in with a placating gesture. "Why don't we just share the bounty? It'll be one silver coin for each of us. That's fair, en't it?"

"Felsith is only offering three silver?" I shook my head in disgust. "What a cheapskate. How is it even worth it for you, to do all this?"

"Easy for you to say, Mr. Fancy Man," String Bean sneered. *Mr. Fancy Man?* "For some of us, that's enough to live off for weeks."

A squirm of embarrassment wriggled into my stomach. Was I really feeling sorry for these greasy men trying to attack and kidnap someone I cared about?

Then Shifty Eyes pulled a knife out.

"If your sister hadn't paid Felsith and his brother off, we'd be coming for you too, giant. So just stay out of our way before you make things worse for yourself. And your family." He flipped the knife in the air and gripped it tight, dirty fingers wrapping around the hilt. It was a jagged, ugly thing, and I watched it uneasily, trying not to let my confident mask slip.

"What are you talking about? Why would my sister—" I broke off. Oh. That's why the bounty hunters have only been after Elikki and not me. My family must have gotten wind of what happened somehow and paid to keep me safe. I felt a wave of gratitude toward them. I don't know how they found out so fast, but I was relieved to have them watching my back.

At the same time, guilt and worry warred together. I really

was responsible for hurting Felsith, even if he was a slimeball. My family shouldn't have to clean up my messes for me. I almost thought I *should* go back now and make things right. This could affect my family's reputation, maybe even our business. Our livelihood.

But Elikki—she had no one watching her back. She didn't have anyone to keep her safe and pay off the bad guys. But how would this play out in the long run? She'd evade capture long enough to get far from this area? A three-silver bounty wasn't enough to keep folks' interest for long.

All of this raced through my mind in moments as Shifty Eyes and I glared at each other across the sharp tips of our blades. Out of the corner of my eye, I saw String Bean rooting around for his weapon, looking a bit flummoxed. I refocused on his partner.

One of us had to make a move. I still couldn't see El from where I was, but if I could get between them and the lake, I could try to maneuver the men away from here and back up to the main road.

I braced myself. "Last chance. Turn back now," I said, forcing menace into my voice. "I don't want to hurt you. Are your lives really worth a few coins?"

String Bean gulped, but Shifty Eyes seemed to harden. "You know nothing about our lives, dickhead." With that, he raised his other hand—when had a dagger slipped into that one?—and flung it toward me.

I dipped down in the saddle, digging my heels in Pebble's sides hard. She leaped forward. The dagger whistled past my ear, and we charged in between their horses, pushing them apart. I swung my sword at Shifty Eyes, intentionally pulling short so that I didn't hit him. While I didn't love that he'd just tried to stab me, I wasn't going to hurt anyone today.

If I didn't have to, at least.

Cursing, he threw himself to the other side of his horse to avoid my long blade, losing his balance and falling most of the way out of his saddle.

I felt a ripping flash of pain in my left arm and cried out, but didn't stop. We were through—I pulled Pebble around to block off the path and we began to corral the bounty hunters' weak, submissive horses forward toward the main road.

Shifty Eyes was still trying to right himself in the saddle, made harder by his horse's movements. His partner seemed shocked at his own actions. Looking from his bloody knife back to my arm that he'd slashed haphazardly, String Bean gaped, skin going pale under the dirt that lined his face.

The three of us flooded back out onto the main road. I cut a long slender branch from a nearby tree with my sword. Though I hated to hurt an innocent animal, if I flicked their horses' flanks with this they'd be galloping away for a long time before these fools could get them back under control.

Testing the bend of the branch, I fixed both men with my best attempt at a furious glare.

"Listen, mate, I'm really sorry!" String Bean said, holding his hands up in the air. "It was an accident. Didn't mean to stab you."

"Don't apologize to 'im, you idiot! We're bounty hunters! Doin' what has to be done." His partner had finally regained his seat, pushing his oily hair out of his beet-red face.

"I never even wanted to be a bounty hunter, Stan! This was all your idea!"

Shifty Eyes huffed and turned to his partner. "Well, we

wouldn't *hafta* resort to this if you hadn't gambled away our LIFE SAVINGS, *Ronald*!"

Ronald looked abashed for a moment, but quickly fired back, "Oh and I suppose all your floozies at the tavern paid for their *own* drink and rooms! That deffffinitely had nothhhhing to do with our empty money chest." He waved his arms about, and a bloody drop from the knife flung onto my forehead. Great.

"For the love of the goddess, how many more times must I apologize! For! The! FLOOZIES!?" Stan yelled, waving his own knife in the air. "I promised you it wouldn't happen again, and I haven't touched anyone since!"

Tears forming in his eyes, Ronald yelled back, "Try once, you beast! Just one *authentic, SINCERE* apology would be nice."

Stan stared at him for a long beat and then dropped his head with a long, deep sigh.

"Uh, guys—" I cut in, "maybe—the knives—how about putting them away now?"

Ronald looked at the glistening weapon still in his hand, as if surprised to see it again. "Oh, ick, gross." He flung it over his shoulder into the woods, then wiped his hands on already grimy trousers.

Stan sheathed his own blade. Taking another deep breath, he said, "Yer right. Yer both right. I'm sorry. I dunno what I'm even doin' anymore.

"Love, I'm so sorry about the floozies. The men. The women. The men and women together, and all the orgies we had while you were home waiting for me to return. It was wrong, so wrong, and it will never happen again."

Ronald pressed one hand to his chest, tears spilling over. He nodded frantically at Stan. "Oh, darling. That's all I wanted to hear. I can forgive you. As long as you can forgive me for losing all that coin on the turtle races. And for selling your lucky gold teeth to pay off the debt collectors. And for losing our house when I tried the races again to win them back."

Stan smiled back at him. "Of course, Ronny. Of course I forgive you."

In the silence as they gazed lovingly into each other's eyes, I coughed.

"Look, I'm really happy that you two are working out your issues. It's…heartwarming," I said as they beamed at me and then each other, exchanging heart-eyes from atop their horses. "But where do we stand now on the whole hunting-Elikki-for-bounty situation? Am I going to need these?" I raised the stick, my hefty sword, and an eyebrow.

Stan had the grace to look embarrassed. He said, "No, no. Think our days as bounty hunters are over."

"We weren't going to 'urt 'er or anything," Ronald added. "But it was basically this or being bandits. At least this is legal. Or semilegal."

"Oh well. Banditry it is, then. Good honest work, I suppose," Stan said with a shrug.

"Wait, wait, wait," I said. "There are plenty of other options than becoming a criminal. That'll just get you sent to prison." At that, Ronald shuddered.

"Take this," I said, passing them a few silvers from my coin purse. "And you know that colorful inn back up the road? Find the owners, Legus or Saho, and let them know I sent you. And maybe, um, try to wash up a little in a stream before you get there. If you're nice and don't bother the customers, they're likely to help get your feet under you again."

Stan tucked the money into his boot. He said quietly, "Thank you. That's very kind."

"We'll repay you someday!" Ronald said, looking a bit overcome with emotion. "Sorry again about the stabbing."

I tossed my stick back into the woods and waved them off. "Just—take care of yourselves. And good luck."

They waved farewell, and I watched as their tired horses plodded away down the dirt road. When they were out of sight, I let out the huge breath I'd been holding. After sheathing my sword with relief, I shook out my wrists and rolled the tension out of my neck. That could have gone very differently. I didn't feel great about sending another of our problems to Legus and Saho for them to clean up, but I knew they'd want to help. I'd do the same for them.

And—dammit—I really had been stabbed. Now that the adrenaline from the fight was fading, I was fully conscious of the sharp, throbbing pain in my left upper arm. I forced myself to look at it. Blood had soaked through a good bit of the sleeve, though it looked to be slowing down now. Grimacing, I moved my arm around gently to test it.

Painful, yes, but it didn't seem to be deep. I'd have to clean and bind it soon to be safe, or Ma Wren would scold me for weeks. But first things first.

Where the hell was Elikki?

17

Elikki

Floating, floating. Hair drifted around my head. The water was freezing cold, but the top bit was just sun-warmed enough to manage.

Besides, I needed the shock of the icy water to wake me up. Now that I was on my own again, I had to be alert. Constant vigilance. It wasn't safe to be tired, or even look tired. Or take midday naps in lovely lakeside patches of grass, however much I wanted to.

I let my body bob horizontally, savoring the feel of the hot sun on a few frigid parts that broke the water's surface—the top of my tits, my belly, the curve of my upper thighs. This really was a beautiful little lake.

Closing my eyes against the bright sky, I tried to focus only on the way the water moved over and around my skin. *Don't think about him. Barra.* His name brought a sharp jolt to my chest.

Stop it. You need to wake up and smell the seaweed. He's gone.

I'd probably never see him again. And I needed to get over it.

The jolt stabbed harder, and I ground my teeth. A few tears leaked out, but that was fine. They mingled with the lake water on my face. It was all just lake water.

My toes were starting to go a bit numb. I should probably head back to shore. Get dressed, pack up, figure out my next steps.

I sighed up into the clouds, thinking of the long walk ahead of me to Old Orchard. A long, quiet, boring walk with no sexy half-giant at my side to talk with, laugh at my clever jokes, flirt back and forth with, and give me those shy little smiles that made my heart go all warm and gooey. *You really screwed this one up, girl.*

Maybe another bounty hunter would attack me on the road to break up the monotony. Sighing again, I let my body fall under the lake's surface and dunked my whole head. Sputtering, I rose and pushed the thick wet strands of hair out of my face.

"—ikki? *Elikki!*" I heard a voice calling. Wow, did I just conjure a bounty hunter from thin air? A bit earlier than I'd like—hard to fight when you were stark naked. Not impossible though.

"What are you *doing* out there, you madwoman!"

I started to swim back to shore, but stopped in shock when I saw who was waiting for me. Pulling his hair, looking like he had half a mind to throw off his shoes and come into the water to get me.

Barra.

"I'm not giving back the blanket!" was all my mind came up with to shout back.

Exasperated, he threw out his arms, stepping closer to the lake's edge, to me. "You daft mermaid, I'm not here for the ruddy blanket!"

I swam toward him slowly, thoughts whirling. When my feet touched rocky sand and we were within normal talking distance, I stopped again.

"What are you here for, then?" I studied him, holding back from rushing through the water to close the distance between us. He didn't break my gaze.

"You," Barra said, swallowing hard. "I'm here for you."

It suddenly felt very hard to take full breaths. Warmth spread through my chest despite the water's chill. I kept motionless, the lake's gentle waves lapping over me.

"You left," I said.

"I know. I'm sorry."

I'm sorry too, I wanted to say. *I'm sorry I suck at explaining what I'm feeling. I'm sorry I kissed you when you needed to talk. I'm sorry I didn't even try asking you to stay.*

Moving steadily, I stepped toward him. As the lake water sluiced off my skin, revealing me bit by bit, Barra made a choking sound, his eyes roving over my body before pulling skyward.

"El," he said weakly. "You're naked."

"Oh. I guess I am," I said, a hint of cheekiness slipping into my voice. He let out a shaky laugh, keeping his eyes averted, to my amusement.

It was hard to be sexy when freezing though. Once I reached the shore and the breeze hit my bare skin, my teeth began to chatter. I hugged myself and looked for my clothes. Barra, probably hearing my teeth rattling away, jumped to help. He grabbed my long skirt from where I'd tossed it on the ground and guided me to step into it. He shrugged off his huge brown coat and wrapped it around me, bundling me tight. I burrowed into the warmth it held from his body.

"You're ice cold," he said, his voice tinged with worry.

"W-worth it," I said, "V-very refr-freshing dip. Oh dear. Are my t-t-toes blue?" I peered down at them. Yes, definitely light blue. How annoying.

I moved to where the infamous wool blanket was still spread on the grass and plopped to my knees awkwardly, wrapped in the bulky coat. I remembered yanking off my socks here. Where were they? Searching around, I spied them behind the big basket.

My hands were shaking. I couldn't pull them on. Frustrated, I flung them away. So cold. So, so cold…

Barra was suddenly kneeling over me. He held my feet, wiping them dry with a piece of the blanket, then tucked the thick socks over each one.

"We need to warm you up more, El. Can I…?" He moved closer, gesturing with his arms out, a question in his eyes.

I nodded, shuffling closer to him. His arms surrounded me, and I pressed into the heat of his torso. This felt so familiar, safe. I breathed in his minty, woodsmoke smell and let myself enjoy this. It felt surreal that he was back. It couldn't have been more than an hour or two, but I'd already been trying to mentally force him into the "Past" box in my mind. To shove away the memories and move on.

Now he was here, solid and real. He'd come back.

I reached for the blanket and tried pulling it around my legs for more warmth. Barra saw and carefully shifted me so I was lying down, then moved to wrap it around me.

"No—st-stay here. You're warm," I said.

He looked at me for a beat, brown eyes liquid and dark, and then nodded. Lying down facing me, he pulled the blanket over both of us, tucking in the corners as best he could. I tangled my legs with his.

"This reminds m-me of that first night. I moved closer to you once you fell asleep because it was chilly."

Barra wrapped his arms around me again, rubbing warmth slowly into my back. I ducked my head under his chin, burrowing in.

"Was that really just two days ago?" His chest rumbled against my cheek.

"Hard to believe," I said. The feeling was coming back to my toes. I wiggled them in my socks with relief. My fingers, pressed between our bodies, felt more like fingers again. I wiggled them experimentally too. "Yay, I can feel again!"

"Huzzah for that," Barra said dryly, but I could hear the relief in his voice.

A comfortable silence fell. I wanted to stay wrapped up in this big blanket cocoon with him forever.

"Barra. I'm sorry." He held still. It was easier to say this into his shirt than his eyes. "I'm not always great at—well, at talking. About important things. Feelings. But I have them. About you. And I should have at least tried to explain. Instead of letting you leave."

"You have feelings about me? For me?"

I squirmed a little, suddenly feeling far too hot.

"I suppose. I mean, yes. I do." Barra's breath hitched a bit, and I rushed out, "I care about you. And when I realized it… honestly, I think I just freaked out a bit. Growing up the way

I did, never truly feeling like I was wanted by my parents, by anyone—"

I let out a shaky breath, feeling uncomfortably exposed, and he squeezed me tighter. After a few moments, I went on, "I'm starting to realize how much it kind of fucked me up. You know, they forgot my birthday three years in a row? *Three*. I know they never planned to have a kid. They both are so obsessed with their work, it's like nothing else exists. But I—I *existed*. They made me exist, and then it was like they just…couldn't be bothered with me. And I remember so *desperately* wanting their love. It was like this constant belly pain that wouldn't go away.

"As I grew up, I found that the only thing that worked was to pretend it wasn't there. I didn't need them. I didn't need anyone else in that town. And once I left, after a relationship mishap or two, I decided that I also didn't need anyone else I met. I was enough, and I was happiest on my own. That's what I told myself, over and over until I believed it."

I squeezed my eyes shut, pressing into his warmth. "It was so wonderful not to feel horrible all the time anymore. Freeing. And I have loved my life on the road, truly. Parts of it anyway." Swallowing hard, I tried to rally my nerve. "But I shouldn't have pushed you away. That's not what I want. It's not your fault I had shitty parents and a crappy childhood. And I—I'm sorry if I hurt you."

Barra's lips brushed the top of my head. I could almost feel him thinking. Quietly, his voice a reassuring rumble, he said, "I care about you too, El. So much."

I smiled against his chest, blinking pesky tears away. "Well, good. That's settled, then. We care about each other. And I'd rather we stay together for the foreseeable future. Until you need to return home." My mouth tasted bitter as I formed the word "home," picturing him being welcomed joyfully back by his mothers and sisters. But I scraped that feeling away and focused on him here, now.

"I'd like that," he murmured against my hair. "And I'm sorry too—I should have waited. Given you more time to think. Now that I know…it makes sense. But in the moment, it had really seemed like you just didn't want me around anymore. Except to fuck. Which is a dynamic I know isn't healthy for me."

"I'm sorry I made you feel that way," I said quietly, snuggling closer into him. We lay there for long minutes, just breathing, taking comfort in being together again. This felt so perfect, I almost wished we could stay here by the lake, wrapped in each other's arms, and doze peacefully all day.

On the other hand…

"But now that we're talking and being all emotionally mature and everything…" I said coyly, shifting my hips slightly closer to him. "We *could* still have sex. If we wanted…right?"

I could feel his limbs tense, his cock harden against me. His warm, low chuckle rumbled through me again. In answer, Barra slipped one of his thick thighs between mine and nudged up my skirt a bit.

Rising on one elbow, he stroked my cheek, then dipped down to kiss me. His lips were soft and full, and something unclenched in me when I felt them press against mine again. He kissed me not urgently, not frantically, like how I'd tried to claim his mouth a few hours ago—but relaxed and slow, letting us explore each other.

A kiss that calmed my heart but also sped up my pulse, saying "there's no rush" and "yes, yes, *yes*."

Barra pulled me on top of him. I let out a surprised laugh and pressed a dozen quick kisses over his face and neck. My legs spread, slipping to either side of him. The blanket had fallen away long ago. But I didn't feel cold anymore.

It was still a beautiful day, golden afternoon light now sparkling over the lake's surface. Crickets were beginning to chirp their music, joining the gentle sounds of wind in the distant trees and waves lapping the shore. Everything was peaceful, soft. The fresh scents of crushed grass beneath us and the pear juice I spilled earlier touched my nose. I dipped down into Barra's neck and inhaled, replacing the aromas with his smoky minty musk that I loved.

"Are you...smelling me?" he asked with a smile, one hand stroking my upper back. His other reached under the folds of his coat that I was still wearing, tracing his fingertips along the sensitive skin of my side.

"Maybe," I said, sniffing again. "You just always smell *amazing*."

Looking embarrassed, he pulled a small tin out of a jacket pocket and opened it. It was half full of little green leaves.

"Mint!" I plucked one out and rubbed it between my fingers. "So that's your secret."

"I chew them often. A habit I picked up as a child when some folks in town were...less than kind about my presence at first." He picked up a leaf too, twirling it. "I suppose I became a bit paranoid. About how I smelled, looked, talked, walked—everything."

"It's hard to feel comfortable when it seems like everyone is watching and judging you," I said gently.

"Yes. It is." Barra placed the leaf back into the tin and tucked it away. "It's one of my habits that's hard to break."

"Well, I love it. And if your worst qualities are that you're self-conscious and addicted to mint—"

"—and have some intimacy issues," he added.

I rolled my eyes. "Who doesn't? Same, apparently. But if that's the worst, I'll take it in a heartbeat."

Barra watched me with that warm, unguarded look that almost made me want to squirm away. But I wasn't going anywhere this time, and neither was he.

He gently tugged me down to him again. Bending, I pressed all my twisty, fuzzy feelings into his lips. I shrugged out of his coat, letting it fall. Deepening the kiss, he ran both hands over me, palms trailing fire wherever they touched.

Barra broke away for a moment, both of us panting with need. His eyes were dark, pupils blown. Holding my hips on both sides like I was a life buoy and he had fallen overboard, he gripped me tight and tugged up toward his head.

Realizing what he wanted, I wiggled happily and shifted my body up his broad chest until I was kneeling over his mouth. I hovered, let him take the lead.

He gathered up my long skirt and flung it behind me. Grabbing my hips again, he pulled me to his mouth with a pleased grunt, burying his face in my hair. I was already a little wet and seeing him moving below me sent a surge of pleasure down my body.

When he began to lick me, I was lost. Running my fingers through his hair with one hand and gripping one of my breasts with the other, I just tried to not writhe around too much.

Barra held me fast, moving my hips possessively to reach whatever part of my pussy he wanted to lick. I felt his tongue dip inside me, trace along my lips, tap against my clit—I held on as long as I could, swearing into the blue sky. But I came fast and hard on his mouth, so hard it swept my breath away, chest gasping for air.

"Ohh, fuck fuck fuck *ohhhhh*," I mumbled as I slid down his body, lying down chest to chest on top of him, limbs like jelly.

After a couple of minutes of Barra rubbing languid circles on my back, I propped myself up on my elbows and fixed him with a sly look. I could feel his cock below me, still hard, touching my right thigh through his breeches. Shifting just the right amount, I moved down his body until I was sitting on top of it.

I began to grind, moving over his length through the fabric, sighing at how it brushed against my sensitive skin. Barra never broke eye contact. He held my hips again, tightly.

"Do you want to be inside me?" I asked, voice unsteady. My orgasm was already building again. I wanted him so badly I ached, my abdomen clenching with need.

I'd seen last night that he had the standard rune for protection against sexual diseases and a ward against pregnancy tattooed near his hip. I had the same on my own body. Most people I'd encountered got them as a teenager; it was a smart practice that was safe, cheap, reversible, and lasted decades.

Barra swallowed, still watching me steadily with his intense eyes. "Yes. Yes, I really do."

Sitting up, he held me to him with one arm and untied his breeches with the other, shucking them and his boots. When his bare cock touched me, I shivered in anticipation.

He hesitated. "I'm a bit…much for most people. Tell me if we need to stop."

I nodded, nuzzling his chest, but said, "Oh, trust me, I can handle you." Barra hummed in pleasure, hands roaming over my body, squeezing my ass reflexively. He kissed me—my cheeks, my lips—before nipping gently at my neck in a way that made heat pool low in my belly. I whimpered, reaching between us.

His low laugh teased me. "You want to be fucked, don't you, El?"

"Yeah, I want it—please, Barra." I was almost whining, beyond embarrassment.

He lifted me, positioned himself, and lowered me carefully down on his cock, letting me guide our slow pace. He was huge. But I took him in, inch by blissful inch, moaning at how full he stretched me.

Barra paused, his breath catching. Our foreheads pressed together.

"You okay?" I ran a hand over his chest, kissed his large nose. My legs shook with the effort of not moving on top of him, taking him deeper.

In a strained voice, he said, "Yes. Yes. You just feel so fucking amazing."

"Can I have more?" I whispered, massaging the back of his neck.

Almost growling, Barra thrust his hips up at my words, plunging deep. I cried out. He moved inside me, and I held on, fire building steadily in my core.

We found a rhythm together, moving frantically in time. When he dipped his head down to my breasts, I leaned back, propping myself up on his legs. His tongue found each nipple in turn, sucking hard. I swore at him, scratching his legs with my nails, and pulled his head back to do it again and again.

We were frenzied, gone—our bodies came together again,

close and hot, sweat mingling on our chests. I licked the crook of Barra's neck, tasting him, his sweat and burning skin.

His gigantic cock reached the deepest part of me over and over and over, for goddess knows how long, and I was near crying in utter ecstasy as I climaxed. Stars scattered across my vision. I squeezed my eyes shut, and he held me close.

With a few more pumps, drawing out my orgasm further, he came too. I relished the feeling of his cum spilling into me, his shattered breath, the way he gripped me fiercely, as if I'd both wrecked and saved him.

We flopped back down to the ground, and Barra turned on his side toward me. I nestled my head on his biceps. My limbs were loose, liquid, and his gentle fingers felt lovely against my face as he brushed wet strands of hair back, pressing light kisses as he went.

When his sigh rumbled lightly through my body, my eyes snapped open as I remembered how significant this was for him. Twisting to see his face, I was relieved to see he was smiling softly back at me.

"Feeling all right?" I asked. "This wasn't...too much?"

"I feel incredible. *You* are incredible." He pulled me closer, and I nuzzled in.

The sun was dipping lower in the sky, and though I didn't want to, I knew we had to get moving.

Barra apparently was thinking the same. "We should probably head out soon if we want to make it to Old Orchard by nightfall."

"Guess it wouldn't be smart to camp here, what with all these rogue bounty hunters running around after me," I joked.

He grimaced and sat up, seeming to realize just how exposed

we were. I groaned in protest. Barra jumped to his feet with an energy I definitely didn't have, then reached for my hands. I let him pull me up.

"Just a bit farther, and then we'll find a nice inn where you can rest," he said as he swept around, gathering our belongings and packing them away in Pebble's saddlebags. I patted her nose fondly, happy to see her again. She searched for the apples I've been sneaking to her over our journey, snuffling at my hands and skirt pockets, and then nudging my right boob.

"No snacks for you right now, I'm afraid. But you're right—I should probably get dressed."

I found the rest of my clothes where I'd strewn them over a rock before my dip in the lake. After shimmying into my shirt and corset and adjusting everything into a comfortable position, I started to tighten the strings a little. Barra came over and placed his hands over mine.

"May I?"

I nodded. His large fingers deftly moved along the laces, tightening them perfectly so that the corset supported me but didn't squeeze. He tied the ends with a bow. Brushing the knuckles of one hand softly across the top of my breasts, he dipped down to kiss the crook of my neck.

"Beautiful," Barra murmured against my skin, sending tingles through my chest. I smiled against his hair.

He gave me a boost up onto Pebble's massive back, and with one last look back at the shimmering lake, I nudged her on the path forward.

18

Barra

We made good time on the main road. As the light faded around us, treetops darkening overhead, I recounted my run-in with Stan and Ronald to Elikki. She gasped and giggled through the story, and I found myself laughing along.

This light bubble of happiness that had filled my chest since we opened up to each other beside the lake was still there, making me almost giddy.

When I got to the part about being stabbed in the arm, she insisted on seeing the wound herself and dressing it "properly" from her perch atop Pebble. Before I knew it, she'd grabbed some clean cloth from her pack and she was pulling my shirt away from the sticky wound, heart-shaped face tight with concentration.

I protested a little at first, tried to brush her off. But truthfully, it felt wonderful, if a bit strange, to have someone tend to me like this. I was so used to being the sole caretaker in my relationships. The way Elikki insisted that I let her care for me in return—it did something to me.

When she finished her work, tying it off with a neat knot, she made me promise to clean the wound fully and bandage it again once we found a room in town. I smiled at her use of the singular "room." She smirked back, expanding the bubble in my chest even larger.

Still, part of me kept expecting someone to leap out and attack her again. Both of us stayed alert for more bounty hunters—peering around into the forest's shadows and halting randomly to listen for footfalls—but all was normal.

As we walked, my thoughts kept coming back to what Elikki had shared by the lake. It was hard to make sense of the type of neglect and emotional abandonment she'd described in her past. She'd been ignored by the very people who were meant to love her the most—it made me sick to my stomach. I began to see that Elikki had been hurt more deeply, more viscerally, than I had ever experienced. She'd grown up feeling unwanted by her own parents, her communities. Unloved.

I didn't realize until this moment how much more scarred than me she probably felt, all these years later. She'd just buried the hurt deeper. Covered it with layers of charm, wit, and charisma. Protected herself in the ways she could. Hardened her heart to everyone, so that no one could hurt her like that again.

As these realizations struck me in the chest like blows, I felt a surge of understanding and love for this elf. That she'd been through so much and still started to open up, let me see *her*—that was nothing short of miraculous. Not only was she strong, charming, and mind-shatteringly gorgeous, but Elikki Sunstorm was the bravest person I'd ever met.

We reached Old Orchard just as the last bit of daylight slipped away. Restaurants and taverns spilled light into the street. Folks called to one another, shouting and laughing merrily, and everyone scrambled out of Pebble's path as they caught sight of her. The golden magefire lamps, which illuminated larger towns and cities across the Willowisp Woods at night, shone brightly along the sides of every road here, a welcoming entrance. Like all folk, mages had to live where they could find work, and most opportunities were in places like this. Not small villages like Nepu, so we usually just made do with candles at home. But goddess, if this wasn't a beautiful sight. Cheerful dancing flames shone about us, reaching tendrils up to the darkening sky from their lampposts and tinting El's auburn hair golden.

So beautiful, I thought, reaching over to twirl a loose strand around my finger, just for the sake of it. She smiled sleepily over at me, and I pressed a kiss to her hand.

We stayed on the main cobblestone road as it curved to the right and up a gentle hill. It was a little quieter up here, fewer folks carousing and more weary workers heading home for warmth, supper, and a good night's rest. I'd visited this town several times before for work, and I hoped my preferred inn had space for us tonight.

Following the bend of the high street, we finally came to my destination. The Oak & Spoon was a tall, jaunty building set on a street corner, its door the classic turquoise shade Old Orchard inhabitants were so fond of using. Large windows glowed warmly, beckoning us inside. I helped Elikki down before passing Pebble's reins to the stablehand slouching nearby. Hefting both of our packs, I followed her inside.

The comfortable front room was filled with soft light, every chair and sofa strewn with pillows and colorfully knit blankets. There were no performers here, but the gentle clinking of cups and murmuring of voices provided their own soothing music. Elikki beelined to the squashiest, biggest sofa by the fireplace and plopped down with a sigh. I followed, placing our packs on the floor. With a quick kiss on her hair, I went to the bar to arrange our accommodations.

Luckily, one of their larger rooms was available. The barkeep sent a young lad to bring our packs up as we rested by the fire. Soon two steaming plates arrived on the table, along with a lavender-chamomile tea for me and a spiced wine for Elikki.

I looked around the room, trying my best to be unnoticeable. Difficult, when you tend to attract folks' attention. After a quick check, it seemed we were in the clear. For now, at least.

"So," she said in a low voice as we tucked into our meals of roast chicken, potatoes, and garlicky greens, "I've been watching everyone in here. No one gives me a whiff of bounty hunter." She munched on a golden-brown potato, casually scanning the room. I breathed a bit easier. She'd know better than me how to spot one, and I trusted her instincts.

"He'll probably give up soon. That cheap bounty can't pull many people who would be willing to do a four-day round trip—especially for such a 'dangerous criminal,'" Elikki said with a grin, eyes glinting devilishly in the firelight.

I tried to ignore the voice in my head filling me with worries. She was probably right. Everything would be fine.

But—what if we were wrong? What if Felsith decided to raise the bounty price? What if someone caught her off-guard again? Should we have been running farther, faster?

Or maybe not be running at all?

That option, of simply facing the music and resolving this

with Felsith and the law head-on, had never seemed like a real possibility. Everything had happened so fast. Though she hid it well, I saw how shaken Elikki was—and I was scared for her—so we had just kept moving.

If Felsith didn't lose interest, though, we could be dealing with more bounty hunters here in Old Orchard. How long would it take before the local constables got involved? I didn't have enough experience with the law to know if that was likely, but chances seemed good that one way or another, Elikki would have to move on again soon, with or without me. We should make the most of our time here together.

I took a steadying breath. "You're probably right. Legus and Saho will also be keeping an eye on anyone who comes through their inn. Let's just stay on our guard. Wait and see."

"And in the meantime," Elikki said, taking my hand, "we can have some fun!"

I squeezed her fingers gently. She looked exhausted, still needing a solid night's rest after her magical exertions today. The long day of travel, the frigid swim, and the strenuous—though incredible—sex by the lake had all probably taken a toll on her energy.

"Definitely. To start, I could really go for a bath and a deep sleep," I said as I forked up the last bite on my plate. She had finished her meal a while ago and was sipping sleepily at her spiced wine. I drained my tea, then stood and stretched.

"No dessert?" Elikki yawned.

"We can have some sent up to the room," I said, carefully guiding her around the furniture and toward the carved wooden stairs. Her eyelids were already starting to droop closed. Small hand in mine, she clomped up the stairs with heavy steps. When I unlocked our door, she immediately went to the wide, sleigh-style bed and fell into it face-first with a groan. I bent slightly under the doorframe and followed her, taking in the ivy-patterned wallpaper, sturdy worn furniture, and soft glow of the fireplace. This should do nicely for our time here. I lit a couple of squat candles and stoked the fire so that she would be warm enough, before pulling the dark brown wool curtains closed.

"Can you unlace me?" Her muffled voice came from the pillows. "I don't think I can move."

Chuckling, I sat on the edge of the bed and began loosening her corset. When that was done, I got her boots and socks off too.

"El? Can you sit up for me, love? You don't want to fall asleep in your traveling clothes."

A tired grunt answered me. With an effort, Elikki dragged herself upright. Her eyes were shut, wavy hair awry. "Not going to sleep. Time for more sex."

I smothered a laugh and said, "Right. Well, either way, you'll want to get out of these clothes."

Eventually, we got her corset, shirt, and long skirt off. I folded them neatly. Down to just her light shift, Elikki snuggled close to me, her breasts and stomach pressing warmly against my side. Moving slowly, I got her lying back on the bed, settled among the fluffy pillows. But when I tried to let go and stand, she held on to my arm, saying, "Noooo. Stay."

After a second's hesitation, I stretched out next to her, making sure my boots hung over the bed's edge. Elikki turned over, wiggling her butt against me before settling into the soft linen duvet again with a contented sigh.

I stroked her hair lightly. She was already falling fast asleep. My heart clenched watching her gentling breaths, her fingers scrunching the sheets, glinting with the beautiful artistry of her rings.

The magic that she wielded astounded me. It was both beautiful and fierce, practical and playful—just like Elikki. Who knew what else she could do?

When her breathing was slow and steady, I finally shifted inch by inch off the bed, pressing a light kiss against her hair. Turning to the waiting bathtub, I shed all my clothes—folding them on a table, of course—and stepped in, sinking down with relief. It wasn't exactly the kind of luxurious bath one found at Legus and Saho's place. The water was unscented, and the tub itself a bit too tight for comfort. But it did the trick all the same, leaving me refreshed and clean as I scrubbed away the dirt and sweat of the day's adventures.

Wrapping myself in a too-small towel, I sat by the dying fire and tried not to think about all the worries hovering at the edges of my mind—the bounty hunters who might be searching at this very moment; my future, or lack thereof, with Elikki; the stress and concern that my absence might be causing my mas and sisters. It was hard to ignore the internal cacophony.

But then I looked over at Elikki, curled up like a cat in our large bed. From what she's said, she's been through far worse than this. She barely seemed shaken.

We could handle it all together. Tomorrow, I resolved, I'll write to my family and explain. Reassure them that I'm all right. And Elikki and I would take things one day at a time.

For now, though, I needed to get some rest. I untied the dark red ribbon from my hair and placed it carefully atop the bedside table. After pulling on my loose sleep pants, I slid into bed beside Elikki and threw a thick blanket over us. She wriggled a little again in her sleep and shifted closer. Tucking one arm gently around her soft body, I fell asleep with a smile on my face.

19
Elikki

The next few days passed blissfully. Barra and I would wake, sunlight peeking in through the curtains, and come together under the covers for sleepy morning sex. Either twenty minutes or two hours later, we'd dress and head downstairs for breakfast with silly grins. After filling up on fruit-laden pancakes or eggy toast, we strolled through town for a light morning walk.

On the first day, I'd decided to seek out Old Orchard's local Artisans Guild and found a metalwork station to borrow while I was in town. I was determined to follow through on the promise I'd made myself after the encounter with Maerryl—I would hone my control over my powers, slowly but surely learning how to sink into that calm frame of mind that allowed me to exert full dominance over my metals. And that meant practice, practice, and then some more practice. For this, I needed the resources found at a guildhall, where I could make some new pieces to work my magic on. So now, each morning, Barra and I would end our meanderings there, parting with a head-turning kiss at the door before he went off to take care of his own business.

We knew we should probably be laying low, but his seven-and-a-half-foot-tall lavender form was near impossible to miss anyway. *Might as well give people something to stare at*, I thought as we approached the guildhall hand in hand on the fourth day.

When we stopped, I pulled down the back of Barra's neck, bringing his mouth firmly to mine. I loved the way his breath huffed out a little whenever I surprised him with my intensity—the slight pause before his body won out over whatever concerns his mind was feeding to him.

I knew he worried about passersby staring, of being judged for who he was or how he looked. And I also knew the joy and freedom he felt when he was able to let that all go for a while. When he threw his arms around me, returning my kisses fiercely, lifting me up to my tiptoes to bring us closer together, matching my brazenness—I saw the light in his eyes as we drew back and said our goodbyes. The looseness in his gait as he walked away smiling, so different from the rigid, contained posture he normally carried. Something was changing in him, and I blazed inside to see it. I would kiss him a million times in public, act a fool if it opened him up like this.

For the first time, I thought—*How might he be changing me?*

Pushing that irksome idea away, I entered the guildhall and resolved to focus only on my work for the day.

Old Orchard's guildhall was designed in an open-air layout, at least four times larger than the charming but cramped guildhall in Povon. Once you passed through the magically protected front gate, you entered a courtyard with smooth gray rock underfoot. Arranged in a semicircle around it was a low, long building, also made of gray stone, with wide eaves to protect the dozens of workstations tucked along its curving length.

Inside the main hall, through wide turquoise doors at the building's center, was a large gathering space, a mailroom, and an exhibition room where local artisans could display one item each of their craft. Along the outer walls were spare bedrooms, bathrooms, and a small kitchen. Spaced along the inner walls were the more elite workshops for each artisan specialty—everything from calligraphers to cobblers, potters to painters. You had to reach a certain rank within the guild, or be an apprentice of a high-ranking member, to have access to those more private and permanent workspaces. Though I'd found that with the right amount of charm and flattery, I could usually convince someone to lend me the tools or materials I needed.

In any case, I actually preferred working at one of the floating stations in the courtyard. They were all about the size of a street vendor's cart, and several were outfitted with what I need to make my jewelry. As long as the weather was pleasant, I'd much rather be out in the fresh air, surrounded by the hustle and bustle of the guildhall's constant activity. Made it easier to people-watch and pick up gossip also—two of my favorite pastimes.

As I walked through the courtyard and found an unused station, a few people shouted greetings to me. I chirped back to them, enjoying the warm buzz of friendliness on a bright, sunny morning.

"Hello, Sera! Sounds like you've got the pitch just right on those lovely wind chimes!"

"Feeling spicy today, Filippe? Those hot peppers are burning my nose hairs from here!"

"Wow, wow, wow! That self-portrait is really coming along, Mabal—you look stunning."

I settled into my spot, unrolling my bulky jewelers kit and laying out the tools I would need first. Then I lit a fire under the small stove and placed a crucible on top to heat.

While I waited, I took out my notebook containing all the recent sketches I'd made. In these past few days, I'd been more inspired than I'd felt for years. Designs popped into my head constantly. It was almost more than I could manage to get down on paper before something new came to mind.

The pieces were of a simpler physical design than I normally created, yet magically more intricate than I'd ever attempted before. Most were quite elegant, spare shapes—such as brass interlocking circles woven together into a cuff bracelet, or a shiny silver four-pointed necklace pendant inset with a smooth piece of sea glass—and I reined myself in from adding my usual extravagant flourishes. With the new, more difficult enchantments I'd been working on, the second, magic-imbuing stage was taking so long that I'd need days to finish just one piece if I didn't scale back on the details.

As it was, I spent most of my mornings metalsmithing, working to carefully melt, mold, shape, and transform the designs in my notebook into real, solid jewelry pieces. Sometimes I drew on my powers a tiny bit—to reheat a section more easily or force a curve into the metal when it acted stubborn—but that was instinctual, small stuff. I had to conserve most of my energy for later. After an extended lunch break with Barra, I usually went right back to our room at the inn. He attended more meetings after our meal, so I had the space to myself all afternoon.

Once I chose a piece to work on, I sat down in the comfiest

chair and closed my eyes. Holding the freshly made jewelry in my hands, I forced myself to do the breathing exercises my old mentor had taught me. Four seconds breathing in, hold for four seconds, then four out and four holding again.

When he caught me doing this one day, Barra told me he does something similar when his anxiety spikes. For mages like me, it's a technique that can also be used to focus our minds and allow us to access and more easily control our magic.

I've known about this skill for ages, of course. My mentor used to hound me constantly about practicing more. But I had hated the tedium…and was awful at it too. Most of the time I tried, it felt completely fruitless. My magic was always like a snarled, pulsing ball inside me. Whenever I struggled with it, breathing as carefully as I could, the magic still wrestled out of my grip. The feeling that my mentor and others in the guild had described to me over the years—of their power coming into balance, of connecting with and calming it within themselves—I never reached that point. Try as I might, I couldn't get there. It drove me mad with frustration. My magic and I remained at odds.

Ultimately, I had given up. Stopped trying. And I just let my magic be, avoiding it most of the time. I could draw on it a little when I was metalworking, as I fell into a focused state of sorts that calmed it into mild complacency. Creating jewelry and working with the comforting physicality of metal centered me, taking all my concentration. It seemed to help.

Other times, it burst out of me, uncontrollable, when I was angry or upset. And almost always caused a problem and a mess to clean up. I hadn't realized until my recent adventures with Barra, and all this bounty hunter nonsense started, just how out of control it had gotten.

When things went sideways and a strong emotion raced through me, my magic came with it. It flowed right to my fingertips, thrumming *do it do it DO IT*, and I used to just let my magic take over. But if I could control my emotions, I could control the magic. So now I sit in our room every afternoon, recalling the way it felt on that forest road with Maerryl, when I imbued the golden bracelets with my intentions. I was steady, collected. The willing metal leaped in my mind, responding to my determination and eager to receive my energy.

I practiced by channeling that feeling often now, reaching inside myself to find the snarled ball of light that is my magic. Every day, I sensed it untangling, relaxing. Bit by bit. I was trying not to get too excited. Eventually, my magic might flare up again. Unpredictable, chaotic, fierce—the force of it was bound to catch me unawares again at some point. It almost made me wish for someone who could teach me more, guide me in this work. If only my mentor could see me now—I'd definitely earn one of her rare smiles. We could finally make progress, move forward. So much more was possible now. She could show me the secrets of wielding that I'd once dreamed of learning. I wouldn't give up like before.

Still, I was doing fine alone. I had my friendly metals, my deft fingers, and a new calm that was settling in me with each day that passed. Maybe sometime in the future, though, I could find a master to teach me again. The vision of myself as an official mage of Kurriel popped up from where I'd hidden it long ago. Perhaps it wasn't too late…

But I didn't want to get ahead of myself. The most important thing, for both Barra's safety and my career, was to hone my control little by little until my own will was as strong as my magic's force. Before, the thought of that kind of long-term, drudging work would have driven me to frustration. Now I felt a tingle of excitement and anticipation. I'd already improved more in these past few days than I'd ever thought possible. Somehow, it was so much easier to work like this when the rest of my time was filled with such…happiness. Mornings tangled up in bed with Barra, our meals and walks each day, the long evenings of conversation and fun—everything felt simpler with him around. Lighter.

Sitting in our quiet inn room now, breathing evenly, I gently touched the core of my magic. It brightened and danced within me. Slowly, ever so slowly, I drew one strand out. Focusing on the four-pointed silver pendant cupped in my hands, I set my intention for it firmly in my mind. Twining that intention around the strand of my power, I carefully fed it into the metal. It knew me. We've been together for years, and I concentrated on that connection while slipping my magic into its solid, welcoming form.

The silver glowed, warming the already hot, sweaty skin of my palms. *You are a shield. You will protect your wearer from harm*, I told the pendant. *You will let no spells touch your wearer's mind. You will deflect curses, charms, and invasive spells. You are strong and solid. You are a shield.*

Over and over, I repeated this sentiment to the pendant, imagining my power and will filling every tiny part of it. The silver agreed with me. It *was* a shield. It would protect its wearer from harm. It was happy to do as I asked.

Thank you, I thought to my creation as the final bit of my magic's strand slipped into the pendant. I opened my hands. It glowed softly, pulsing with the most beautiful light.

My magic did this. Created *this*. It was still hard to believe, though this was the fourth powerful piece I'd made in as many days.

I slipped it onto a long, sturdy chain and drew it over my head, pressing the hot metal gently against my heart. A quiver passed through me. The pendant's protection covered me now, so lightly that I probably wouldn't even notice if it wasn't my own magic. I'd wanted it to be strong but difficult for other mages to detect, and it seemed I'd achieved that.

Joy burned in my chest, and I blinked sudden hot tears away.

This was real. I'd had an idea, and I used my metalworking skills and this new, unrefined grasp on my power to make something unique. Something that was not only beautiful—and goddess, it was *stunning!*—but also useful. It was leagues beyond the pieces I'd created before, painstakingly etching rudimentary runes into metal for hours on end to give the wearer some mild power—more confidence, a lessening of aches and pains, protection from bees, and such.

But this—what I'd unlocked within myself these past days—this was real magic. Badass, big money, *Hey, have you heard of that mighty elf mage Elikki?* kind of magic. The sort that my mentor had always said I possessed, usually shaking her head in disappointment at my latest tantrum of frustration. Now, though, who knew what I could do?

Rings that made the wearer invisible? Earrings that let one hear sounds a mile away? Bangles that could give the power of flight?

I brushed my fingertips over the smooth sea glass in the center, a deep amber with a hint of red that had reminded me of the ribbon I'd tied into Barra's hair. That felt like a lifetime ago. Tracing over each of the pendant's metal curves and four distinct points, I could sense the thrum of its power—*my* power—coiled contentedly within.

I couldn't wait to find out.

20

Barra

There were only so many fake meetings that someone could invent at the last minute. With everything that had been going on with Elikki and me, and the bounty hunters, I'd somehow forgotten that I'd made up a reason for us to travel together to Old Orchard. I was supposed to have business in town. Now that we were here, I found myself scrambling to come up with that "business" during the day while Elikki was working for real.

After I dropped her off at the Artisans Guild on the first morning, I'd walked—a bit dazed from the kiss she'd laid on me—toward an area where a few shops sold swords. Old Orchard was a good-sized town, with a thriving economy fueled by, as you'd expect, its prized orchards and vineyards that sprawled for miles around, as well as its central location in the Willowisp Woods province that drew in traders and merchants of all stripes. It was well worth the lengthy seasonal trips

I took, and over my past journeys here for actual business, I'd connected with most of the middle- and high-end shop owners, showing them Ma Reese's handiwork and building relationships. They placed orders on behalf of their customers, and sometimes arranged one-on-one consultations with me for folks who needed more complicated repair or customization work done. I collected all the pieces that I'd be bringing back with me to Nepu, along with half of the payment.

Our armory business had grown quite the reputation over the years. Ma Reese's skill was legendary, and most folks were willing to wait the weeks or months that it took for their weapons to be completed. So, although this was an unplanned journey, there was still plenty for me to do in town at first. I visited all my contacts and picked up all the new orders that had come in. Had a few productive meetings with potential clients. One in particular would excite my sister Telen. She loved doing custom design work on daggers—the more intricate the better—and this rich client had ordered four for his teenage children.

But by day three, I found myself at a loose end in the afternoon. I hadn't been able to schedule any new meetings, and I didn't want to distract Elikki. She'd been focusing intensely on her magic in our room every day after lunch, coming up with incredible creations that she showed off when we met up in the evening.

I thought often about telling her the truth. That I hadn't actually been headed to Old Orchard. That I'd lied because I was—what—worried about her safety? So smitten that I didn't want her to leave? It seemed silly. Knowing her now, I didn't think she'd really care that much. I could see her bubbling with laughter, teasing me for it.

But it still sounded uncomfortably close to pathetic, the lengths I was going to to stay near her. And we likely would have to part soon anyway, though a wrench tore through my chest whenever I thought of that. Any day now, whenever Elikki decided it was time for her to move on. If I told her, there's a chance it could hasten that day along.

I also didn't want to distract her, shake her focus. Ever since we arrived, she'd been so concentrated on her art, both with jewelry making and magic. I could tell it was draining—particularly her afternoon mage-crafting sessions—but she was absolutely brimming with cheeriness. And she always seemed to revive with every meal we had together...and every night we spent making love and snuggling in our sleep.

Everything was good. Better than good—marvelous. Perfect. And I couldn't risk breaking this spell of happiness we were in together.

So that's how I found myself on a long, winding walk through one of the town's infamous orchards on the afternoon of our fourth day here. I'd spent the morning semiproductively at a nearby pub, sipping cup after cup of green tea while I worked: organizing all my notes from the past few days' meetings, sketching out a timeline for each of the orders, and sorting them by priority. I wrote and mailed another letter to my family; the first one I sent via messenger hawk should have arrived by now.

Ambling slowly through the ordered rows of apple trees, I let my feet wander and lost myself in thought. There was a fantasy that I'd been letting myself imagine sometimes over the past few days, when I was alone and feeling a bit overcome with the bliss that was my life right now. As I walked along, lifting my face to the sun's soft rays, I pictured my gray stone house in Nepu, with its tidy thatched roof and window boxes spilling with cheerful blue and yellow flowers. I walked through the door into the large front room.

It was a modest home, nothing extravagant, but had very high ceilings for me, which made it feel grander than it was. Today it was a bit messy, and I tidied while making my way through the room and down the hall—folding a blanket here, righting a teetering stack of books there—before I reached a doorway.

In my real house, in real life, this was a spare bedroom, most often used by one of my sisters when they visited me. In my daydream, however, I pushed the cracked door open to a workroom, unkempt and a bit cluttered. The wide windows that looked out into the back garden were pushed open as far as they could go, a gentle breeze lessening the heat coming from the small forge set in a corner of the room. One whole wall was filled with shelves containing every manner of handicraft items: boxes labeled with different metals, jars of jewels and stones, trays of hooks, wire, and countless tools. It's warm, but not unpleasantly so, and my heart fills with the feeling of being home. Being exactly where I'm supposed to be, with the person I yearned to see whenever I'm away from her for more than a minute.

Because at a large workstation in the middle of the room sits Elikki, her pointy ears perking up at the sound of me coming through the doorway. I stepped close, careful not to jostle her as she finishes setting a stone into a piece of bronze. Brushing the auburn tendrils of hair away from her neck, I press a soft kiss just behind her ear. When the setting is complete, she turns in my arms with a wide smile and kisses me, pulling me closer to her.

My dream ends there, us holding each other tightly in the studio we built for her together. In the peaceful, snug home we shared. Sometimes it seems impossible, a ridiculous fantasy concocted by my most desperate desires.

Other times, like today, with the sun shining down and Elikki's post-lunch kiss still lingering on my lips, it didn't seem silly at all. It felt like the most real, true version of my future that I'd ever let myself imagine. It felt like love.

I halted at the thought.

I loved her.

"I love Elikki," I said out loud to the silent trees lined around me. No one was around for miles. It was just the orchard, the occasional bird, and my heart pounding in my chest.

"*Fuck.*" Head in my hands, I stood there until I could think clearly again.

I was a fool. This is exactly what I'd told myself I couldn't let happen. Daydreams were one thing, but Elikki had made it clear from the beginning that we don't have a future together. This was just supposed to be fun. She was always going to leave, and she'd never pretended to want anything different.

But—what if her feelings had changed? Mine had, over the course of our time together. From lust to affection to infatuation to now, a ridiculous all-consuming, head-over-heels love. We spent every spare moment together. I trusted her more than any other sexual partner in my life. We talked and made love late into the night, every night, and woke up tangled in each other's arms every morning.

She kissed me like she was marking me, making me hers. And she still hadn't mentioned anything about where she planned to head next. Or asked me when I was returning home.

Was it outlandish to think that she'd changed her mind?

If I was picturing a possible future for us together now, maybe she was too.

A glimmer of hope sparked, and I tried to squash it down quickly. I couldn't assume anything. She'd been honest about what she wanted from the beginning. Sex and a traveling companion. Did I really want to confess my feelings to yet another person I'd naively fallen for, just to have them reject me?

I continued walking, now heading slowly back in the direction of town. Mind full of Elikki, I tried to sort out my thoughts and decide what to say to her, if anything. Breathing slowly in and out, counting my inhales and exhales, helped to calm my racing heart and leech the stress from my body.

I needed to wait for some kind of sign from her. An indication that this was more than just fucking and friendship. More than likely, she'd get bored of me soon and want to leave for the next town, the next person, and the next adventure.

The thought left a dry, acrid taste in my mouth. It didn't ring true—but if I believed it now, it would hurt less when she left me.

Maybe.

Reaching the edge of town, I went down a side street that was a shortcut to the main road. The best bakery in Old Orchard was tucked along here. Drawing up to its faded turquoise door, I ducked inside and found it mercifully empty. It was a tiny shop, and my height and breadth tended to make things uncomfortable if there were other people in the small space.

Elikki and I had come here yesterday on our morning stroll, and I ended up having to stand outside as she got our treats. Once she'd come out, a heavy bag tucked in one arm, she'd fussed over me while she dug through the baked goods. *Such a small space—they should just use a takeout window so everyone can place orders,* she'd said. *And that door is ridiculously short. I barely fit through! Good you waited out here anyway. A guy in line had terrible BO.* Then she'd passed me a braided chocolate pastry and took my other hand, weaving our fingers together and tugging me along the road with an easy smile. I don't know how she could tell when I'm feeling self-conscious, but she always knew what to say.

Now the bell chimed cheerily at my entrance. A bit hunched, I took a deep breath, inhaling the comforting scents of vanilla, sugar, and yeasty bread. The remaining baked goods of the day were laid out in baskets on the wide counter. An elderly man shuffled out of the kitchen, and I ordered one apple strudel for me and the last big cinnamon roll for Elikki. She'd devoured one yesterday and had declared it "the most magnificent damned pastry" she'd ever eaten.

The baker rang up my purchases and waved me out the door with a wheezy "Enjoy, sonny!" I meandered down the cobblestone street, feeling surprisingly at peace. There was still a chill at night, but it didn't bother me. The air smelled fresh and crisp, even here in town, and the sun was beginning to set, casting a golden glow on the rooftops and windows. A mage was scurrying along, lighting the lampposts on each street with yellow-orange flameless fire. More and more townsfolk walked to and fro, heading home after work or to the pubs for an evening drink and some entertainment.

It was week's end. Tomorrow was a Resting Day, when most folks took off from work and relaxed or shopped or visited the bathhouse. Elikki was planning to set up a stall and sell her jewelry down in the main square.

As I thought of it, the memory of the first time I saw her flashed in my mind. She was so charming and vivacious—to me, it seemed like she drew everyone in her radius in toward her booth with sheer charisma. I couldn't wait to see her back in action tomorrow.

My steps quickened as I approached our inn. It was still relatively quiet inside, just a handful of patrons and a fiddler tuning their instrument in a corner. I stopped by the bar for a large pint of cloudy cider—Elikki's favorite—before making my way to our room.

My stomach buzzed when I drew closer, as it always did when I was near El.

I unlocked the door, then entered quietly in case she was still focusing on her magework. But she was slumped in one of the large armchairs by the fireplace, eyes closed and face a bit drawn. I set everything down and knelt, softly petting her hair and rubbing my thumb across her forehead the way that she liked. Elikki let out a long, tired groan.

"I could sleep for a *week*," she said, sliding down farther in the chair. "Today's casting really took it out of me."

I pulled the bakery bag closer and opened it up. After a moment, Elikki cracked one eyelid open.

"I smell sugar," she said, lips curving into a small smile.

"Have enough energy for a little treat?" I said, pulling out the gigantic cinnamon roll. Her eyes widened.

"I'll try to muster my strength." She reached for the pastry, taking a big bite of mostly frosting. Groaning again—this time in pleasure—Elikki swallowed and then licked the frosting off her lip with her quick tongue. I stared, going still at her side.

She knew what it did to me when she licked her lips like

that. Sure enough, she flicked her gaze over mischievously before drawing my head toward her for a deep, sugary kiss. I moved in front of her and leaned into it, placing my arms on either side of the chair, letting Elikki pull me as close as she wanted. The buzzing in my stomach fanned into a full bonfire. Her tongue swirled against mine, lips chasing lips. She was sweeter than anything I'd ever tasted. It had only been a few hours since we last kissed, but this quenched a longing I'd had since we parted after lunch.

Her free hand trailed down my side, dragging up my neatly tucked in shirt and drawing her nails lightly against the skin of my back. My breath stuttered, and I could feel her lips turning upward against my mouth.

I drew back just enough to murmur, "You scamp."

Elikki drew an innocent face. "Who, me?" she said, before smearing a dollop of frosting on my neck and sucking it off. My cock stiffened.

"You seem much revived," I said wryly, pulling down the neck of her blouse to reveal more of the ample breasts that spilled out of her yellow corset. Kissing down her collarbone, I swiped some of the frosting for myself, smearing it in her cleavage before diving in, long licks of my tongue making her pant hot breaths against my neck.

"Yes, I'm feeling—ohhh—ten times—ooOO!—better now." Elikki squirmed underneath me, fighting to remove her corset so I could tend to her nipples. I sat back on my heels.

"Here, love, let me," I said. I picked the cold cider up from the floor and passed it to her, then I stood and knelt behind the chair. She beamed and took a deep gulp.

"Ahh, this is bliss," she said, taking another bite of her cinnamon roll and washing it down with cider. "Now I am officially recovered! What a day." She placed them on the table and sighed with deep contentment.

I kept loosening the corset strings. I was getting quite quick at it with all the practice I had this week. The anticipation, the time it took to unravel the strings and undress her, always left me rock-hard by the time I was done.

After lifting the garment over her head and placing it off to the side, I leaned forward and scooped each of her soft, heavy breasts into my hands. Elikki hummed happily. Kneading them gently first, I then found her taut nipples through her linen shirt, rolling them each between my thumb and forefinger. Her breath quickened, as I knew it would.

I pulled Elikki to her feet. Our gazes locked on each other, heavy with need.

"Take off your shirt, Barra," she said, voice low and demanding.

I didn't have to be told twice. With one hand, I pulled the hem up and over my head, throwing the shirt across the room instead of folding it. I'd noticed Elikki loved it if I did things like that when we were heating up. And it wasn't hard to override my normal neat-freak tendencies when she looked at me like this.

I needed her body against mine as soon as possible, tidiness be damned.

Her gray eyes flashed. She stepped toward me—slowly, too slowly—and I felt my pulse race faster with every inch she drew closer. When she reached me, she tugged her own shirt off and flung it across the room too. I drank in the sight of her. Plump, beautiful stomach and full breasts, her strong arms reaching for me.

Sitting on the edge of the bed so we were face-to-face, I pulled Elikki close in between my legs, running my hands along the smooth length of her back. I tangled myself in her thick hair and tilted her against my lips, desperate to taste her again. "El," I breathed, my chest full, heartbeat roaring.

She met my kiss fiercely. We moved against each other, exploring, savoring. Her small bites on my bottom lip got progressively sharper, making me moan.

Suddenly, she drew back. "Wait, I have an idea," she said. Darting back to the table, she grabbed the remaining half of the cinnamon roll and stalked toward me again with her most mischievous grin.

"What are you…" I began to say, before Elikki smeared some of the thick frosting on my collarbone. Her quick tongue swiped at it. She was back between my legs, and I locked my ankles together, tucking her tightly against me. Like a cat, she lapped at the frosting, moving from my left shoulder along my collarbone to the base of my neck. When she reached that spot and began kissing and nipping lightly, my head lolled back. She'd recently discovered how sensitive I was there, and ever since had delighted in driving me to a frenzy at her whim.

Inconvenient when we're, say, eating lunch in public and I had to hide my boner under the table until it goes down. But here, locked in our cozy room, smelling of sugar and magic and *her*, I could let myself go completely.

I rucked up Elikki's skirts and found her ass, squeezing its fullness with both hands. She squeaked against my neck, and I couldn't help chuckling. She moved her lips to my throat now, licking the hollow below my Adam's apple once.

Two could play that game.

Slipping her underwear down, I let them drop to the floor. I reached between our bodies, knowing exactly where to go.

Letting my forefinger slide along the length of her slit, I waited for her to do her hum of pleasure and arch into me before I plunged it in up to my knuckles. Her breath caught. She was wet, soaking for me, and I felt myself get impossibly harder.

Curling my finger inside her and rubbing near her clit with my thumb, I used my other hand to lift her right breast to my mouth, sucking lightly on the hard nipple. My legs braced her. She was losing herself to my movements. Eyes fluttering closed, her weight leaning on me, breath loud and fast.

"*Fuck*, Barra," Elikki huffed out. "That's perfect. You… arghhhagagagh…" I felt her tense for a beat, nails sharp in my shoulder blades, before she came undone. Limbs warm and loose against me, she let me hold her. I kissed her forehead, nose, shoulder. Untied her skirts and let them fall so I could hold her flush against my chest, legs wrapped around my hips on the bed.

We stayed like that, torsos pressed together like two pages in a book, until her heartbeat slowed. After a while, she pulled back slightly and whispered, "I made you something."

"Let me guess—is it edible or dirty?" I said. "Edible *and* dirty?"

She swatted me playfully. "No and no."

Slipping down to the floor, Elikki pranced over to her rucksack, shamelessly showing off her nakedness to me. She returned holding a small velvet pouch. With an almost nervous energy, she offered it to me.

I took it, but said, "El, what is this?"

"Open it and see!" She laughed, nudging me. She crossed her arms under her chest and waited, watching my hands instead of returning my gaze.

I untied the pouch and upturned it on my palm. A long, thick silver chain spilled out, glinting in the candlelight. At its end was a four-pointed pendant with dark, amber-colored sea glass set in the middle. It was beautiful.

She made this for me?

As I continued to stare at the necklace, mind struggling to catch up with what I was seeing, Elikki jerkily shifted her weight from foot to foot. She burst out, "I know it's not perfect. I'm still honing this new style. And I mainly wanted to make sure the enchantment was strong. So it's a bit rough." She gnawed on her lower lip.

Stunned, I said, "Your magic is in this?"

"Yeah. It's a protection spell, of sorts. It should keep you safe from any nefarious magic. If you want to wear it, I mean. It's fine if you don't."

Elikki reached out as if to pick up the necklace, and I broke out of my daze. Trapping her hand between both of mine, I held it firmly.

"This is the most incredible gift anyone has ever given me," I said quietly.

Her eyes finally snapped to mine. Relief in them, strangely, but happiness blooming as well.

"You like it?" she asked. "I used that lump of silver that I gave you to make the pendant. May have snuck it out of your pocket while you were sleeping. I wanted it to be a surprise."

"I love it," I said, bending forward to say it again with a kiss. "El, I love it so much." *And I love you*, is what I wanted to tell her. Instead, I asked, "Why did you make this for me?"

"I just…I wanted you to have some part of me. And to keep you safe," Elikki said. "I want you to know you mean a great deal to me." She lifted the chain up and over my head. The pendant settled, a reassuring weight against my bare chest.

My heart squeezed. "Are you leaving, then?"

"*No*," she said, gripping my shoulders. "No. But it's only a matter of time, isn't it?"

I wanted to say, *It doesn't have to be. We could stay together. Make a life together.*

But Elikki kissed me fiercely, and I let her.

Her kisses tasted like *let's not waste time* and *this is what I can give you*. She met my mouth with hunger. The pendant pressed between us, metal warming from our heat. I made myself focus on the feel of her soft lips, her hair wisping against my cheeks. Her smooth full body, my hands filled with her, and the sweat forming between us. The pleasure we were about to have together, again and again and again.

21

ELIKKI

When we were finally sated and breathless, having tried a couple of new, slightly acrobatic positions, Barra and I readied ourselves for supper.

"So, I guess it's safe to say you really do love my gift," I teased with a coy smile as I rebuttoned my skirts. "Three orgasms is quite a show of appreciation."

Barra stalked over to me, smoothed down my tousled hair, and tucked a lock gently behind an ear. "It could have been four if that nightstand hadn't given out on us." He bent and kissed the tip of my nose.

"Ahh, yes…we should probably pay for the damages. And get a sturdier replacement so we can try that move again."

"Agreed," he rumbled, straightening his shirt and overcoat. An uncertain, thoughtful look came into his eyes. But he turned away, righting a potted plant we'd knocked over.

"What is it? I'm not paying for the nightstand, if that's what you're thinking," I said with a laugh.

He fussed with the dirt that had spilled out, sweeping it into his palm and returning it to the pot. "It's nothing," he said, "Let's get some supper."

"Barra—" I came closer, concerned now. "Tell me?"

He turned, swallowing. "I was thinking," he said, then hesitated again. Looking down at me, he brought his hand to where my pendant rested on his broad chest. He took a breath, then said, "I was thinking that I have a very sturdy nightstand in my bedroom at home."

I stilled.

"If you wanted to—to visit. You could stay as long as you wanted. And my mas, my sisters, they'll all love you, I know it—"

"Barra. Stop." My voice was quiet but sharp as an icicle.

His mouth snapped shut. Hurt reflected at me from those smoky quartz eyes.

I crossed the room to where my cider sat, long forgotten. It had gone warm in the past hours, but I chugged down every drop. Wiped the back of a hand across my mouth. Buckling on the worn brown leather belt that carried my coin purse and favorite knife, I moved back to Barra and took his hand.

"Let's go eat, okay?" I tugged him gently toward the door.

For a panicked second, I thought he would refuse. But he simply gave a small sigh that stung my heart and let me lead him stiffly out, down the staircase, and through the crowded inn tavern to the fresh air of the street below.

I linked an arm with his, and we wandered downhill, following the curve of golden magelights deeper into the thick of Rising Night revelry. I waited until we came to a tavern full of merrymakers and loud with music before pulling us inside. Barra lingered uncertainly near the door, scanning the room. But I darted ahead through the crowd and snagged an empty back table with a sturdy-looking bench. Waving him over, I plastered a smile on my face as he came near, moving his bulky body carefully through the scrum.

It seemed like everyone was out on the town tonight—drinking, laughing, and dancing to their heart's content. Folk tended to get a bit foolhardy in Kurriel at the end of each month, a swelling energy that was released through the night's celebrations. Supposedly in honor of the goddess, our kingdom's dual-souled deity. For as much as I liked the idea of the goddess and her open-hearted mysteriousness, on Rising Nights I usually just felt grateful, like most people, to have an excuse to go a bit feral once a month in whatever random town's pub I frequented at the time. I hadn't felt that swelling pressure in my mind over these past days, but it hit me hard now. Goddess, I needed a drink.

Barra slid onto the bench next to me, keeping a wary few inches between us. "El, are you sure you want to eat here?" He raised his voice a bit to be heard over the music. "I feel like we should go someplace to talk."

I scooted closer to him, eliminating the space between our bodies. Yelled into his ear, "This place is great! I'll get us some food!"

With another fake grin, which he didn't return, I bounced up and shimmied through the crowd to the bar. I could feel his gaze on my back. I didn't dare turn around.

After placing our order—two house specials, one cinnamon tea for Barra, and a large pint of ale for me—I dawdled there for a bit longer, taking in the scene and thinking of anything I could to *not* let myself think of his words in the bedroom. His offer.

I downed that pint quickly and ordered another. Suddenly, I spied a couple of friendly faces from the Artisans Guild nearby. Screaming our hellos at each other, we hugged and began to talk over one another about our days, the performers, the cute bartender.

One of them—Cookie, I think his name was? Toffee?—bought shots for the three of us. Some local specialty he called sapsa, deep green and herbal smelling. It burned my throat, squeezing tears out of my eyes. I ordered another round.

We toasted again—To the night! To new friends! To our skilled fingers and to sexy bartenders!—and tossed them back, laughing riotously through the searing sting, pungent green liquid clinging to our fingers.

In the corner of my eye, I could see Barra still seated at the back, watching me. A server had dropped off our meals at some point. I flagged down the bartender and got one more pint, telling myself that this would be the last one. After saying my goodbyes to Cookie and Mera—Sera?—I turned, keeping that smile fixed on my face as I wove over to our table. Pecking a kiss on Barra's cheek, I slid in close to him on the bench.

"Mmm, this looks delicious," I said, picking up a fork and diving into the plate of roast potatoes, honey-glazed carrots, and some kind of mystery meat.

"El," Barra said, a warm hand rubbing my back. "Are you all right?"

"Of course I am!" I said. Spearing another potato, I grinned wildly and held it up to him. "You should try these! Eat, eat. Look at you, you're wasting away."

He opened his mouth and accepted the food, chewing slowly as he watched me with steady, dark eyes. I broke our gaze. Focusing on my plate, I sawed into the meat with vigor.

"I want to explain," he said. "About what I said earlier. El, can we please just talk about it—"

"Actually!" I said, leaping up, my silverware clattering to the table. "Actually, I'm pretty full! I'm going to dance for a bit. Back soon!"

"Wait, you've hardly eaten—" Barra reached out to me, but I pretended not to notice and shimmied away into the crowd.

He wouldn't follow. The people, all moving together, packed close—I knew it was the last place he would want to be.

Some better, smarter part of me said, *What are you doing? This is all wrong.* Working my way to the main dance floor tucked next to the far corner of the bar, I chugged the rest of my pint and slammed it on the counter. *Shut the fuck up*, I told that voice. It faded to a distant whisper, drowned out by the loud instruments, the shouts and laughter surrounding me, the pleasant buzzing in my head that told me the alcohol was doing its job.

I found my new guild friends again and we danced, and danced, and danced. Laughing about nothing, I spun around, flung from one set of arms to the next. It was a reel, then a jig, and then I was twirling my skirts alone in the middle of a circle. Around and around. Faces blurred, colors smearing into a whirlwind, the fiddles scratching in my ears.

Around and around and around. I couldn't feel my feet, and my body was something else entirely, but hands grabbed at mine, sweaty and hot. This was fun. This was fine. Hair was plastered on my face, in my eyes. I tried to fling the strands away, the movement sending another dizzying jolt through my pounding head. The music was a wall of sound that pressed against me, hard and fierce. More hands grabbed at me, cackling laughter spiking my ears.

I should stop. I should stop. I needed to get away.

Hot bodies surrounded me, pushing me along with their rhythm. Their mad joy. I twisted now, searching for an exit with eyes that couldn't focus. My throat was tightening, chest heaving. I was alone. How to get out. Had to get out.

Strong, cool arms encircled me. A pocket of air. People moving away.

The arms held me lightly, not close. One on my back, just touching. One brushed the hair out of my eyes with gentle fingers. Someone peering worriedly into my face. Barra.

The crowd of drunken revelers had quieted a bit around us, but a new lively song struck up, and everything carried on again. It was as if there was a bubble around the two of us. Everyone kept their slight distance from the tall half-giant, and for once I was glad of their wariness.

I took deep breaths. My racing heart slowed.

Barra held me steady, hands roving quickly once to make sure I was all right. His chin jutted toward the exit, eyes questioning. *Do you want to leave?*

I clung to him. Shook my head slightly. *Not yet.*

Wrapping my arms around his waist, I rested my cheek against his chest and let my hazy eyes drift closed. He was so steady, solid. The music faded away. His arms stayed snug around me, where they belonged, his chin just grazing the top of my head.

I swayed us gently, ignoring the rhythm, and Barra followed

my lead. Everything stopped spinning. I could feel the hard wooden floor beneath my boots and hear the calm pounding of his heartbeat.

It was just the two of us, alone. Alone together.

I don't know how long we stood there. But at some point, I reached up on my tiptoes, teetering for a moment before his arms tightened around me. I kissed him hard, greedy. As if I could keep him with me like this forever if I just kept my lips against his. As if this wasn't a goodbye.

Eventually, we pulled apart and headed hand in hand to the door. Coming outside was a relief after the heat and noise of the tavern. The night air was fresh and sweet, stars sparkling above in the inky black sky. We made our way slowly back to the Oak & Spoon, me stumbling and cursing the tricksy cobblestones a bit as I went.

After a while, Barra broke the silence. "Would it be so bad—coming back to Nepu with me? We could find you your own place there if that's the issue."

I kept walking, watching the moths tapping uselessly against the golden magefire streetlamps. I tried to order my scrambled, tipsy thoughts. "It's not that I think badly of it. I know you have a beautiful life there," I said, swallowing hard. "But it's not what I want."

And instead of saying *You could want it. You'll like it. I need you, please,* like so many before him, he just said, "Then what do you want, El?"

Heart in my throat, I sighed and said, "I don't know. I really don't know. But it isn't that. Not now."

I dared a glance at him, walking steadily beside me. His expression shuttered, mouth tight.

"I do want *you*, though," I said softly. "And I wish I could want the kind of future you want for us, Barra. I just don't think I have that in me. That way of loving someone. Being with them." The drink had loosened my tongue too much.

"Couldn't we just try? Together?" His deep voice broke a bit.

I didn't want this to happen, to hurt him like this. Hurt myself. He should have disappointed me, should have done something by now that made me feel like I needed to get away.

Instead, I'd only grown more attached with each day that passed. The warm, shy smile whenever he saw me. His sleepy eyes and soft kisses in the morning. How he could light fire in my veins, my core, with just a look. How he always thought of me, considered my needs, made his care clear beyond a doubt. The way he'd begun to absentmindedly brush a palm across my hair, down my arm, when we came back together, even if we were only apart for a few minutes. When he let me see more and more of him—his vulnerabilities, anxieties, past scars on his heart—and how he made me want to share some of my own too, for the first time.

We should have let each other go when we first got to this town. Everything seemed so clear now, walking side by side in the cool, quiet night. I never should have convinced him we could keep this casual fling going for a few days. I'd been lying to myself then. We'd been lying to each other ever since.

And now I was going to be just another person in his life who hurt him. Rejected what he offered. Rejected him. After he'd braved opening himself up again. And I hated myself a little bit for it.

But what he offered me—going back with him to Nepu, living there, being a part of his family—almost everything in me cringed at the idea. I tried to imagine it. Settling down in the village. Meeting his neighbors, family, friends, everyone who had known Barra since he was a child, now judging me, seeing if I would fit in.

It was too much. Far too much pressure.

His many sisters and mas—maybe they'd welcome me, maybe not. They all have an established dynamic together. A long history, inside jokes, strong bonds woven over years that tied them tightly together. Where would I fit into that? I had no frame of reference. My own family hadn't liked me, wanted me—why in the goddess's name would complete strangers ever welcome some wandering, aimless elf into their homes, their lives?

They might try. For Barra's sake, they probably would. I would too, desperately. From everything he'd said, they sounded kind, like him. But eventually I would say something wrong, do something awful. I wouldn't fit. They'd turn on me. Or I'd make myself leave before things imploded. And if that were months, or years, down the line—it would only cut me deeper. Cut Barra deeper.

Better to end this now. He would get over me, probably sooner than he expected. And I'd keep moving, as I always have. Traveling on to the next towns, cities, villages. Exploring my newfound powers and continuing to hone my metalsmithing skills. Making friends along the way, causing some drama, having adventures.

Not taking any new lovers though. Even the thought made me queasy, reminding me that I'd had several drinks on a mostly empty stomach. No…not for a long, long while. Until Barra was many hundreds of miles behind me, and I could think of him without wanting to travel straight back into his arms.

So now I slipped my hand into his as we walked. To his question, I said, "I'm sorry. But I don't want to try for something that I know won't work."

I could practically feel the sadness rolling off Barra, but he kept his face forward. Shoulders stiff and only a gentle squeeze of my palm acknowledged my words. My jaw clenched. I forced the tears that threatened to rise back down. I wouldn't make this even harder for him.

We reached the inn in silence and went up to our room. I gathered my belongings and packed them away, hefting the rucksack onto my back. Barra stood leaning against the far wall, arms wrapped around himself. He didn't watch.

"I'm going to sleep at another inn tonight, then set off after the market tomorrow. But I'll see you in the morning, right?"

No reply. I let myself gravitate closer to him, reach a hand up to his chest. He flinched when I touched him, and I pulled back quickly.

"Barra, will you come by my stall? To—to say goodbye. You can show off that necklace, make my customers wild with jealousy." I smiled weakly, trying to joke.

His eyes finally dragged up to meet mine. Pain swirled in their brown depths: bleak hopelessness, embarrassment, and so much pain. I found myself stepping back, suddenly gripping the metal doorknob.

In a hollow voice, he said, "I love you, you know."

My windpipe clenched. I couldn't get enough air. I was back in the hot tavern, spinning, spinning, spinning. Before I knew it, I had slipped through the door, closing it gently behind me.

I ran.

Soon I stumbled out of the inn's front door. The stones of

the street, the lamplight, the townsfolk moving along—it all blurred in front of me. Light and colors smearing together from tears swimming and spilling. The drinks were catching up to me. I set my feet down a side street shortcut toward a nearby inn with a Vacancy sign that I'd spotted earlier on our walk back. It felt miles away, and I was tired. So tired.

Lost in my thoughts, I almost didn't notice the figure that stepped from the shadows of an alley. But he walked right in my path. Faced me with a cold sneer and said, "Having a bad night, sweetheart?"

I froze, my brain trying to take in the person before me. That familiar, unsettling voice.

Felsith.

My lip curled. I blinked furiously to clear my vision. It was darker here, the main road half a block away. No one around.

Reaching for my belt knife, I took a breath to bite back at him.

Something stung, sharp and cold, into the side of my neck. My fingers found a small dart there as the edges of my vision quickly darkened, fading to black. From a far distance, I felt myself stumble and slump to the ground. Someone behind me caught me low before I smashed my head on the cobblestones.

"She's out," a woman's satisfied voice said close to my ear. And then, as everything slipped away, "Told you that I'd make you pay…"

"Good," Felsith replied, a distant oily purr. "Let's move her fast."

A response from the other person, indecipherable. My numb arms thrown around shoulders.

Then everything went dark.

22

Barra

Elikki was gone.

Just a few short hours ago we'd been together in this room. Talking. Fucking. Laughing. And now she'd left.

I thought back to that moment when I asked her to come stay with me. I had truly believed that her gift—this beautiful necklace that she had poured so much of her time and magic into for me—meant something.

Not just that she valued our time together. But that she wanted *more*. More of me. More of our…relationship? What I had started to hope was the beginning of a relationship, at least.

The way Elikki had looked when she gave me the necklace, when she kissed me—a sadness like she was mourning the loss of me while I was still in the room. I'd thought she might want another option. A future together, or at least the possibility of one.

I had been so fucking wrong.

Inviting her to Nepu only hastened our ending. It was the

same story I'd written for myself time and time again with previous people, just in a different font. I'd put myself out there again. Scared off someone wonderful again. Got my heart broken. *Again.*

When would I learn? Elikki had been completely honest with me from the start. She didn't do serious. This was supposed to be short-lived, just fun. Two travelers on an unexpected road trip, fighting bounty hunters and having some amazing sex.

I should have kept my mouth shut. Swallowed my feelings and enjoyed the time we had, whatever days were left. It still would have broken my heart when she eventually moved on, but all those extra memories...I could have had so much more Elikki to think about, hold close, in the months and years after I returned to my monotonous life.

Who invites someone home to live with them after a week? Who tells someone that they love them as that person is actively leaving you, rejecting you?

She was right to go, I berated myself as I dragged a palm over my face, rubbing away tears. I had to get out of this room. Maybe I'd go see Pebble. It had been a couple of days since I checked in on my horse at the inn's stables. Dragging myself to my feet, I took a few steadying breaths, then headed downstairs.

When I entered the inn's main room, still half full despite the late hour, the innkeeper behind the bar looked over. She was talking to a cloaked figure who leaned forward, listening intently.

I stopped abruptly. Bounty hunter.

We thought they'd given up. There hadn't been any sign of one since we'd arrived. Thank the goddess Elikki was gone, safe somewhere else for the night.

The innkeeper nodded and jerked her thumb at me. I tensed. There was nowhere to go. I'd have to deal with them here. The cloaked person looked over to where the innkeeper pointed, to where I stood like a seven-and-a-half-foot-tall statue by the stairwell. I desperately wished I'd strapped on my sword before leaving my room.

Their face was partly in shadow. Shaking their hood back, they peered across the candlelight room at me—

"*Telen?*" I cried in disbelief.

My eldest sister's dark brown face broke into a wide grin. She strode toward me, hands in her pockets.

"Well, well. Glad to see you're alive, little brother."

"What—what are you doing here?" I returned her tight, quick hug, bending down to her shorter human height.

She gave me a bemused glance before flagging down the innkeeper from across the bar. "Looking for you, of course."

"But…why? Oh no—is everyone all right? What happened?"

"Everyone's fine, fine. No, I want to know what happened to *you*," she said, then paused, eyes tracking across my face and likely bloodshot eyes. "But first—I know you don't often drink, Bar, but let me get you something. You look terrible."

"Wow, thanks," I grumbled under my breath. Telen truly had no filter. But I didn't protest as she got two hot toddies and led us to a quiet table in the corner.

"Now sit," my sister said, placing a massive, steaming tankard in my hands, "and tell me why I found you here, days away from where we thought you were going on business, looking like someone just cut down all the flowers in your precious front garden."

I stared into the amber depths of my tankard, not knowing where to start. The spiced lemon-honey scent lifted to my nose, the heat of the mug a welcome comfort. Telen waited patiently, sipping at her own hot toddy and watching me as she played with one of the short braids that framed her face.

In starts and stops, I began to recount what happened. I told her everything, from the charged encounter between Elikki and Felsith in the market, ending with her breaking his wrist, to the mass fight that we kind of accidentally started in the bar later, when I broke his *other* wrist. I explained our flight from the town, how I pretended to El that I had business in Old Orchard, our tumultuous and exciting journey, the bounty hunters, falling for her, and the blissful days we'd had together here.

Choking out some of the words, I told her about everything that had happened tonight. How I'd messed up. How she'd run away from me, and she was going to leave town tomorrow. At some point Telen had taken my hand, or I'd taken hers, and she held on with her firm, steady grip, strong from years of apprenticing with Ma Reese in the forge.

When I finally finished, we sat together in silence. I felt raw, empty. Though it also felt good, somehow, to get it all out. I slumped back in my seat, wiping my face again with the handkerchief Telen passed me.

She had finished her drink while I talked, and now reached over for mine, still untouched on the table. She took a long swallow, then leaned back too and said, "Well, why don't you go with her?"

"…what?"

Fixing me with her look—the one that said *don't act dumb, dummy*—she said again, "Why. Don't you. Go with. Her. This Elikki woman—if she can't come back with you, why not travel with her?"

My brain whirred. "I can't…I can't just set off…traveling, for—for who knows how long! I have all of you at home. Our mas, and Monty, Sassura. And our family business. I need to be there to do the books, do the orders, keep things run—*why do you keep shaking your head?*"

Telen barked out a laugh and said, "Bar, I love you, but we're not exactly going to fall apart if you leave. I know how to do the books. You taught me yourself. I already handle them when you're out of town on customer trips. We'd be fine."

"But—I have a house. The garden. My—my plants."

She shrugged. "I'll stay there if you want, in the spare room. Keep an eye on things. I've been meaning to find my own place and move out of our mas' anyway. And I bet Ma Wren would be happy to help with the garden. Will keep her from fussing over Monty and the pregnancy." She snorted, taking another gulp of my hot toddy. "Goddess knows she needs a new project, or Monty is going to combust from the overattention one of these days."

"I can't ask you all to do that. I should be there, taking care of you too. Monty's baby is coming in a few months. I wouldn't see Sassura off for her next performing season. I'm already going to be so behind on work as it is…"

Telen just said, "The girls will understand. Our mas will too. Stop trying to come up with excuses, Bar." Softly, she added, "We've watched you be unhappy for so long. Giving up on love when it's something you've always wanted—throwing yourself into work and pointless tasks—it's been hard for me, for all of us, to see you drawing in on yourself these past years."

I closed my eyes, letting my head fall back on the wall behind me. Tried to let myself picture it, what the reality of what she suggested would look like. Traveling with El. Leaving my home behind.

Somehow, the idea didn't scare me. It didn't feel like a

sacrifice. I just couldn't believe it hadn't even occurred to me. I was so sure that after a life of no real home, no real family, this was something substantial that I could offer her. That she'd want stability, comfort, and a place of her own because that's what *I* knew and *I* understood.

And when she said it *wasn't* what she wanted, I didn't bother to fight for her. I just let her walk away.

Releasing a long sigh, I said, "I doubt El would even want me to go with her now. She probably never wants to see me again."

"If that were true, I doubt she'd have asked you to come see her at the market tomorrow morning. Besides—if there's even a slight chance that she'd accept, don't you have to at least try? I certainly will never forgive you if you come back to Nepu with me without talking to her." At that, Telen drained the last of the hot toddy and burped lightly in my face.

Waving the stink away with a grimace, I said, "I suppose you're right. Disgusting, but right."

"I always am," she said with a smile, then stood, stretching out limbs tight from the long day's ride. "I have more to tell you about my journey, but I'm exhausted. Going to get a room here. Meet in the morning for breakfast?"

"Yes, but early. At dawn. El said she was going to try and get to the market as soon as possible tomorrow, to get a good spot."

"All right, all right. Night, little brother." She yawned.

"Good night," I said. "And Telen—thank you."

She waved me off and went in search of the innkeeper. I headed up to my room, head spinning with everything I'd realized tonight. Going over and over my plans for what to say to El when I saw her.

This could go terribly. Again. But like Telen said: if there was any chance, I had to try.

And if we were completely wrong, and El just wanted nothing more to do with me, I swore to myself that I would let her go. Even if it ripped my heart apart irrevocably.

After a near sleepless night, I finally gave up just before dawn. Dressing and gathering my belongings in the feeble candlelight, a memory of Elikki's rapid, silent packing last night flashed across my mind. The pained look on her beautiful face.

I kept moving. No matter what happened today, I wouldn't be returning to this room. I'd either be with El on the road to some unknown destination or shuffling home with Telen.

Downstairs, no one was awake yet. I made my way out to the stables. Pebble was a welcome sight, and I took my time feeding, watering, and brushing her as the sun slowly rose. She didn't really need it—the inn's stablehand had taken excellent care of her—but it was a relaxing ritual that calmed my frantic pulse.

When everything was done, and Pebble was saddled and loaded up with my bags, I headed back inside. Only my good manners, long ago engrained in me by Ma Wren, kept me from knocking on every room at the inn until I found Telen. If she slept in late, I wasn't going to wait for her. I could not risk missing El at the market. Although a grain of common sense in my mind tried to remind me that market setup wouldn't happen until nine o'clock, at the earliest. Everyone liked to sleep in on a Resting Day.

A kitchen lad poked his head out into the room. Spotting me at a table by the door, arms crossed together, he crept out and warily asked if I wanted any breakfast. I tried to wipe the scowl off my face and fixed my posture to look more approachable. Less intimidating.

Then I stopped. I was in a foul mood. If El were here, she'd tell me I didn't have to pretend to be happy and harmless for a timid human. *Don't be an asshole*, I could almost hear her lilting voice say. *But you can feel your feelings, Barra.*

I straightened a bit and looked the lad in the eyes. He winced slightly but didn't scamper away. In my normal gruff morning voice, I said, "I'm having a rough time of it this morning, kid. Could you get me a large pot of the strongest black tea you have? And two full fry-ups, if you can. Extra portions on one of them, for me."

He softened a little and nodded with a nervous smile. "Aye. Went a bit too hard last night, did you, sir? We've all been there."

"Something like that," I said.

"Well, I'll get those started for you, sir." He disappeared back into the kitchen and returned a few minutes later with a steaming pot of tea just as Telen stumbled down the stairs. She dumped her bag on the ground and half fell into the seat next to me with a groan. The server fetched an extra cup.

"Remind me again why we have to be up at the ass crack of dawn when everyone sensible is still in bed?" She dribbled cream into her tea and slurped it down, eyes half-closed in sleep.

"For love," I said, patting her back while I drained my own cup. Telen murmured something that sounded like "stupid love is stupidy stupid" and rested her head on the table.

Luckily, she perked up when our food came out ten minutes later. We tucked in, inhaling the greasy eggs, beans, thick bacon, mushrooms, and tomatoes in record time. I munched on a triangle of toast, dipping the charred bits into my tea, while she downed another cup.

Once she looked a bit more alive, I clapped my hands together and stood, pulling her up with me. Dropping our payment on the table, I called our thanks to the serving lad and strode outside. Telen grumbled but followed me.

She'd stored her own bag in the stables with her horse, and we set off in the direction of the main square where the market was held. It was just a short walk downhill and into the center of town. I rehearsed again what I was going to say to Elikki. And then one more time for good measure. Then, to distract myself and calm down, I did my breathing exercises, counting in and out while I tried to focus on my solid steps over the worn cobblestone and the grumpy chatter of my sister.

When we reached the large square, I paused and did a slow scan around. It was still fairly empty, only a few vendors setting up their wares on the side of the street that would get the best shade once the sun fully rose.

Elikki hadn't arrived yet. I let out a heavy breath.

Telen and I sat on the wide edge of the central water foundation to wait. I tried to refocus on what she was saying, asking questions and making noises at the appropriate times, but it was difficult to think about anything other than El.

My sister recounted her journey here, which was relatively quiet, except for a run-in with a remarkably loud singing troupe that begged her to let them perform one song...which turned into six. She told me about her stop at Legus and Saho's inn, and the strange new pair of bickering employees they'd hired. I smiled to myself at that. It was good to hear Ronald and Stan had made it there and were trying to give up their untalented attempts at a life of crime. Though from what Telen said, they may not make it as a couple—Saho and Legus had to keep them working in separate parts of the inn every day so their squabbling didn't annoy the guests.

She also mentioned a surly but hot dwarven woman named Maerryl was working the bar. Telen had tried unsuccessfully to pick her up, and she'd disappeared later that night. According to a peeved Saho, she'd left them in the lurch without any explanation—seemed to have hit the road again, though surprisingly only swiped a loaf of bread and some apples on her way out. That caught my ear, and I filled Telen in on the details of our encounter with Maerryl in the forest on our travels. The memory of her scowling face, the thinly veiled sense of desperation about her, tugged in my mind again like a hangnail on knit gloves. I wondered, not for the first time since we encountered her, what it must take for someone like that to become a bounty hunter. Stan and Ronald had turned to the work because of money problems—maybe she had too?

It was solitary, dangerous work—a strange calling for dwarven folk. And Maerryl wasn't anything like the usual type, those hulking and muscled brutes I'd occasionally seen hauling someone into a constable station. Armed to the teeth and cold in the eyes. For all that she had her own sharp toothiness, the woman hadn't seemed to remotely enjoy hurting Elikki or revel in their fight.

An odd person indeed. Over and over, the image of her vexed face, pinched and cursing over one shoulder as Elikki's charmed bands tugged her down the road, replayed in my thoughts. Somehow, I didn't think we'd seen the last of Maerryl the half-dwarf.

The sun rose higher and higher. More vendors settled into booths for the day's work, and townspeople began to trickle through the square to get their shopping done before the crowds. And yet, no sign of Elikki.

The nervous, shaky feeling that had sat in my stomach since last night was rapidly turning into a heavy, worried queasiness. Telen could see I was starting to spiral a bit.

"I bet she just slept in. Maybe she's hungover from last night," my sister said.

I didn't respond. Spotting Elikki's two friends from the tavern last night at a row of Artisans Guild booths, I went over to ask if they'd seen her.

They hadn't. Not last night after the tavern, not at the guildhall, not this morning. My stomach dropped further as I thanked them and walked back to Telen. The clock tower rang out ten clangs.

Ten o'clock, and Elikki was missing.

"Bar," Telen said, putting a bracing hand on arm, "I hate to suggest this, but do you think she may have...left town?" I shook my head slowly, looking around the square again. She went on, "Maybe Elikki changed her mind about the market and decided to—you know—cut and run without an awkward conversation?"

I thought about it. The way she'd looked last night when I confessed that I loved her. Her face stricken, miserable. How she disappeared through the door as quickly as she could...

Maybe. Maybe she had left town altogether this morning. A large part of me immediately accepted that and all my worst insecurities agreed. But in my gut, it just didn't ring true.

"Something doesn't feel right about this," I said. "Maybe I'm being naive, but I don't think she'd leave without saying goodbye. And she'd been planning for this market for days. Working so hard on her new pieces, her magic—pouring her soul into them. Even beyond her just needing the money, I know she'd come to show off her work."

Telen still looked skeptical, but she didn't argue for once.

"Let's head back up the road. Elikki said last night that she was going to stay in a different inn. She can't have gone far. We'll just check in with the few near ours." I knew I probably sounded desperate to my sister, but my concern was real. Something felt very wrong. But I forced myself to say, "If we don't find anything strange at the inns, I want to check back here one more time. And if we still can't find her after that…we can head home."

A brisk walk later—Telen huffing and red in the face—we decided to split up to cover ground faster. Or, I guess, she decided. Shouted "Your legs are twice the length of mine, you knob! I'm taking this street, and you can speed off fast as you like *that* way!" before stomping off. Fair enough.

I strode to one, two, three inns on the streets surrounding where we stayed. All smaller travelers' spots, they were usually just a couple of rooms above a pub. But I checked everywhere that had a ROOMS FOR LET or VACANCY sign up. No one had rented a room to an elf with reddish-brown hair last night.

After the third "sorry, mate," my stomach was in knots. I was about to head back and see if Telen had had any luck, when I spotted another wooden sign in a dirty window across the road. It was just a dubious scrawl reading ROOMS HERE, but I made my way over and pushed open the creaky front door. It was dark inside, despite the bright sunny day, and empty but for the sole obligatory drunk slouched at the end of the bar.

"Hello?" I called into the back room. "Anyone here?"

After a minute, an elderly man in a stained apron shuffled out to the bar. "You wanting a pint then, son?" he asked.

"Oh no, but thank you. I was wondering if you'd seen a woman last night, with red-brown hair and gray eyes? She's white, curvy, and about this tall." I motioned with my hand. "An elf. You may have rented her a room?"

"Yeah, I saw her. Certainly tied one on, she did," he replied with a chuckle.

My heart leaped into my throat. Rushing my words, I said, "She was here, drinking? Did she stay here?"

"Oh no, her friends brought her in. Already passed out, she was. They said she'd had a few too many. Let her sleep it off in their room."

"Who were these friends? Are they still here?"

The barman, bleary-eyed though he was, was starting to look a bit suspicious. "Eh, what's it to you, then?"

"She's my—she's someone I care very deeply for. And I just need to make sure she's all right." I kept eye contact with him, putting every ounce of sincerity and worry into my words that I could.

After an assessing moment, he said, "Aye, prob'ly good of you too. I didn't love the look of this one fellow who rented the room."

"What did they look like?"

"The woman, half-dwarf I think, was fine. Grumpy, but fine," he said. "The man, though—greasy fellow. Bit of a dick. Got a face only a mother could love. Always sneering, sticking up his nose. But they paid good coin in advance. Fesmit was his name. Or Feltsim?"

My blood iced over.

"Felsith."

"Aye, that's the one."

And Maerryl, from the sound of it. The bounty hunter was still working with that scab of a man, and it sounded like they'd found Elikki last night and knocked her out. What were they planning to do, cart her all the way back to Povon so she could be sentenced and do time? If they hurt her...

I already knew the answer but had to ask. "Have they left yet?"

"Yeah, must have been early this morning," the old man said. "I didn't hear a peep. Just came down here myself an hour ago to let Jerod in." The drunk raised his pint glass shakily.

"I saw the lass," he croaked. "Was waiting outside when they left. She didn't look too good."

Pacing closer to Jerod, I said, "What do you mean?"

"The pretty elf, she was hanging between the two of 'em. Head all bopping around, feet dragging, like. I'm not one to judge, I'm not. Still, seemed a bit of a mess. They piled her into a carriage and set off toward the main road."

Hanging on his words, I motioned impatiently for him to continue. He took another sip and said, "The short dickhead said to the other one, the dwarven lass, 'Just shut up and do what I'm paying you to do.' Then she looked *right* steamed. But just climbed up and rode them away." He shrugged and took a long draw on his pint.

I thanked them both and rushed out of the pub. Felsith and Maerryl had El. Drugged, knocked out, or worse. They were in a carriage, probably hours ahead on the road by now. I had to get Telen, get to the stables, and go, *now*.

I was going to find El. No matter what.

23

Elikki

I awoke groggy and confused, my body jostling uncomfortably against a hard surface. *This was some fucking hangover. Way to go, dumbass.*

My head pounded like my brain had doubled in size and was trying to burst out of my skull. The left side of my neck had a dull, throbbing pain, and my limbs felt a bit useless.

Water. Needed water, a nausea tonic, and a bacon egg bap before I braved the market. Barra would get it for me. Maybe he already has, bless that sweet hunk of a man. Just need to open my—

Oh. Wait. No.

Barra was gone. I'd left.

In a rush, it all came back to me. The mad frenzy of the tavern, dancing with Barra, his face as I left our room, running out into the night, crying in an empty street, and then—

Felsith.

My stomach dropped. Felsith slipping into the dim lamplight

in front of me, a satisfied smile fixed on his shiny face, was the last thing I could remember. That absolute *turd*. He'd attacked me. Or, at least, his henchperson did. He wouldn't have a chance against me on his own, and I bet he knew it.

Although—shit. As I took stock of my body, I realized my hands were tied together behind my back. Not just the wrists. They'd wrapped heavy rope or something all the way down my hands, so that I couldn't move so much as a pinkie.

Well, that was…not great. I couldn't wield my metal magic without my hands. And arms too, usually, if I was being honest with myself. Proper mages, the kind with years and years of training, could wield with any part of their body. Some of the most powerful ones could even use just their mind, I'd heard.

But that wasn't going to help me. Even with my newly deepened connection with my magic, I was still essentially a beginner. There was a lot of metal nearby—including my own jewelry that called out to me, disgruntled and unhappy—though it wouldn't do me any good. And as I scanned my body, it seemed all the bits I normally stored on me had been removed. My usual rings, the thick chain bracelet I'd been wearing yesterday, my various daggers—all gone. Even my backup hairstick, sharp and reliable steel that I always kept stored in my braid or my corset, had been found and taken.

It appeared I was a bit fucked. *Stay calm, girl. Breathe. You've been in worse scrapes than this.*

Had I though?

Opening one eye just a crack, I blinked a few times to clear my bleary vision. A carriage. I was in a carriage. Quite basic, but with brocade curtains and a few plump pillows. I tried to keep as still as possible, letting my body stay slumped against the hard wall, the road bumping me about whenever our wheels hit a rough patch. A metallic clang sounded near me, followed by a pleased murmur. My pulse spiked. Someone was in here with me.

Switching eyes, I took in the other side of the carriage. *Felsith*. That conniving worm was seated diagonally across from me, rooting through my rucksack like a pig snuffling for food. I let my gaze fall and focused on not panicking.

Could I really go for a hot coffee and custard pastry right now? Yes.

Did I desperately want to kick my boot into Felsith's chin? Yes.

But I had to keep it together. At least until I knew where exactly I was and how many assholes I was up against.

We continued driving for some time, bumping along the uneven country road, until finally I heard Felsith slide back a window and call out, "Let's stop for a pee break!" before slamming it shut again.

The horses slowed. I heard someone clamber off the driving seat and open the carriage door. Felsith bustled out and headed, I assume, into the woods on the side of the road to do his business. There was a long, long pause. And then they closed the carriage door, sliding something through the handle, presumably to keep me in.

Footsteps padded away. I let out a careful sigh.

And then I moved.

Hopping across to the opposite seat, I ducked my face into my rucksack. Felsith had made a mess of everything. But I knew I had a couple of sharp knives tucked into the front side panel. If I could just—

Tense voices sounded from outside the carriage. I froze and strained my elven ears to catch their words.

"What do you care, you daft girl? We have her. Just stop your nagging."

"You know that's not the issue. I don't think it's right, that you steal her life's possessions."

"It doesn't really *matter* what you think. You are *nobody*. And I deserve some payment for my pain."

"Your payment will be justice. That's why we're bringing her back to town, to serve her sentence."

A laugh, low and cold. "Oh, of course. *Of course*. But would she really feel true justice if she did not lose something she loved? Or, perhaps, everything she loved?"

I scrambled in the rucksack. C'mon, c'mon…it must be here somewhere.

Yes. I gripped one thin utility knife in my teeth and flung it across to my corner of the carriage. Sliding back over to that side as silently as I could, I tried to maneuver it with the very tips of my fingers that weren't tied tightly with rope.

"This isn't right," the woman's voice said quietly. "She's already going to pay for her crimes, and dearly."

"*Not enough*." Felsith's oily voice turned harsh, hard. "Do you even know what she did to me? Do you? She made a *fool* of me. Crushed my wrist with her power without a second glance, then set her giant on me to finish the job. The healers were barely able to salvage both of my wrists! And they cost so much coin, I had to go to my brother for help.

"That nitwit," he said almost under his breath. "My dimwitted Lord Brother! *He* had to bail *me* out. Our parents, my wife, our neighbors…everyone knows. They all think of me—me!—as an idiot. A laughingstock. And this elf—this *bitch*—just got to saunter off into the sunset, la-di-da. Well, I don't think so. She is paying her dues—however I see fit."

There was silence after Felsith's speech. Even I was

motionless for a moment, chilled by the visceral hatred in his voice. This was much, much worse than I'd thought.

I kept maneuvering, trying to get the knife into a good position to cut the ropes on my hands and wrists. For a moment, I thought I had it—and then a sharp pain sliced into my arm. I bit down on my lip, willing myself not to cry out in pain.

A sudden jostling of the door, and a weight stepped back into the carriage. I was suddenly being shaken. Felsith had me by the shoulders, jolting me hard back and forth. My shoulder slammed into the wall, and I yelped.

"Wake, wake! Time's up, girl!"

He pulled me from the carriage before I could react. I stumbled, missing the step, and fell hard onto my knees in the dirt road. My head spun viciously, and I blinked at the sudden bright daylight.

"Careful! What are you doing?" a woman shouted. I swung around to see who else I was up against.

Maerryl. Goddess damn her. Of course that wiseass dickhead had joined up with him.

The half-dwarf strode closer. Her tanned skin was flushed deep red, strong eyebrows slanted in a glare. Well, that wasn't anything new. She was always pissy—but at least this time it didn't seem directed toward me. Maerryl's narrowed eyes flashed at Felsith, fists clenched at her sides. She stopped halfway between Felsith and me. We were almost in a perfect triangle, and I had a sudden absurd desire to laugh. The three of us were facing off in the middle of nowhere. I had no way to defend myself. And the kicker was—I'd put myself in this idiotic, goddess-forsaken predicament. If I hadn't run away like a coward from Barra, none of this would be happening.

Barra probably thought I'd ditched town this morning rather than face him after last night. I might never see him again. And he'd go about the rest of his life thinking I was a cold, cruel monster who'd strung him along for a week and then was too heartless to even say goodbye.

At that thought, I forced myself to my feet. My body screamed in protest, aches and fatigue weighing me down, but I ignored it. No matter what happened, I'd face it standing. Blood dripped slowly from the cut on my arm into the dirt behind me.

"She's bleeding! Are you all right?" Maerryl's eyes cut to me, assessing. I returned her look coolly. I didn't like her, but I needed her on my side. Or at least not on Felsith's side.

"I've been better," I said, letting some of my pain show in my eyes.

She nodded, hard and decided. "Let's get you back in the carriage."

"I have a better idea," said Felsith, who had been watching our exchange closely. "Why don't we mete out justice right here?"

"What are you talking about?" Maerryl said, her voice flat.

He crept closer, and I took a step back. The carriage was behind me. I was boxed in by them.

"Well. I find that I don't wish to wait to see her punished anymore. The whole rigamarole with the legal system, keeping her in our jail, the extra drama and gossip it will provoke in town, perhaps across the queendom—it's all a bit much, isn't it?"

Felsith stepped closer again, and my back was against the carriage's side. I could see his every oily pore, the flash of madness in his eyes.

"We could take care of this right now. I'll keep most—not

all—of her belongings. Her precious *jewelry*," he spat to Maerryl, keeping his stare trained on me. "But I'll leave her tools, a few coins. You'll get triple the coin I promised you. And then we'll cut her loose here to go on her merry way."

Maerryl looked dubious, conflicted. I could tell she wanted to be done with this business and cut ties. She seemed to regret aligning herself with him out of anger toward me. Or perhaps it had been simple desperation. I knew what it was like to be penniless and out of options. "I suppose…I suppose that's an acceptable solution. If not entirely legal."

"Of course…" Felsith continued, eyes locked with mine. I didn't look away. He said softly, a hint of a wicked smile beginning to spread across his face, "Of course, we'll have to break her wrists first."

My throat plummeted into my stomach, a cold cement weight.

"You're insane," Maerryl breathed.

I burst to the left suddenly, running as fast as I could while trying to stay balanced with both arms tied tightly behind my back and my vision still tilting slightly.

Which, as it turned out, is not so fast. Even with my natural speed, I was too slow and Felsith caught up and grabbed me by the hair, unbalancing me further so I had to scrabble to keep my legs under me. Laughing manically, he let go and shoved me hard into the road. Rocks dug into my side, ribs and hip on fire from colliding with the hard, packed dirt. I fought to catch my breath.

"Good try, elf. But not quite quick enough!"

"I am going to kill you, you filthy, disgusting toad," I said, injecting my voice with icy venom as I struggled to rise. "Untie me now or I will slice you up with a thousand shards of rusty metal."

Felsith just laughed again, pinning my bound wrists to the ground with his boot. He loomed over me, satisfaction gleaming in his beady eyes. I thrashed violently like an animal, kicking for him, trying to knock his legs or knees out. Straining my neck to bite him, to get at him in any way I could.

He leaned more weight on my wrists, making me cry out in agony. I stilled.

"Maerryl, STOP HIM! This is madness!" I yelled. She stood frozen, face a stony blank.

"Not madness. This is fitting, no?" Felsith said, delighted with how perfectly his plans had fallen into place. I could hear his smarmy smile, feel his need to crush me like I'd crushed him.

"An eye for an eye. So to speak. Too bad for you, however, there are no healers for miles. Tsk-tsk. A few good stomps should do it…"

No, no, no no no no NO. This wasn't happening. Without my hands…

"Stop."

I squinted my eyes open. Maerryl had stepped closer. She held a long dagger in each hand and said, "Get away from her. Now."

"Or what? You'll attack me?" Felsith laughed incredulously. "You have no money. You *need* me. *And* the huge amount of coin I'll be giving you when this is done."

"This isn't right," Maerryl said, her mouth in a tight, firm line. "Last warning. Back away. Let her go."

"Shut UP, you useless DWARF!" Felsith shrieked, patience lost. The unrelenting heel of his boot ground harder into my wrists, making me cry out.

Maerryl flung one of her daggers, hard and fast. It whistled past me, and Felsith screamed, so loud the birds in the trees above flew from their perches.

The heavy weight on top of my wrists lightened. I tore free, throwing my body weight forward and rolling away from him. Frantically scrambling to my feet, I hurled myself near Maerryl. She caught and steadied me, sturdy arms gripping tight. Her glance held none of the flippant irritation I'd seen since we met. Now she was all business, with poorly disguised guilt pinching her forehead as she checked me over quickly.

"You *bitch*! How DARE YOU?!" He would have stormed toward us, certainly, if it wasn't for the dagger firmly embedded in his left foot.

Maerryl's eyes met mine, holding an apology that I knew she wouldn't say. She swiftly cut the bindings off my wrists and faced Felsith again, pointing her second dagger toward his chest. Tears sprang to my eyes at the relief in my shoulders, my arms. I shook the numbness out of my fingers and massaged them gently. The bones of my wrists, thank the goddesses, didn't seem to be broken, but they ached terribly.

"Get your pack," she told me. To him, she said, "You and I are done. You're clearly unhinged. No amount of money is worth being an accomplice to torture and maiming of another person. No matter how annoying that person might be." She cut her wry gaze to me, and I rolled my eyes. Surprised as I was that Maerryl was helping me, I was more surprised to find this wiseass bounty hunter apparently had such moral fiber.

Clambering into the carriage, I willed my arms back into movement and grabbed my rucksack, tucking in the items Felsith had strewn across his seat when he was rooting through it.

Last, I picked up the thin blade where it still lay on my seat, the edge coated with my drying blood.

I jumped down from the carriage. Filled with cold rage, I stalked toward Felsith. My blood pounded in my ears.

No—that was real pounding. Horse hooves riding toward us along the road. Witnesses. I'd better make this quick.

Felsith saw my murderous eyes and turned to flee. I lifted my empty hand—weak, but power flowed through my veins again—and clenched. Felsith screamed as the knife in his foot dug deeper.

"Okay. Okay, that's enough," Maerryl said at my side. "Let's get him up on the carriage and leave."

"We can't just let him go! After what he did to me?" I stared at her in disbelief. Sweat dripped through my brow, into my eye. I was wrecked, but I would have my revenge.

"Elikki, think. He's a noble. The lord's brother. His cousin is a constable of the queendom. A dozen people saw what you did to him, but only you and I can attest to what happened here. And now he's injured." Maerryl sighed. "Who do you think will be believed, us or him?"

"Us! Obviously us! Look at him, he's gone off the deep end!" I pointed to where Felsith was trying to crawl-hop behind a tree, practically foaming at the mouth in fury.

The hoofbeats grew closer. Around the bend in the road, two horses flew toward us. One, a brown mare carrying a serious-looking woman, and the other, a familiar, truly massive gray horse. My heart leaped.

Barra galloped up on Pebble and had barely slowed her to a stop before he dismounted, unsheathing his sword.

"El," he said, breath ragged. Scanning the scene, he took in

Maerryl, dagger still drawn, Felsith muttering to himself on the side of the road, and me, covered in dirt and clutching my thin blade in one fist for dear life. I saw him notice the bruises and blood on my hands, my clothes and hair in disarray, the rage—and maybe some lingering fear—in my eyes. He stepped toward me, but I could see his internal battle as he held himself back from reaching out.

"What happened here?" His deep voice was so full of worry and anger, I was seized with the sudden intense need to touch him. I clenched my blade tighter and broke our gaze, turning again to Felsith. The mystery woman dismounted but kept her distance.

"Him," I spat. "That little shit attacked me. Poisoned me with something"—I skipped over the part where Maerryl had done the poisoning—"drove me out here, and then tried to…he tried to…" My mouth dried.

Maerryl cleared her throat. "He was going to break her wrists, steal her belongings, and leave her here."

In two steps, Barra was in front of me, looking over my body frantically for other signs of injury. "Are you all right? Please tell me you're all right," he said hoarsely.

I lifted my arms up for him to inspect, rolling my wrists. "I'm fine," I said, only wincing slightly. "Nothing a few days rest and some salve won't fix. Full arm function still intact. Speaking of—"

I turned and flung my knife straight toward Felsith's face. At the last millisecond, I stopped it with a twitch of my finger.

Felsith's face slackened, his mouth a gaping hole. The tip of the knife *just barely* touched the skin between his eyes, drawing the thinnest cut.

"I wouldn't move if I were you," I said to him. My blood blazed. Magic coursed through my veins, desperate to be used.

"El…" Barra cautioned.

My steely gaze bore into Felsith's shocked eyes. Just minutes ago, he'd been laughing at the prospect of hurting me—now he looked like he was about to shit his pants.

I raised both arms, shaking but determined. My power called to the metal around me—my full rucksack on the ground; all the hooks, chains, and nails of the carriage and horses' gear; the nose ring and dagger on Maerryl, two meager coppers in her coin purse; Barra's large sword and the necklace I'd given him; the still-sheathed broadsword and boot knife on the mystery woman; Felsith's glittering belt buckle, heavy coin purse, and my jewelry, stolen off my unconscious body and stuffed into his pockets.

To the trembling man before me, I snarled in a voice I barely recognized, "I'm going to crush you like the bug that you are."

His panicked eyes widened, darting around for any possible escape, before coming back to me. I could see white all around his irises. He knew what was coming. Pinned by my razor-sharp blade, he shook pathetically.

Before I could move to attack, a small voice piped up in my head. *Is this really what you want?*

Yes. He deserves it. I tried to squash the part of me that was trying to rethink this.

To become a cold-blooded killer? Play into the stereotype that people like him *think? You really want to let your anger take hold of your magic again, after finally,* finally *gaining control over it?*

No. No, I didn't. But the temptation to relinquish that control again felt so, so good. I wouldn't have to worry or fight anymore—my anger-fueled power would make these hard decisions for me. And oh, how it desired that. I sensed it just below the surface, ready to take over. My magic wanted to slice, to punish, to explode. To melt away how it *felt*—the pain of leaving Barra, the helplessness of being kidnapped and hurt, the anger at Felsith and everyone like him. Melt it until I felt clean and powerful again.

The possibility was tantalizing. But I wasn't that person anymore. I didn't need to be. I could choose for myself, my future. Closing my eyes, I tried to clear the blind rage from my mind and focus. I breathed hard until the fog cleared a little.

I looked up at Barra. His strong jaw clenched in worry. Smoky eyes watched me—unafraid, just filled with concern and love. Love for *me*.

If I did this, if I let my power consume me again like I used to, there was no telling what would happen. I wanted to destroy Felsith with every fiber of my being—but not at the risk of Barra or anyone else being caught in the crosshairs. He would probably do something noble and stupid, and I might accidentally hurt the only person I truly loved.

At that thought, I blinked. My arms fell. The buzzing tension of my power faded to a dull hum. The thin knife dropped into the dirt.

A wave of tiredness washed over me, but also a rush of exhilaration. It was as clear to me as my own name, as right as the perfect clang of hammer to metal. I met Barra's eyes in bewilderment.

"Holy shit, I love you," I said.

Barra stared at me for a moment. Then a tentative smile touched his lips.

"You do?" he asked, hope glimmering. He reached for my hand, and I gripped back as hard as I could.

"Very much. I think…I've loved you for a while now."

In my side vision, I distantly noticed Maerryl ducking around to a now crawling Felsith who was attempting to make a turtle's pace getaway. She stepped firmly on his back. He fell onto the ground with an "oof!" and she efficiently began to tie his hands with rope.

"But I didn't—or I couldn't—let myself see it. Or fully feel it." I shook my head slowly, looked away. "I didn't want to lose you."

"You won't."

"And I thought you'd be happy alone. In the long term."

"I wouldn't be."

"I don't know what I'm doing—I have no idea how to be in this kind of relationship. How to deal with families, live in one place, build a life with someone, any of it. I have no fucking clue!"

"You don't have to. We'll do it together."

I laughed, exasperated. "So simple, huh?"

"Simple," he said, drawing my hand up to his mouth. He pressed a kiss into my palm, sweaty and dirt lined. "Chaotic." He kissed my sore wrist. "Ridiculous." His lips moved up my arm. "And lovely." I reached for him, coming close and pressing against his stomach.

"A life together," he said.

I went on my tiptoes and met his kiss as he leaned toward me. Our lips enveloped each other, soft and sweet.

Shiny bubbles of golden light fizzed through me, setting my senses ablaze. I pressed closer, grabbing his muscled arms tightly. Bending, Barra lifted me up, laughing softly against my lips, and spun me around. My laughter erupted out of me, joining his, and then we were just two utter fools gasping for breath through their mirth, spinning in the middle of the godsdamn road.

When we finally slowed to a stop and caught our breath, Barra regained a touch of seriousness. "El, I want to travel with you."

"What do you mean?"

"I don't think we should go back to Nepu. It's not right for us, not now. Maybe not ever."

"But your whole life is there—and you can't just *leave*. What about your job, what about—"

"I know it seems like a big change. But honestly, I think I've been needing some major change for a long time now. I'll still work for our business on the road. Extending our customer base, sending orders back home, and doing some much-needed exploration to learn about new techniques, styles, and materials. I've thought it all through," Barra explained steadily. He seemed so sure. But…

"And your family? How do you know they'd be all right with all of this? I don't want them to resent me."

"We won't," a smooth voice piped up from behind me. I whirled. It was that woman who'd arrived with Barra. I'd nearly forgotten about her in all the turmoil. She'd been so quiet, practically blending into the background as everything unfolded.

Now I took in her thoughtful face, searching for dislike or distrust and finding none. For all her seriousness, she had laugh lines around her eyes and mouth.

"This is my older sister, Telen," Barra said. "My family was a bit, uh, concerned. So she rode out to find me."

24

Barra

"Oh! Your sister! Um, hi. It's so nice to meet you!" El hesitated, then threw herself at the other woman, wrapping her shorter body in a hug. "I'm Elikki."

"I know." Telen chuckled, returning the hug gently.

Releasing her, El turned back to me. "But why would they be concerned? Something you wrote in that letter? Was it...were they worried about me stealing you away or something?"

"*No*, no. Telen had already set off before that letter even arrived. When I didn't return from Povon." I scratched the back of my head, feeling the weight of everyone's eyes on me. "You see, I wasn't exactly on my way to Old Orchard like you."

Her brow furrowed. "I don't understand."

Telen watched the two of us, looking suspiciously like she was enjoying my discomfort. I cleared my throat.

"I was only meant to be in Povon on business for a day or two and then return home. But then everything happened with that worm"—I threw a look back to Felsith, now trussed up on the road with Maerryl sitting placidly on top of him—"and we had to run out of town, and then we had that, um, morning together"—I could feel my cheeks flush at the memory—"and I just found myself lying about my travel plans so...so I wouldn't have to say goodbye yet."

"But why not just tell me?"

"Maybe I should have. But you didn't know me then, not really. You were a woman traveling alone, and I was a huge man who suddenly wanted to drop my plans and follow you into the woods for days...wouldn't that have seemed creepy?"

Elikki crossed her arms, eyes twinkling. "Ahh. Yeah. I guess so."

I rushed to explain, trying to stay calm. "I kept telling myself I would leave soon. That I should turn back and let you continue on alone. But then Maerryl attacked you—still a bit confused about why she's here and helping us now, to be honest—and you were weak from the fight. One thing just kept leading to another. And then when you finally told me that you wanted me to stay—there was no way I could have left your side after that. Not while you wanted me."

"Well," Elikki said, cocking an eyebrow, "I can't honestly say that's even in the top five oddest things a person's done to try and get into my skirts over the years."

"Wait, you aren't weirded out by that *at all?*" Maerryl said.

El shrugged. "Not really. I'd probably have done the same thing. It's actually kind of romantic. I hadn't wanted to part yet back then either." She reached up and kissed me again, quick and sweet.

My chest was full of air. She didn't hate me for lying. The

relief was so intense that I was a bit lightheaded, dizzy with her kiss and her understanding.

"Two weirdos made for each other," I heard Telen mutter to herself, mystified.

Suddenly, El's pointed ears twitched, and she looked west down the road, in the opposite direction we had traveled from. "I hear hoofbeats. Someone's coming," she said. "Or a few some-ones, by the sound of it. We should try to move the carriage over a bit."

"Well, what're we going to do with this lump?" Maerryl stood and nudged Felsith with her toe. "Had to drug him a teensy bit so he'd calm down. We could knock him out more, dump him in the carriage, and let him sleep it off while we get away? He can drive himself home once he comes to."

Telen came closer, inspecting his prone body with a frown. "That won't do. He's seen all of us anyway, and he knows me. I may have, uh, bribed him not to press charges against Bar or put a bounty on him…"

"I can't believe you gave that asshole your hard-earned coin. I'll pay you back, sis," I said.

"I know, I know. But we weren't sure what was happening! It seemed like you were in danger. And we have the money. It's my job to protect you, so just shut it." Stubbornly, she threw a hand up in my face and continued, "I'll take Felsith back. I'm passing through anyway, on my way home. I'll explain the situation to the lord and act as witness to this worm's crimes. The Draos family is well-respected—they should listen to me. And, if not, I'll send for our mas to back me up."

"But you weren't here for the attack," Maerryl pointed out. She began to haul Felsith by his bound feet to the carriage door.

Telen came over to help, covering up the spots in the road where his foot had bled with a few kicks of dirt.

"Those nitwits in Povon don't know that. And if Felsith tries to dispute it, I'll just say I was hiding, looking for a moment to intervene on his deranged attack," Telen said with a flinty smile. Maerryl smiled tentatively back at her, which was a strange but cute sight.

I could hear the approaching horses now. Three mounted figures came around the bend. Spotting us, they shot down the road and halted suddenly. One, a woman in a guard's leathers, swung down and walked closer, inspecting Felsith as he drooled into the dirt.

"We got 'im, sir!" she called. "Seems fine, just a bit out of it. Did you knock 'im out?" she asked, looking around our group.

"In self-defense, yes," Telen said stiffly, stepping forward with her chin raised an inch. "This man attacked us with violent intent. He also kidnapped our companion, drugged her, and attempted to maim and rob her. We were forced to make a citizen's arrest, on behalf of the High Queen of Kurriel, and we are transporting him to his town's authorities now. Who, may I ask, are you?"

From atop his horse, a tired-looking middle-aged man sighed and said, "Oh, Felly, what have you done now?"

El and I blinked at each other. *Felly?* she mouthed, nearly making me burst out laughing in the awkward silence.

Pinching the bridge of his nose, the man said, "I apologize. It's been a long and—erm, stressful—journey. I should introduce myself. I'm Lord Renalo of Povon, and this"—he gestured to Felsith—"is my younger brother. I expect we arrived a bit too late to the party, so to speak. It took us some time to track him down, the wily little fellow."

"You can say that again," Elikki grumbled, rubbing her still-sore wrists. I glared at the pompous man—still shorter than me, even on horseback—and began brushing soothing circles on El's back with my palm.

She leaned into my touch a bit, letting me hold some of her weight against my body. I fumed internally at Felsith, and these newcomers, but didn't let my anger seep into my touch. She needed rest—a warm bath, a pot of tea, and a soft bed to sleep off the pain and awfulness of this morning.

The lord let out another, deeper sigh. "You must be Mistress Elikki, the jeweler. My brother has been on quite the tear about you lately. I apologize for his actions here." He inclined his head to her. "That being said, you did severely injure him as well, when you were visiting my town."

"Allegedly," she said flatly. "And if you had investigated the matter before putting a call out for my arrest—and allowing him to put a bounty on my head—you would have discovered that *he* laid his hands on *me* first."

"I actually didn't call for your arrest. Or encourage the bounty. I called for you to be brought in for questioning, as is proper procedure under Kurrielan law. But you and your—uh, companion's—actions complicated things somewhat. I'll admit, however, that the situation got rapidly out of hand on my watch." The lord sighed yet again and slumped in his saddle.

"You didn't? Oh, well…right. You still could have handled things better," she said, looking like she was struggling to maintain her wrath in the face of this absolute soggy roll of a man.

He nodded. "Yes. I know what my brother is like, and I should have intervened sooner. Unfortunately for all of us, he's surprised even me with his atrocious behavior this time. You know he stole my carriage and horses here too? Do you have anything to say for yourself, Felly?" he called down.

Maerryl prodded Felsith with her boot, and his eyes slit open. "I'm just a baby worm...don't know whosits from whatsits... just sleep in my worm hommmme..." he moaned woozily before zonking out again.

"Right you are, Felly." Another heavy sigh, and Lord Renalo motioned to his guards. "Please put him in the carriage and secure the door. One of you drive that back and we'll put your horse on a lead." The two guards came forward to collect Felsith and tossed him on the floor of the carriage with barely concealed looks of disgust.

"We'll be off, then. I want to make good time back to town before we camp," the lord said with a sniff. "This matter is settled. My brother will be punished, that I promise. He won't be bothering you again. Between you and me, it's high time he was also placed into mandatory therapy and anger management, which I will also arrange."

Privately, I didn't think it would do much good for that rotting slimeball. But I suppose you never know. Elikki said, "Um, good luck with that. And what about us?"

"You are both free to go, of course. Legally, as the lord of my township, I cannot give you financial recompenses for your, um, troubles. But I can say that if you were ever to visit my fair town again in the future, I will welcome you into my home and treat you as my family's most honored guest. Any of you." He bowed at the waist to our ragtag group.

Like any of us would be caught dead spending a second more with that disaster of a family. El exchanged a look with me that said she was thinking the same, but she told the lord, "Thanks, I guess. Good luck rehabilitating that one."

"Thank you, Mistress Elikki." A final long-suffering sigh, and he turned his horse around and trotted away, guards and carriage following.

We watched them disappear quickly down the road and around the bend. A last spark of fury burned inside me as that odious man was carried away, along with any hope of getting revenge for the way he'd treated Elikki. I tried to let it fizzle out. She was safe. That's what mattered.

"Wish I could have gotten one good slap on that toad's face, don't you?" I asked. Her gaze was still trained on the now-empty road.

"*Yeah*. Something like that," she said, smiling wickedly.

"You're imagining slicing him up with sharp metal pointy things again, aren't you?"

"Maybe…" she sighed, sounding eerily like Lord Renalo. "I can't believe he did all this *bullshit*, and he just gets carted back home by his fancy-pants big brother. Fuck, I wish I knew how to cast *curses* on people."

Maerryl pulled something from her boot with a flourish. "Does it help that I stole his coin purse?"

"HA! A bit, yes," El said. The other woman handed the heavy pouch over, and she rifled through it.

"And the 'teensy' drugging I gave him…maybe wasn't so teensy after all," Maerryl added.

"Oooh, what did you do?"

"Let's just say old Felly won't exactly be himself for a few days…or weeks," she said, looking extremely pleased with herself.

"You sly dog!" Elikki grinned.

Face sobering, Maerryl continued, "I'm glad you're all right.

I didn't mean for everything to...to escalate like that. Met him at the Painted Dragon the other night, and when I told him about our encounter, he offered me a lot of coin to be his muscle on this, um, mission."

Maerryl shifted from foot to foot, quickly looking around at all of us before dropping her gaze. She almost looked as if she thought we'd take our revenge on her now that Felsith had been snatched away. Despite myself, despite everything she'd done, I found that was the last thing I wanted. A glance at El and my sister told me they felt the same.

Shoulders tight, Maerryl mumbled, "I didn't know what he was planning. I swear."

"I know," El said. She dropped Felsith's coin purse into Maerryl's hands. "Keep this. And don't argue. I know exactly how much coin you have on you, and it's certainly not enough to keep you out of mischief for long. Besides, you did kind of save me. Even if you took your sweet time about it."

Maerryl scowled but seemed relieved, gripping the purse tightly before tucking it back into her worn boot. Then El moved in, trapping the other woman in a tight, quick hug before releasing her with an affectionate pinch on the arm. Taken aback, Maerryl let it happen. A small smile fought its way out of her typical stormy expression.

I watched this whole exchange, baffled. I really had to get the full story of what happened from El at some point.

25

Elikki

"So...what now?" I said, looking around at Barra, Telen, and Maerryl.

Barra came to stand by me as if he was drawn in, metal to a magnet. "Now I suppose you and I go wherever we feel like. I'm not quite sure—I've never had an open-ended adventure before."

I smiled up at him, finally feeling the last ember of my rage fade away. "I'll show you. As long as you're sure about this," I said.

He kissed me in answer, dipping me back so that my world went sideways and he was nearly bent in half at the waist, keeping me steadier than I've ever been held. I blazed at his touch, loving the gentleness of his arms and the heat in his eyes.

"Oh yes. I'm sure," he whispered.

Telen's quiet cough broke the spell, and Barra pulled me up with an easy spin that left me laughing. "Excellent. And you'll take my horse, Elikki." Holding up a firm finger when I opened my mouth to argue, Telen said, "No, don't bother. You are taking him. His name is Dewdrop, and he positively craves adventure. Feisty, excitable. Good luck to you."

"That's very kind, Telen," I said. "But I can't—how will you get home?"

"It's only a few hours walk to the inn, I expect. I'll stay there tonight and buy or borrow a horse from Legus for the journey home. Want to come with me?"

This last she directed to Maerryl, who blinked as if she'd heard wrong. "Me? But you hardly know me."

The other woman shrugged. "What I do know, I like."

Telen seemed incapable of blushing, but Maerryl's cheeks tinged pink at the compliment. "Fine by me," she said, shrugging with careful nonchalance.

"Great!" Telen moved to Dewdrop and began collecting her belongings. She also lowered the stirrups for me a bit since my legs were much longer. Such an eldest child.

"All set," she said, hefting her pack. "Now, this is just a loan. Take him for as long as you need him. But if your travels lead you back this way in a few months' time, we'd love to see you two in Nepu so you can meet Monty's new baby."

I nodded, no hesitations. "We'd love to visit. Thank you so much. I'll look forward to it."

And I found that I truly would. This woman—according to Barra, the prickliest of his family, seemed to genuinely like me, and I liked her too. She'd stuck up for me with the lord. And even gave me her horse! Maybe this could work. Fitting into a family, bit by bit. For the first time, I could kind of imagine it for myself.

I put all my tender feelings into a hug, squeezing Telen tight. To my surprise, she squeezed back this time. "Take care of my brother," she murmured. "He doesn't actually know how to use that godsdamned sword."

After a hug to Barra and a final wave, she set off west down the road. Maerryl paused before following, standing a few paces away and looking distinctly awkward.

"Well, goodbye, then," she said. "Watch your ass—there might still be hunters around who don't know the bounty's been called off."

I fake gasped, teasing, "Wow, is this *concern*? For my safety? Barra, call a healer, I think our new friend must have a fever."

She flipped a middle finger at me and threw her usual scowl, an oddly endearing sight now. Barra just chuckled. Somehow, this prickly, irascible woman had grown on us. I found myself hoping that she'd be okay. All she carried was a thin satchel. But did she have anywhere to go? Anyone to help her?

Before I could open my mouth to ask, to learn more about this unusual person who'd crossed my life's path, she was stepping away. With a final disparaging smile, Maerryl tossed a hand in farewell and said, "See ya, elf."

I swallowed my words and stuck out my tongue. Laughing, I just said, "Hopefully *not*, dwarf!"

Moving closer to Barra, I watched her walk away, jogging to catch up with Telen. Hopefully she'd be all right. But something told me Maerryl had more problems than a handful of gold and a snarky attitude could solve.

Barra and I held each other's hands for a minute, taking in everything that had happened in the last chaotic hour. Then we moved together, checking on our horses. Barra secured my rucksack while I introduced myself to Dewdrop with a sugar cube. We swung up into our saddles and turned east toward Old Orchard.

"Ready, love?" he said.

I looked at the open road ahead of me. Clear. Exciting. Ripe for adventure. With Barra at my side and possible futures abounding ahead of us, my pulse leaped.

"Ready."

Epilogue

One year later

"Look what I found!"

I yawned and stretched, trying to wriggle out from the heavy woven blankets that covered our bed. Barra perched on the edge. His weight sank the mattress, and I rolled toward him, squealing. He caught me and pressed a kiss against my forehead, then waved a colorful blur in front of my face.

"Uillos! There were only two left, but the vendor said they'd still give me a good deal." Barra handed me one and I sat up, rolling the vivid purple fruit in my hands. *And they probably charged him double the cost*, I thought. Uillos weren't rare in this part of the world. They were a little out of season, though I was sure the vendor would be back with another full cart tomorrow.

But I didn't say anything, of course. He was so excited. And is there anything sweeter than a man bringing you breakfast in bed?

Barra cut into the large, richly colored fruit with his belt knife and held the first slice out to me. I opened my mouth. He placed it on my tongue, a fire sparking in his eyes as I chewed and swallowed, licking the zingy tang off my lips.

He cut another piece and fed me again.

"Did you intentionally try to match our breakfast?" I asked, holding one of the uillos up to his lavender skin.

He placed the knife on the nightstand and took a ferocious bite of the half he held. "I *tried* to find something that would taste nearly as delicious as you do, love. But I fear I failed again."

"Hmm...perhaps we should compare? Just for the sake of fairness," I said, sliding fully out of the blankets. Coming up to my knees on the bed, I kissed him deeply, savoring the sour-sweet taste of his mouth. His skin was still chilled from being outside, and I cupped his face in my hands to warm him.

With a pleased rumble, Barra wrapped his arms around me, picking me fully up before landing us back among the cushions. His body was a heavy, comforting weight. After a few more kisses, he pulled away, moving down my body. I protested at first, missing his lips, but stopped as he bit at my underwear and dragged the flimsy fabric down with his teeth.

When his tongue delved into my folds, I let my eyes—still hazy with sleep—fall closed and drifted into this waking dream of his hot breath against my most sensitive skin.

Firm fingers wrapped around my thighs and hips, pinning me in place even as I writhed, chasing that delicious need. He licked me until I was begging him. "Don't stop, don't you *dare stop.*"

My fingers gripped his long tied-back hair, a green ribbon hanging on for dear life as I yanked, eventually gasping my way into a most beautiful morning orgasm. "Oh, goddesssss," I groaned as I fell back, sinking into the plush pillows.

Barra came up to his elbows and crawled toward me, kissing his way up my soft stomach, giving double kisses to the two rolls in my belly. Lifting for a few seconds, he quickly ripped his clothes off and tossed them away.

"Well?" I asked. "What's the verdict?"

He pressed a kiss into my jaw. "No contest. Not even close."

Barra's chest rumbled against me as he spoke, and I could feel the hard length of his cock against my leg. I shifted my body a bit, rubbing against him. With a groan, he grabbed me with both arms and flipped us over so that I was straddling him.

I let the straps of my nightgown fall, revealing my breasts, and Barra surged forward to claim them one by one. Tracing the thick, cool links of my necklace around his throat, I guided myself onto his cock and began to ride him, slow and steady.

"*Fuck*, El," he breathed against me, leaning back on the headboard. I wrapped one hand around the long chain, tugging experimentally. Barra's pupils flooded his brown eyes. His large hands grabbed as much of my ass as they could and massaged mindlessly.

"Can you—can you do that tighter?" he said, staring at me intensely.

"Safe word still 'blueberries'?"

He nodded, muscles tense in anticipation. "Or I'll pinch you."

"All right, then," I said with a vicious smile, tightening my grip a little. He gasped in pleasure and said, "*More*."

I obliged, feeding a slip of my magic into the metal chain. Willing it slightly tighter around the sides of his neck, my hands were free to roam across his broad chest, his shoulders. Power flowed through me, perfect and filled with light. I felt invincible, complete.

Grinding into him harder, I released the chain's hold for a moment. His hips kept rising to meet me in perfect rhythm, again and again. I closed my fist, choking him lightly once more. Hands that palmed my ass stilled abruptly for a split second, squeezing hard. With a roar, Barra came, releasing himself into me.

I let my magic flow back into my body, emptying the necklace's hold, and slid forward onto his chest with a satisfied smile as he panted.

When he'd caught his breath, Barra reached up to brush soft circles on my back and thighs. He kissed me gently, eyes sparkling.

"That was new," he said, beaming and looking slightly bashful.

I nibbled his earlobe and said, "You are full of surprises, my dear."

"Oh, speaking of—I found a perfect place for us to stay next week."

"Really?!" I bounced on top of him, making him chuckle and nuzzle my neck. We'd been winding our path back south for the past month. In this northern land, cold and filled with welcoming but very small halflings and humans, it often proved hard to find accommodations that Barra and I could fit in comfortably.

Luckily, over our past year of travel he'd discovered a useful network that has accepted him into their ranks, made up of half-giants, orcs, dragonborns, and other larger-bodied people who were passionate about traveling the world. Whenever we crossed paths with one, they were able to give recommendations on the inns, rentals, and restaurants that could accommodate their size well. He compared maps and notes with them, learning and sharing valuable information that allowed us to have restful, comfortable travels.

"Met an orc at the smithy who had just come up from central Kurriel. Bit of a prickly fellow, but he was full of information. Pinpointed a few inns for me, so we can take that longer route back to Nepu along the coast if you still want to."

"Definitely! It's beautiful this time of year. I can't wait to see you swimming in the ocean," I said, reaching for the uillo on my nightstand and taking another delicious bite. Barra licked a drop of stray juice off my chin.

"Want to try that little café before you start working today?" he asked. "I've heard they have this rare northern drink called ice tea. Not *iced* tea—it's still hot. But it's made from these tiny white flowers that only grow deep in the ice caves, hundreds of miles north of here. It's a delicacy."

"You're such a loon for tea, and I love it," I said, giving him a peck on his nose.

Rolling off him, I padded over to our chest of drawers and rifled through it for something to wear. We'd been staying here in the city of Iwwo for about a week and a half, and despite Barra's best efforts to keep things tidy in our room, my belongings somehow always ended up strewn about.

"As long as they also have black tea and those little sugary pastry balls, I'm happy to make a morning detour with you, my dear. Aha!" I cried, finding my favorite red corset hidden underneath the couch cushions.

Pulling on a simple light pink blouse and my warmest skirt—a beautiful creamy wool local style that I'd treated myself to after a huge commission last week—I sauntered back to Barra so he could do up my laces. Once that was done, and he was dressed again, we headed out into the chilly morning.

Wrapped in our thick cloaks and fur-lined gloves, we walked hand in hand along the quiet city streets. I was going to miss this place when we moved on next week, with its ice-lined buildings and kind people.

In our short time here, Barra and I had already become quite well-known. It wasn't hard to become a minor celebrity when almost everyone else was under four feet tall. Our innkeeper, a fellow half-giant, confessed once when they were in their cups that locals had begun calling Barra the "Lavender Lover" because of how he doted on me as we cavorted around town—which had me howling in laughter and him blushing and scowling for the rest of the night.

It was a lovely city, and I found myself wishing we could stay for at least a few more weeks. Barra adored it too, silly nicknames aside. He'd even come back from the shops the other day wearing a cream wool shirt that was embroidered along the buttons in a popular floral Iwwon design. He said the shopkeeper had bullied him into buying it, that he'd asked for his standard brown.

But I knew custom work when I saw it. And I'd caught him checking himself out in our mirror later, with the small, happy smile on his face that always made my heart squeeze.

Sadly, our time here was soon coming to an end. We had to head out next week and begin traveling our way back south and then east, if we were going to make it in time for little Ariane's first birthday.

Over the past year, we'd journeyed back to Nepu twice. Once in the early summer, to welcome Monty's newborn, sweet Ariane, into the world. The next, to wait out the harshest weeks of winter and to meet Sassura, Barra's sister who traveled during the warm months with her dance troupe.

The first trip, I was utterly nerve-racked, sure that his family would reject me. Despite his constant reassurances that they'd fall for me immediately, I barely slept in those days leading up to our visit. Barra kept saying we could put off the trip, go a bit later when I was maybe more ready. But I knew I was never going to truly be ready—I just had to throw myself into the fire and hope for the best.

I pushed us on. And when we arrived at Barra's family home, a large, short gray-haired woman ran out the front door and down the path toward us. Barra got on his knees to hug her—which was as adorable to witness as it sounds—before she finally swatted him away and turned to me where I stood frozen, clutching Dewdrop's reins like they were my anchor in a wild sea.

"So. You must be Elikki," she said with a warm, broad smile on her lined chestnut-brown face. Brushing flour-dusted hands on her apron, she reached for my free hand and gently tugged me up the path toward her house. "I'm Ma Wren. And you look like you need a thick slice of cake and my biggest pot of tea. Come along, dear."

Her hand was warm and strong, and I let myself be led through the front door and into the kitchen, Barra trailing behind us after he tied the horses to the front gate.

After that, it was a stream of desserts and many, many cups full of strong tea. Ma Wren chattered as she bustled around the kitchen—plying us with more treats, opening another window for a breeze, plopping a soft, snuggly kitten in my lap. Before I knew it, I'd found myself relaxing and chatting back. Relief, warmth, and safety crept bit by bit into my mind, and Barra stayed at my side, his presence steadying.

After a while, we left to rest at Barra's house before the big family dinner in the evening. As we said our goodbyes, I gathered Ma Wren up in a hug, bending down to her. "Thank you," I said, my voice thick.

"You're a sweet girl," she said, patting my cheek affectionately. "So strong and lovely—my Barra really lucked out. Finally!"

"Maaaa," Barra groaned as she and I giggled. But he smiled too, pressing a kiss into my hair.

After that, everything felt so much less terrifying. A long nap and a bath helped too, and when we returned to meet the rest of the family later, I was…if not *ready* exactly, at least not scared stiff. Everyone was, as Barra had promised, thrilled to meet me. The evening was nothing but fun, and full of laughs.

In fact, the whole trip went smoothly. Once I started to believe that, yes—these people actually seemed to want me here in their homes, their family, Barra's life—everything came together. I talked metalsmithing with Ma Reese and Telen, helped Ma Wren in the kitchen, and held Monty's baby. Barra and I recounted the last few months of our travel.

And then, to a rapt audience, we retold the now-famous tale of how we got together: road trip, bounty hunters, magic, kidnapping, and all. Some facts of the story had to be reestablished, as it seemed that Telen's version had her heroically rescuing me from an evil wizard while Barra was off looking for a sword he'd dropped somewhere in the forest. Much good-natured arguing ensued, and the night ended with all of us laughing and the baby spitting up on Telen's shirt.

The rest of our week was wonderful, and the second trip was even better. Now, as I walked the streets of Iwwo recalling it all, that new, glowing feeling suffused my chest. The feeling, I was starting to recognize, was the warmth of family, of belonging. I couldn't wait to go back.

Barra and I talked often about the future. What we wanted for our lives. Our dreams and goals. For now we both wanted to keep traveling and having adventures. He had taken surprisingly well to life on the road and had a long list of places he wanted us to visit together. Someday, we thought, we may decide to put down roots in Nepu again, or perhaps a town nearby. Or spend half of the year there and the other half traveling. But for now, it was a time of adventure.

Ducking into the little café, I bought a large black tea, Barra's deliciously scented ice tea, and a bag of my favorite local treat, these small round balls that tasted like almond and burnt sugar. We found a bench near one of the blue magefire heaters scattered around the city's public gardens and sat pressed together, looking out over a quiet pond. The strong tea warmed me from the inside, and I chased it with a sweet almond ball to balance out the bitterness. Barra opened his mouth. I popped one in, laughing as he almost immediately opened up for another.

His arm snug around me, we sat in peaceful happiness, drinking our tea and watching snow rabbits scamper in the frosted earth. I felt a bone-deep contentment. Sugar on my tongue and magic thrumming in my core. We would have a thousand days that felt like this, and we would have joy I'd never imagined.

Acknowledgments

The journey of publishing one's debut book is exhilarating... and strange. Enlightening. Arduous. Consuming. Lonely. Magical. This living, breathing world that you've dreamed up and laboriously translated into words on a page somehow has been chosen. It's being transformed into a new entity that exists outside of myself. And I could not be more thrilled. Or more terrified. The writing and publishing process requires intense vulnerability—not always my strong suit. But I am unfathomably lucky that my life contains so many people who have helped make this book happen.

Here's to my brilliant agent, Brent Taylor, for being such a champion of this story. We clicked from the very start, and I'm delighted to be on this journey with you. And to the whole Triada US team, including intern Sara Aldrich, who gave helpful notes when I was feeling stuck.

To editor extraordinaire Leah Hultenschmidt—I've already said a million thank-yous in the short time we've known each other, but here's another. *Thank you!* I'm so happy that Elikki and Barra's story found a home at Forever with you. And many thanks to the entire Forever team, including Jordyn Penner,

Daniela Medina, Jeff Stiefel, Alli Rosenthal, Luria Rittenberg, Shasta Clinch, Estelle Hallick, Brieana Garcia, and everyone else who works on the book after I'm allowed to make changes here. My deep appreciation to artist Luciana Bertot, whose gorgeous illustrations grace the cover.

To all the assistants, interns, and everyone else working behind the scenes—please know that your work has immense value. You are the ones who keep the wheels turning, the engine running, the wobbly beast that is the publishing industry still chugging along. Thank you so much for everything.

To all my dear friends for your encouragement and support. In particular, my wonderful beta readers—Monica, Megan, and Maddie. Thank you for having such delightfully alliterative names, for being the first ones to read this story, and for helping me make it better while also bolstering my confidence. A special thank-you to Monica, who rightly dubbed herself the godmother of this book. The fairy godmother, I say! And a marvelous one at that. May we never tire of cheering each other on and cheering each other up. Thanks also to my book club ladies and my *D&D* crews, for your friendship, snacks, and creativity, and for getting this homebody out and about.

To my wonderful critique partners, Paula and Alicia—this book, particularly the beginning, wouldn't have been in nearly good enough shape for querying without your insightful edits and feedback. Thanks also to dear Naomi for sharing your metalworking and jewelry making knowledge with me, and for being a good friend. Everyone should go gaze in awe at their beautiful handmade pieces on Instagram at @metalpetaljewelry.

To the dozens of librarians, teachers, and professors who have helped shape me into the person I am: across many years and many schools, I was fortunate to always have kind and supportive educators.

To Margaret, the kindest, gentlest soul I've ever known. We miss you dearly, and I'll always treasure the years that you were in my life.

To my family and parents, whom I am infinitely lucky to have. To my gramma, who has taught me so much about love. Thank you for your warmth, your open mind, and the comfort you bring me and everyone around you. To my sisters, Amanda and Emma—I find myself unable to describe how much you mean to me here. But I think you know.

To my cat, Opal, for always being That Bitch who keeps me forever humble. Thanks for reminding me with every dismissive look that no, I'm not actually cool or impressive.

To my love, Jon—you are my earliest and strongest supporter, the vacuumer of my worries and doubts, and the best partner I could ever ask for. I might never have become someone who could write romance if we hadn't met. Because of you, I see so much hope, positivity, and light around me every day.

Here's to my queer community online, in Chicago, and beyond. To all of the bi badasses. To my fellow weirdos. To anyone who reads this story and connects with it. Who posts about it kindly online, buys a copy or borrows it from their library, recommends it to a friend. Thank you, thank you, *thank you* for taking a chance on a debut author's whimsical cake of a book.

About the Author

KRISTEN VALE writes queer cozy fantasy romcoms filled with sweetness and spice. When not reading or writing, she usually can be found thrifting, playing D&D, or staring lovingly at trees. She lives in Chicago with her partner and her frenemy black cat, Opal. *A Tale of Mirth & Magic* is her first novel.

Connect with her at:
- Bluesky @kristenvale
- Instagram @kristenvalewrites
- TikTok @kristenvalewrites
- X @kristenvale_